# Hot Mail

# Hot Mail

## JANICE MAYNARD

A SIGNET ECLIPSE BOOK

SIGNET ECLIPSE
Published by New American Library, a division of
Penguin Group (USA) Inc., 375 Hudson Street,
New York, New York 10014, USA
Penguin Group (Canada), 90 Eglinton Avenue East, Suite 700, Toronto,
Ontario M4P 2Y3, Canada (a division of Pearson Penguin Canada Inc.)
Penguin Books Ltd., 80 Strand, London WC2R 0RL, England
Penguin Ireland, 25 St. Stephen's Green, Dublin 2,
Ireland (a division of Penguin Books Ltd.)
Penguin Group (Australia), 250 Camberwell Road, Camberwell, Victoria 3124,
Australia (a division of Pearson Australia Group Pty. Ltd.)
Penguin Books India Pvt. Ltd., 11 Community Centre, Panchsheel Park,
New Delhi - 110 017, India
Penguin Group (NZ), 67 Apollo Drive, Rosedale, North Shore 0632,
New Zealand (a division of Pearson New Zealand Ltd.)
Penguin Books (South Africa) (Pty.) Ltd., 24 Sturdee Avenue,
Rosebank, Johannesburg 2196, South Africa

Penguin Books Ltd., Registered Offices:
80 Strand, London WC2R 0RL, England

First published by Signet Eclipse, an imprint of New American Library,
a division of Penguin Group (USA) Inc.

Copyright © Janice Maynard, 2009
All rights reserved

SIGNET ECLIPSE and logo are trademarks of Penguin Group (USA) Inc.

ISBN-13: 978-1-60751-602-6

Printed in the United States of America

*For my wonderful husband, Charles, who wrote me love letters every single day during our freshman year in college when we were three hundred miles apart and missing each other like crazy. Sweetheart, those notes might not have been erotic valentines, but your words made me fall in love with you time and again.*

*Hot Mail*

# One

Jane Norman appreciated men even though she didn't have a clue what made them tick.

She was thirty-two, and her feminist sensibilities were as well developed as the next gal's, but she was willing to ask for help when it came to carpentry projects, plumbing emergencies, auto repair, spider extermination—you name it. Fortunately, at the moment she had no crises, mechanical or otherwise, that needed male intervention.

And though she freely admitted that men were vital to the process of conception, her biological clock wasn't ticking any louder than normal. Motherhood was still a delightful "maybe" somewhere way out on the horizon.

But despite the fact that her life was under control in most areas, she couldn't ignore the truth. She needed a man . . .

For sex. And cuddling. And long walks on the beach. Well, scratch that one. Tennessee was a landlocked state. She deleted the last entry on her mental checklist and continued. . . . She needed a man for sharing meals with. And sex. And laughter. And sex. And playing footsies under the covers. And sex.

Definitely a pattern developing. The trouble was, not any man would do. Jane had a lamentable tendency toward wanting what she couldn't have. Or didn't have. Namely, Ethan Oldham, the tall, self-assured assistant chief of police. He made her heartbeat skitter and her forehead break out in a sweat whenever she saw him in his khaki uniform, his muscular thighs and broad shoulders straining the seams of the standard-issue clothing.

Never mind that she and Ethan had lived in the same community since they were in grade school. Or that they'd shared an on-again, off-again friendship for a decade and a half. Mostly off for the past four years. But hey, that wasn't her fault. Ethan had done the unforgivable. He'd gotten engaged to another woman. And even though he'd had the good sense to rectify his mistake really quickly, she'd told herself it was a sign she needed to eradicate this silly crush.

They were never going to be a couple.

But time heals all wounds, or so she had been told, and when a girl sits alone on New Year's Eve one too many times, she gets desperate. In this instance, really, really desperate. Desperate enough to come up with a plan that was completely beyond her skill set. She was going to become a poet and win the man she loved.

She had never at any previous point in her life aspired to write erotic verse, but in a moment of blinding revelation while standing in line at the supermarket, she'd read a snatch of an article from the latest *Cosmo,* and realized that she needed something original. Something inspired. Something that Ethan Oldham would be unable to ignore.

In a moment of insanity, she'd decided to use bottled ink and a fancy quill . . . as if that would somehow afford her an edge in this dirty-poetry endeavor. Instead, all it had given her was an indelible spot on her favorite robe and a trash can full of crumpled efforts.

She scanned her most recent attempt.

*Roses are red*
*Violets are blue.*
*I'd like to get naked,*
*With you and me, too.*

Not only did her poetry suck—it didn't even make grammatical sense. She sighed and tossed the latest version with all the rest.

It was all Ethan's fault. If he'd reciprocated her adolescent devotion in the ninth grade, things would have been different. But when a girl was almost six feet tall at the tender age of fourteen, it was a cold, cruel world. Sadly, Ethan had been the only boy in the junior high school taller than Jane, and she'd fallen madly in love with him for no other reason than his stature. Of course, his single dimple hadn't hurt. Despite the fact that he barely knew her name way back then, she had yearned for him to notice her.

She pushed the memories aside and looked at the clock in the bottom corner of the TV. Fifteen minutes left in the old year. And good riddance was all she had to say.

She ignored the messy quill and reached for a ballpoint pen and a piece of scrap paper for her next draft.

*There lives near you a lady fair*
*Who wants to play with your hair.*
*She yearns for your touch.*
*She would like it so much,*
*So please take me home to your lair.*

She burst out laughing and moaned, scooting from the sofa to the floor. She crossed her arms on the coffee table and buried her face, wishing she had the confidence to simply walk up to Ethan Oldham and ask him out.

As a healthy, virile young man at the peak of his physical power, he was enough to make any woman's knees weak, but Jane had no clue about how to reveal her not so platonic feelings. She'd tried time and again to move on . . . to develop a crush on someone else. Anyone else. In fact, she had sworn to herself that she was over Ethan . . . for good.

Yet here she was, alone in her apartment on another sad, lonely New Year's Eve, doing her best to compose a sexy, wicked valentine that would bring him to his knees. She knew that one card wasn't going to do it. She'd need patience, and perseverance, and a bunch of valentines.

Maybe six or seven. One for each Friday from now until February fourteenth. Could she do it? Could she court a man using nothing more than creative, erotic verse?

She picked up the quill one last time and retrieved her final sheet of neatly trimmed parchment paper. Her brow furrowed. Her fingers tensed. This was do-or-die time. Delicately, she moved the nib across the paper and watched openmouthed as the pen composed words and phrases with all the confidence and aplomb of a Ouija board.

*A man such as you,*
*A man strong and true,*
*Makes my woman's heart break;*
*Makes my woman parts ache.*

*I'm writing you now,*
*As a sign of my vow.*

*I'm tired of denying*
*This love I've been hiding.*

*So I'll woo you with words*
*And arouse your suspicions*
*Until that fine day*
*When we lose inhibitions.*

*Tonight when you sleep*
*In dreams hot and deep,*
*See me come to your bed and*
*Then dwell in your head.*

*This note's but the first*
*Of a string of my verse,*
*So read this with care*
*And wait for me there. . . .*

Jane's hand was shaking when she laid down the pen. Did she dare send this? Would Ethan be intrigued? And if he was, would she ever work up the courage to reveal her identity?

She thought of his smoke-colored eyes, his flashing smile, the wonderful little rumble of masculine laughter that made her nipples ache to have him nestled at her breast.

She was tired of being a coward. She was tired of wishing for the moon. Most of all, she was tired of watching other people live the life she wanted. Ethan Oldham was on the endangered-species list, and it was time to kick Cupid's fat pink butt cheeks and do some matchmaking of her own.

Soon her oh so yummy, hard-bodied police officer love interest was going to have a bunch of really good reasons to use his handcuffs.

She hoped. . . .

*      *      *

Ethan Oldham hunched his shoulders in his fleece-lined coat and turned the car heater up a notch. Late December in Statlerville, Tennessee, was mild as a rule. Most of the big snows—when they occasionally occurred—came in February and even the end of March. Case in point: Last year on New Year's Eve, folks were out shooting fireworks in their shirtsleeves, the temps in the balmy midfifties.

But this particular January was coming in on a wave of bitter cold that made the thin sliver of moon overhead seem like a pale, icy light against the pitch-black sky.

He didn't have to be out at all tonight. With his seniority, he could be back at the station tucked up in his warm office going over paperwork. But he had no party to go to, and the young pups on the force all had hot dates with their wives and girlfriends.

God. When did thirty-two get to be old? He sighed and turned down the street that ran in front of the high school. He was praying for a quiet night—with no underage drinking—or better yet, no drunks of any age wrapping their cars around telephone poles.

Maybe the weather would keep people inside. Then all Ethan would have to worry about, at least in an official capacity, was domestic squabbles that ended in bloodshed. Something about holidays brought out the best and worst in people. Tonight, on his watch, he was hoping for the former.

Nothing looked out of place on the campus, so he turned his vehicle around in the cul-de-sac by the flagpole and headed toward the middle of town. The courthouse square was a ghost town, the small businesses shut up tight for the long holiday weekend. He glanced at the second story of the brick building on the far corner. In the faint glow of a streetlight he read the familiar name on the sign: PAPER PLEASURES.

Jane's surprisingly successful business. Who knew you could earn a living selling fancy pens and single sheets of paper? She lived upstairs in a small apartment, and judging by the light in the second-story windows, she had elected not to go out tonight. For a brief moment he thought about parking the cruiser and knocking on her door, but then he squashed the impulse. The days were long gone when Jane would have welcomed an impromptu visit from him.

The thought made him sad, and he stepped on the accelerator, eager to get away from the depressing memories. At one time he and Jane had been good friends. But it had been at least four years since she'd given him a genuine smile. They ran into each other from time to time, mostly in social settings, but he had the distinct impression that she avoided him whenever she could.

A sudden burst of staccato conversation emanated from the radio, jerking his thoughts from the past. He called in and then headed toward the interstate, where a semi had flipped over while coming off an exit ramp.

By the time the mess was cleaned up, thankfully without injury, it was after one a.m., which was a damn good sign. That meant that most of the New Year's Eve revelry was over without incident. Statlerville wasn't New York City. At midnight, most people watched the ball drop, shot off a few bottle rockets, and called it a night.

Ethan drove back toward the station, ready to turn over the night shift to someone else and head home to bed. But when he rounded the corner of Grove and Vine, he frowned. His sister's lights, at least the ones in the back of the house, were still on.

Damn. That couldn't be good. Sherry was an early riser and liked going to bed by ten most nights. And he knew she wasn't entertaining this year, because Debra was spending the holidays with her dad in Florida.

Ethan called in his location and pulled into the driveway. His knock might startle Sherry, but she could see his car in the driveway easily enough and not be scared to open the door.

His instincts usually served him well, and tonight was no exception. When his older sibling opened the door and ushered him inside, he could tell she had been crying. Shit. He was no better than the average male at dealing with tears, but he and Sherry were close.

He followed her to the den, where a pile of glowing embers, the real thing, smoldered in the fireplace, still pouring out heat. A lamp burned on one end table, and a book and afghan tossed aside testified to how his sister had spent the evening.

He settled opposite her on the comfy leather sofa. After a moment or two of small talk, he pinned her with a direct gaze. "Tell me what's wrong."

Sherry winced and closed her eyes, her chin trembling as her head fell against the back of the seat. "Debra's not coming back."

The sheer anguish in her blunt words made his heart break. He admired his sister more than anyone he knew. She'd gotten pregnant at seventeen—he was eleven at the time—and she had decided to keep her baby, despite the small-town gossip. She and Barry had married, and both of them managed to graduate from high school.

But the relationship had been a struggle from the beginning, and ten years ago, after a fairly amicable divorce, Barry moved to Florida. Since he and Sherry had joint custody, Debra spent a big chunk of the summer and parts of the holidays in Tampa.

Ethan knew Sherry missed having Christmas with her daughter this year, but his sister had seemed fine when he had dinner with her earlier in the week. He sighed. "What happened?"

Sherry fished a tissue from the pocket of her robe and blew

her nose. "She wants to live with Barry and enroll at the University of South Florida. Says she'll finish her undergraduate degree and then enter the college of marine science to get her master's." The last word ended on a hiccupped sob. "I'll never see her again."

The tears came in earnest now, and Ethan scooted over to hug her. Though she was older than he was, he'd always felt protective of his slender, petite sister. It hurt to see her so distraught.

He patted her shoulder awkwardly. "You can't be too surprised, honey." Debra had worked minimum-wage jobs for a couple of years after high school, because she had no idea what she wanted to do with her life. She finally enrolled in the local community college, and even then she'd seemed bored. But during the past summer while in Tampa, she had suddenly developed a passion for sea life. It was all she talked about when she came home.

Sherry regained her composure and blew her nose again. Now her expression was more resigned than tragic. "I know. I think I knew back in August, but I tried to ignore it. She says that U of SF is culturally diverse and offers things she can't get here."

"True." He was trying not to take sides.

Sherry smiled wryly. "You're not going to give me that speech about letting little birds fly, are you?"

He grinned, moving back to his own end of the sofa. "Do I need to?"

She wrinkled her nose. "I'm going to miss her so much." The chin wobble returned, and Ethan pretended not to notice. He'd miss his funny, outgoing niece as well, and it was hard to imagine a parent's struggle to let go.

Sherry reached for her half-empty glass of wine. "Do you want anything to drink?"

He shook his head. "I'm still technically on duty for another half hour. And besides, I'm wiped out. All I want to do is go home and crash."

She frowned at him. "You should have had a date tonight, Ethan. This is five years in a row you've worked New Year's Eve."

He shrugged. "Are you keeping count?" His immediate boss, the chief of police, was a hundred pounds overweight and ten months away from retirement. He could barely walk from his car to the building without wheezing. Ethan was pretty sure the most exercise he got was handing his paycheck to the teller at the drive-through window.

Which made Ethan the de facto guy in charge. He didn't waste time being resentful of the fact that he did his job and eighty percent of his boss's as well. It would all be worth it in the end.

Sherry still wore her big-sister face. "Don't try to be cute. And I'm not blaming this on anyone else. You volunteered, didn't you?"

He shrugged, far happier to discuss Sherry's life than his own. "It's no big deal."

Her expression gentled. "You can't let one broken engagement make you give up on women."

He stiffened. Sherry had the damnedest ability to hit a nerve. "I haven't given up on women. I date."

She took a sip of wine and eyed him accusingly over the rim. "Maybe twice in six months. For God's sake, Ethan, you're a healthy, virile man in his prime. You should be married and having babies by now."

He peeled out of his coat. "I love you, Sherry, but I'd rather not take romantic advice from my big sister, if you don't mind."

She paled. "You mean because I screwed up my own life so badly?"

He gaped. "Good Lord, no. Don't be ridiculous." He curled

a fist on his knee. "You made one mistake as a teenager—one that isn't all that uncommon, by the way. And you've spent every waking moment since trying to make up for it."

"I can't regret having Debra."

"Of course not. And I happen to know you did everything you could to make things work with Barry. But all of that is in the past. You've got to quit beating yourself up over it. You deserve to be happy. More than anyone I know."

Her smile was lopsided, her eyes moist. "Thanks, little brother. Right back atcha."

He handed her a handkerchief from his back pocket. "Your nose is getting red."

She managed a small laugh. "Okay, okay. I get it. I need to suck it up and quit moping."

He touched her cheek briefly. "Everyone has a right to be maudlin on New Year's Eve."

"Even you?"

He leaned back and spread both arms along the back of the sofa, yawning. "Nah, not me. I'm fine."

She rolled her eyes. "You are so not fine. You need a woman. What about Jane? You guys used to be glued at the hip. Whatever happened there?"

He moved uneasily. "Jane and I were buddies, that's all. Besides, she's not my type."

"What is your type?" Sherry tucked her feet beneath the hem of her robe and settled in for the inquisition.

Now he was wishing he'd taken the drink she offered. "I don't know. Small and blond and cuddly, I guess."

Sherry didn't say a word. She merely raised a very expressive eyebrow as if to say, *Just like your ex-fiancée? Your wacko, drama-queen, duplicitous ex-fiancée?*

The unspoken words hung between them, but Sherry didn't

force the point. She took another tack. "So you and Jane were never romantic?"

"I told you—no. We were pals."

"Explain that to me."

"You know. We hung out, played basketball together. Watched movies."

"Sounds a lot like dating."

"Well, it wasn't," he said stubbornly. "Jane was more like a sister."

"You have a sister," she pointed out, rather acerbically in his opinion. "Are you telling me you felt about Jane the way you do about me?"

*Whoa.* That was a weird thought. He loved Sherry. But Jane had always had a knack for making him feel like a man. She'd cheered his successes and comforted him on bad days. But romance . . . he didn't think so. There might have been times when the thought of kissing her had crossed his mind, but Jane's cheerful, uncomplicated personality had convinced him it was a stupid idea.

She was like one of the guys. She didn't wear a lot of makeup and gunk on her face. She could almost look him in the eye. Definitely not small and cuddly. But on the other hand . . .

Hell, it was pointless to rehash old friendships. That ship had sailed. But he knew Sherry would gnaw at the subject like a dog with a favorite bone if Ethan didn't distract her. Fortunately, he had a legitimate way to change the subject. He hoped.

He ran a hand over the back of his neck and squashed the tiny voice that told him his sister might be on to something. "No," he said slowly. "It wasn't the same at all. You *are* my sister. Jane was just . . . Jane. Can we please leave it at that?"

Sherry wanted to argue. He could tell. But perhaps her emotional meltdown earlier had taken a lot out of her, because she nodded slowly. "Fine." She mimicked zipping her lip and tossing the key.

He chuckled. "Actually, there's one more thing I want to talk to you about. I know it's late, so you don't have to give me an answer tonight. But I was wondering if you might be interested in catering lunches for the police station a couple or three days a week."

"Are you serious?" She looked completely dumfounded, and Ethan shook his head in amazement. She really didn't appreciate her own strengths.

He leaned forward, smelling the wood smoke and wishing he had such a cozy home. "You're a fabulous cook, Sherry. I know you've worked only part-time at the animal shelter because you've wanted to be available for Debra. She wasn't an easy teen to raise, Lord knows. But now with her being on Barry's turf, you'll have some extra time on your hands."

She bit her lip. "You don't have to find things for me to do, Ethan."

He shook his head. "I'd already been kicking this idea around, but now it seems perfect. Most of the guys don't take time to bring a lunch from home, so they end up going out for fast food every day. And you know what happens then, even to the young ones. They start packing on the pounds."

"So you want me to fix diet food?" Her expression was skeptical.

"No. Just healthy, satisfying meals that will be good for all of us. I want to institute some fitness standards, but . . ."

She caught on immediately. "But until the big guy retires, your hands are tied."

He nodded. "Exactly. So in the meantime, healthy eating, especially if it's homemade food they don't have to prepare themselves, sounds like a win-win situation. They'll all pay cash on the spot, and you could determine cost. What do you think?"

Her eyes narrowed, and he could see a flicker of interest on her face. "I do love to cook."

He smirked. "Well, there you go. Problem solved. I'll keep you so busy you won't have time to miss Debra."

Her tears and the wobbly chin returned, and he cursed under his breath. "Hell, I'm sorry, Sherry." He pulled her close for one last hug before he got to his feet and retrieved his coat. He'd love to crash on her couch until morning, but he needed to stop back by the station.

She had risen to her feet as well, and he chucked her under the chin. "Don't worry, sis. It will get easier, I promise."

She sniffed and handed him back his handkerchief. He took it gingerly and stuffed it in his pocket.

When she rose up on tiptoe to give him a buss on the cheek, she smiled slyly. "I'll make you a deal, Ethan."

He didn't trust her sudden smile. It made him nervous. "What do you mean?"

"I'll take on your catering project if you'll swear to me that you'll start dating again."

"I told you," he said, sidling toward the front door for a clean escape, "I date."

"You can't con me, baby brother. I'm talking about a meaningful relationship with an available woman."

He felt the noose tighten about his neck, but he was too proud and stubborn to retract his culinary offer. Surely he could find someone to have dinner with a few times . . . long enough to get his sister off his back.

He realized that he had another weapon in his emotional arsenal. "The same goes for you, then."

Sherry looked blank. "What do you mean? I *was* married. I have a kid."

He grinned at her with genuine affection. "You're also still young and very eligible." The sheer apprehension on her face made him laugh, entirely without sympathy. "Kind of scary, isn't it?"

"It's not the same thing at all," she said, practically choking on the words.

"Think about it," he said, his hand on the door. "If you're going to push me out of the nest into the cold cruel dating world, then I'm sure as hell dragging you with me."

# *Two*

Jane had one entire day to procrastinate. After all, there was no mail pickup on January first. But the following morning, her nagging subconscious started demanding that she mail the valentine that lay on the antique bureau in her bedroom.

Actually, the lavender envelope looked so pretty against her embroidered dresser scarf that she almost hated to send it on its way. The words inside were emblazoned in her memory. She'd finished off the five-stanza poem with a carefully disguised signature.

It was doubtful that Ethan would recognize her handwriting after all this time, but just in case, she had used block letters and signed the card, *Your devoted admirer.*

Was that a bit over-the-top? Or in the world of erotic love notes, were there actually no rules at all?

She'd found a feminine-looking postage stamp in her desk and carefully stuck it in the upper-right-hand corner of the scented envelope. Which left the other corner empty. Well, poop. The USPS frowned on mail with no return address. Already she was feeling guilty, and she hadn't even sent the darn thing yet.

She thought about inventing a return address to make it look more official. But what if falsifying a return address was a federal offense? And if sending pornography through the mail could get you thrown in jail, where did things stand in terms of erotic valentines?

She carried the not so innocent missive downstairs with her and hid it under a large book in the office. Thirty minutes later, she opened the front door at ten sharp and was pleasantly surprised when morning business started off at a brisk pace.

She specialized in stationery, gifts, and supplies for dedicated scrapbookers—archival paper and albums, scissors that cut decorative edges, themed stickers and borders . . . you name it. And if a customer wanted something she didn't have in stock, she was always happy to order it.

The woman who helped out part-time from eleven to three every day was still out of town for the holidays visiting relatives in California. So at lunchtime, Jane put her pretty BE BACK SOON sign in the front window and walked the block and a half to the post office. The naughty valentine lay safely hidden in a pocket of her oversize black leather purse.

She bypassed the box near the street and climbed the shallow stairs to the entrance. All the mail from the boxes around town, even the one just outside, was collected and taken for sorting to a main facility in Knoxville. But inside this local branch, it was possible to deposit a letter in the slot marked STATLERVILLE. That mail was handled locally, postmarked, and then delivered in town without ever leaving the city limits. Which was perfect for Jane's planned seduction.

Barring unseen complications, she could always be sure that

the notes she mailed on Thursdays would be safely in Ethan's possession the following day. Each of the six Fridays between now and February fourteenth.

She waited until a little burst of activity cleared out. She perused the wanted posters, faintly surprised that such things still existed. She picked up an express-mail box and studied it intently. Then finally, the last of the customers loitering in the lobby exited.

With her stomach churning, her heart knocking in her chest, and her hands clammy, she withdrew the valentine from her purse and thrust it in the mail slot before she could change her mind.

Ethan greeted Friday with the wonderful realization that he had Saturday off, and not one damn thing he absolutely *had* to do other than sleep late, be a couch potato all day, and relax. It sounded too good to be true, and consequently, Friday dragged on and on.

He was working another long evening shift, thanks to his boss. The big cheese claimed to have come down with the flu. But Ethan had a strong suspicion that the man wanted to stay home and watch the last of the bowl games.

Ethan yawned and squinted at the numbers on the page he had just printed out. He was working on an end-of-year report about prisoner statistics that was due in to the state by the fifteenth. He still had plenty of time, but he hated this kind of task and wanted to get it over with.

Just after midnight, he wandered out of his office to get some fresh coffee. He happened to be standing near the dispatcher when the 911 call came in, and his blood ran cold when he recognized not only the address but the voice as well. He grabbed one of his officers, and they set off with sirens blazing.

Ethan jammed on the brakes and screeched to a halt four minutes later. Paper Pleasures was dark and showed no signs of activity, but when Ethan and the officer jumped out of the car to investigate, they found that a side window facing the alley had been smashed in. Glass littered the ground, and just inside the window, a display case had been knocked over, presumably when the intruder entered.

Ethan's heart in his throat, he made contact with the dispatcher, who had stayed on the line with Jane. "Tell her we're here," he croaked. "It's okay to come out." The 911 employee had cautioned Jane to lock herself in the office and stay put.

The young officer pulled out his kit and began collecting evidence while Ethan went around to the front and waited. He shifted anxiously from foot to foot until Jane turned on the outside light and opened the door. Her eyes were huge and dark in her pale face.

She seemed shocked to see him, but she backed up and allowed him to enter. "Ethan?" There was a quaver in her voice. "I didn't expect you to show up. Should I be honored to warrant a visit from the assistant police chief?" The transparent attempt at levity fell flat. Her arms were wrapped around her waist as though she was trying to hold herself together.

He wanted to hug her, but he felt the awkwardness of their long separation between them. So he contented himself with studying her face. "Are you okay?"

She was wearing a long, fuzzy bathrobe in baby blue. It matched her eyes, and he remembered that blue was her favorite color. The random thought made him uneasy, so he cleared his throat. "Jane?" She still hadn't answered him.

She clutched the lapels of the robe in one hand and nodded jerkily. "I'm fine."

Her pupils were dilated, and even her lips were pale. He

smiled reassuringly. "Why don't we go sit down and you can tell me what happened?"

It took her a moment to process his request, and he realized she might be a bit shocky. In her crowded office he forced her gently into a chair and draped his jacket around her shoulders. On the long, scarred wooden worktable, Jane had a microwave and tea bags, so in barely more than a minute, Ethan was able to hand her a warm mug and watch as she cradled it in her palms before finally taking a sip. He'd loaded the drink with sugar, and he saw her wince at the first taste.

When she had downed half the contents and had a bit of color back in her cheeks, he finally questioned her. "Okay, Jane. Tell me what happened. Everything you can remember. Even if it seems insignificant."

She licked her lips and brushed her hair away from her face. The style was shorter than he remembered, barely brushing her shoulders, but it was the same lovely caramel color, struck through with highlights of cinnamon and pale honey. She swallowed. "I couldn't sleep. So I came downstairs around eleven thirty to look over some orders and invoices. I lost track of time, but I think it was about thirty minutes later. . . ."

"When you heard something?"

She nodded jerkily. "There was a loud crash and then I heard footsteps in the shop."

"What did you do?"

She took another sip of tea, burying her nose in the steam before meeting his concerned gaze. "I tiptoed across my office and locked the door." She faltered, her eyes brimming with tears. "It couldn't have been more than fifteen seconds, but I felt like I was walking in slow motion. If I hadn't been quick enough . . . if he'd had a gun . . ."

He couldn't help himself this time. He pulled a stool, the only other seat in the room, close to her and laid a hand on her arm. "You're okay, Jane. You did the right thing. Most burglaries happen when no one is home. That's how the B-and-E guys like it. So it was sheer bad luck that you came downstairs. He wasn't counting on that. He probably bolted when he got far enough inside to see the light coming from beneath the office door."

She nodded, the overhead fluorescent light emphasizing her pallor.

She didn't seem to notice that he had touched her, so he withdrew his hand. It was unprofessional at best, but he didn't think anyone would fault him for trying to comfort a woman who was so obviously shaken.

Jane had always struck him as a calm, self-possessed female, not at all prone to hysteria. But what had transpired this evening would upset anyone, and all things considered, he thought she was handling herself pretty well.

She shivered hard. He realized that the frigid air pouring through the busted-out window had filtered to the back of the shop. He could handle it, even without his coat, but Jane was in a vulnerable state. He glanced down at her feet and cursed as he realized for the first time that her slender feet were bare.

He ground his teeth, trying to remember that she had dealt with a lot tonight and didn't need him berating her. Biting back his scolding words, he stood, took the cup from her, and set it aside.

When he scooped her up in his arms, she flailed wildly. "Put me down."

He grunted and nearly dropped her. "Be still, for God sakes."

She continued to struggle, traces of pink blooming on her cheeks. Her expression was mortified. "I'm too heavy, Ethan. Don't be ridiculous."

He had already reached the foot of the staircase leading up to her apartment. "You're tall," he said, breathing heavily. "There's a difference."

Her foot hit the wall as he moved up the stairs. He muttered an apology and hitched her a bit higher in his arms. Her bare toes struck him as sexy, and the thought made him uncomfortable, especially considering the fact that her left breast was nestled against his chest. He could smell her soap and a faint trace of perfume.

Where her head rested on his shoulder, strands of her hair tickled his chin. It was disconcerting as hell.

On the second floor, he thought about setting her on her feet, but he'd made it this far, so he might as well finish his chivalrous posturing. He spotted her bedroom through an open door and managed to maneuver through it without doing any further damage to his cargo.

He dropped her on the bed and ignored his aching back. Instead, he turned to the dresser and yanked open a drawer. "Where are your socks?" He tossed the question over his shoulder and froze when the first thing his hand touched was a hot pink bra.

He dropped it like it was a poisonous snake and moved one drawer down. "Jane?"

"One more," she said. Her voice sounded stronger, and he thought she might possibly be laughing at him.

He sighed in relief when he found a pair of wool hiking socks. As he replaced the drawers, his mind flitted back to a beautiful spring day when he and Jane had hiked in the Smokies. They'd laughed and talked, and at the top of a steep incline, they had simply paused to savor the view.

His chest tightened as awareness slammed into him of how much he missed those fun-filled times with Jane. She was easy to be with, and he had always felt comfortable and relaxed around her.

But somehow . . . not today.

He turned to face her and couldn't quite meet her eyes, particularly when his breathing fractured as he sat down beside her and slid first one sock and then the other onto her icy feet. He tried not to notice the sensual arch of each foot or the pretty pink polish that made her toes look cute and kissable.

Kissable? Holy hell. What was wrong with him? This was a crime scene. He was the assistant chief of police. He had work to do.

He stood and backed away from the bed. "If you have cardboard and duct tape downstairs, I'll cover up the window until I can get someone here tomorrow."

She gave him the information in a low voice and he managed to look at her without flinching. Her wide-eyed stare told him she must have picked up on his agitation. She managed a small smile. "Thank you for doing that. But you'll need your coat back if you're going outside."

He put in on and shrugged, shoving his hands in his pockets. "No problem. Stay under the covers and get warm. I'll be back up to check on you when we're finished."

Jane had never experienced such a far-reaching range of emotions in one short two-hour period. First it was the frustration of insomnia brought on by the sick feeling that her valentine agenda was doomed to failure. Then later terror, relief, joy at seeing Ethan, and bafflement and surprise at his tenderness. Embarrassment as he struggled up the stairs with her. Finally a flood of nostalgia for what had once been and now was lost.

But his concern warmed her heart, made her feel like he still cared for her after all. Maybe not what she felt but something.

She scooted down in the bed and huddled under the covers. For some reason, she couldn't stop shaking, and her stomach felt queasy. She had always felt so safe in her little abode, and she loved being able to walk down the steps to work. The police station was only three blocks away, so that had convinced her she would never have to worry about being the victim of crime.

Hard to admit she had been a naive fool.

Early on she had considered installing a security system, but her shop sold paper and note cards and pens, for heaven's sake. Not exactly the kind of stuff someone could sell for drug money.

She could hear the two men moving around downstairs, and she wondered bleakly how she was ever going to feel safe again. Would she be doomed to sleepless nights wondering if someone was going to climb the stairs and stab or rape her while she slept? She knew her vivid imagination was not going to make this whole thing any easier.

It was almost another hour before she heard Ethan's footsteps in the hall. She scooted up against the headboard and smoothed her hair.

Her first thought when he entered the room was that he looked exhausted. His jet-black hair was rumpled and his gray eyes were dull with fatigue.

Though it wasn't her fault, she felt guilty anyway. Call it the curse of her gender.

Suddenly, she had to know. "Have you been home today?"

He frowned, removing his jacket and tossing it on a chair. "No. Why?"

She waved a hand. "No reason." *I merely wanted to know if you had opened your mail.*

He perched on the foot of her bed and stared at her. "I sent my officer and the squad car back to the station. My shift ended at one thirty. Would you like me to stay with you? As I recall, your sofa is pretty comfortable."

He asked it prosaically. Not a hint of flirting or sexual intent.

Nevertheless, her nipples tightened, and her legs stirred restlessly beneath the covers. *Did she want him to stay? Only for the rest of her life.* She gripped the edge of the blanket with both hands. "That's not necessary. I'll be fine."

Apparently she was a lousy liar. One corner of his mouth kicked up in a wry grin. "No need for heroics, Jane. Anybody in this situation would be spooked."

She sighed. "Not you." She couldn't imagine Ethan being afraid of anything. He was strong and confident, and even the benign arrogance he sometimes displayed could be discounted in light of the fact that his assurance was backed up with the ability to handle a crisis.

He ignored her last comment. "Tell me where to find a blanket and pillow."

"In the hall closet."

He disappeared, and immediately her bedroom felt colder, more lonely.

She heard water running in the bathroom across the hall, and then he poked his head in the door a few moments later. "Good night, Jane."

"Good night."

When he turned off her light, she slid down beneath the covers and curled into a ball. As soon as she closed her eyes, she was suddenly back in the midst of that terrifying few minutes. Her stomach rolled, and she broke out in a cold sweat. Oh, God, she had never been so scared in her life. There was no way to know if the intruder had been armed, but if he had, she could be dead right now.

Finished. Over.

She sat up quickly and reached for the lamp beside her bed. Her breathing was rough and jerky, and she didn't pause to weigh the risks of what she was about to do.

"Ethan?" She called out, her voice just short of shrill. She hated the panicky, needy wave of emotion that tightened her chest.

He didn't bother answering. In a nanosecond, he appeared in her doorway, his hair tousled, his chest completely bare. "What's wrong?" The urgency in his voice matched the speed at which he stumbled into the room and came to a sudden stop within feet of her bed.

She surrendered the last of her pride. Gave up any remnants of poise. "Will you talk to me . . . until I fall asleep?" It was a stark request borne of the need for comfort and a desperate urge to be close to him.

Something flashed across his face. Lord, she hoped it wasn't pity. In all her imaginings, she had never envisioned fate bringing Ethan back into her life like this. She—the poor, rattled female. Ethan—wondering how he had been unlucky enough to get saddled with a semihysterical crime victim.

He ran both hands through his hair, and in better circumstances, Jane might have swooned. The muscles that rippled in his arms and torso were even more impressive than she remembered from those long-ago times at the lake, or on the court at the YMCA, playing shirts and skins. But not in bed. Not in intimacy. He shrugged, his face impassive. "Sure."

He retrieved his pillow and blanket and brought them back to her room. For the first time, she saw his confidence waver. He clearly didn't know how to proceed.

She took pity on him. "It's okay to lie down. I know you must be exhausted."

He took her at her word, settling on his back on top of her

comforter, flipping the blanket out to settle over his legs, and tucking his hands behind his head.

She felt breathless, as if he had sucked all the air out of the room. But she also felt something else—peace. With Ethan by her side, the bad guys were exiled to some other place. She'd been standing on her own two feet for a long time. But tonight, just this once, she needed to lean on someone.

She couldn't believe she wasn't hyperventilating. Ethan Oldham was in her bed. And he hadn't even received her first erotic valentine. She closed her eyes, feeling the inexorable pull of fatigue. All her adrenaline had winnowed away, and she felt battered in mind and body.

Ethan stirred beside her. "Do you want me to turn out the light?" His voice was husky. She kept her eyes closed, unable to summon the strength to look at him. It was enough to sense his warm, hard body so close. To know that he was there.

She curled on her side, facing him, moments away from sleep. "Do you mind if we keep it on for a while? Will it keep you awake?"

*Will it keep you awake?* Jane's voice was slurred. Ethan shifted his hips and found a comfortable spot, one that carefully maintained a sizable "no-touching" zone. The lamp was the least of his worries. He had never felt less like sleeping, even though he was damn tired.

She had asked him to talk to her, but he sensed it was going to be unnecessary. Already her breathing was steady. She had her hands tucked beneath her cheek. Like a little child. But there was nothing childish about Jane. She was soft and sweet-smelling, and the boorish male inside him was in danger of kicking the gentlemanly Ethan's ass. The urge to spread her long legs and mount her throbbed in his gut.

He had a massive erection, and it both shocked and dismayed him. He'd never lusted after Jane. They had been friends. Good friends. But somehow that familiar relationship, the one he'd thought long since destroyed, had evidently been lying dormant, ready to reappear in a newer, definitely more alarming manifestation.

He closed his eyes and courted sleep. For the first time, his brain clicked over from a professional assessment of what had happened tonight to a far more personal realization. Jane might have been badly hurt. Perhaps killed.

The thought shook him. Even in a quiet town like Statlerville, violence was a reality. Humans did unspeakable things to one another at times. But he knew the value of keeping a one-step-removed perspective.

In order to do his job, he had to keep his emotions in check. He might react to a crime scene with pity, or sorrow, or occasionally even shock and horror. But those human feelings, if he allowed them to take precedence over his instincts and his training, would merely get in the way of doing his job.

But nothing about tonight seemed familiar. Not his reaction to the initial 911 call. Not the strangling rush of fear he'd felt for a woman from his past. Not the urge to protect and care for Jane.

If anyone had told him yesterday that tonight he'd be in Jane's bedroom, in her bed, he'd have laughed.

But at the moment, humor was the last thing on his mind. He moved restlessly and grunted when pain shot through his lower back. He was going to pay, no doubt, for his Rhett Butler imitation.

He sighed and pulled the blanket up to his chin. If he'd ever felt more out of his element, he couldn't remember when. He was the assistant chief of police. Nowhere in his job description did it list "spending the night with a victim." He could have called his sister. She and Jane knew each other.

He could have suggested Jane go to a motel for the night until the window could be replaced. He could have offered to park a squad car at the front door. To deter any further mischief.

But no. He'd had to be all gallant and macho and offer his services as a babysitter. And tomorrow, when Jane was once again her usual confident, assertive self, this two-on-a-mattress scenario was bound to be embarrassing for both of them.

He abandoned his perusal of her ceiling and turned his head to look at her. Her skin was creamy in the soft lamplight, her bare lips blush pink. . . .

She still wore the blue robe, but without her death grip at the collar, the material had gaped open to reveal a V-neck sleep shirt, which offered him a mouthwatering glimpse of her firm, curvy breasts. He gulped and dragged his gaze away. His unintentional voyeurism smacked of taking advantage of Jane's vulnerable state.

He closed his eyes and inhaled, noticing the faint mix of scents that were so uniquely Jane. Suddenly, the conversation with his sister came back to him. The one where he had promised to date seriously.

Of course, he'd had his fingers figuratively crossed behind his back. He had every intention of weaseling out of that agreement. But it seemed like an odd karmic twist that Sherry had mentioned Jane just a few days ago, and then—bam . . .

He had reason to know that karma could be a twisted bitch with a sick sense of humor, and he had learned the hard way to proceed with caution in matters of the heart. A philosophy that in the last four years had translated to keeping his relations with the opposite sex infrequent and impersonal.

Jane was a wonderful person. They had once been very good

friends. But that was a long time ago. And just because being here in this apartment—hell, in this *bed*—made him feel some really odd but kind of sweet emotions. . . . Well, that was probably nothing more than a potent cocktail of nostalgia and bone-deep weariness.

He reached out to brush a strand of hair from her cheek. His hand froze in midair. *No. Don't go there.* Deliberately, he lowered his arm, turned his back on her, and closed his eyes. He didn't need more complications in his life. He needed sleep.

## Three

Jane surfaced slowly from a night of deep, almost drugged sleep. Even trapped by the lingering mists of weird dreams, she was aware that light filtered into the room. But it was the weak, chill light of a winter's day.

She huddled under the covers, savoring the warmth of her comfy bed. Before she opened her eyes, she took stock. In barely the time it took her to draw a breath, everything came flooding back. The break-in. Ethan showing up. Ethan staying.

She lifted one eyelid a fraction and checked out the bed. Ethan's side was empty, the covers smooth, his blanket and pillow nowhere to be seen.

Had she dreamed the entire thing?

She listened intently. Outdoor noises in the distance were familiar, but the only sound in her apartment was the quiet ticking of an antique mantel clock that had been her grandmother's.

She reared up on one elbow and saw a note on her night-stand. With trembling fingers, she opened it.

*Dear Jane:*

*I'll send someone over first thing to get the window replaced. We were able to recover a few partial fingerprints. I'll keep you posted on the investigation. Let me know if I can be of help in any way.*

*Sincerely,*
*Ethan*

That was it. Short and sweet. She swallowed her disappointment and forced herself to get out of bed. Her body felt old and tired, as if she had done hard physical labor yesterday. Her aches and pains were no doubt the remnants of stress and fear. In the light of day, her behavior embarrassed her.

When Ethan had offered to stay last night, she should have turned him down. Her apartment had a sturdy lock on the door. Even with an open window downstairs, she would have been perfectly safe.

It was impossible to forget his kindness, the gentle way he comforted her and took command of the situation. But she didn't want to be seen as a victim. The whole point of sending the erotic valentines was to woo him with the image of a sexy, take-charge woman. One who wasn't afraid to go after what she wanted.

Instead, Ethan's first real contact with her in four years had shown her in a less than confident light. She'd had just cause to be shaken, but even so . . . She didn't want to be listed in his mental Rolodex as "police business." She wanted to be his "personal business"—very personal.

Had Ethan opened her valentine yet?

His home was walking distance from downtown, but on the opposite side of the courthouse. A long time ago, while he and Jane were still close friends, he had bought a lovely condo. It sat in a development of a dozen or more that had been built to blend in with the ambience of the historic district. He'd even enlisted Jane's help with some of the decorating.

Without a car at his disposal, he'd probably walked the mile and a half or so home this morning. If he'd gone home at all. Maybe he'd gone straight to work. The station had a locker room with showers, so he might have cleaned up there.

She stared at her reflection in the bathroom mirror and made a face. *Quit obsessing about Ethan and show some gumption, Jane, my girl.* The woman in the mirror was unfortunately not inclined to be cooperative. All the while she was dressing and eating breakfast, her heart was flipping and skittering all over the place.

Ethan had slept in her bed last night. That had to be a good sign . . . right?

She made it downstairs on time and was relieved to get a phone call from Mrs. Fitzhugh. She had come home a bit early and was ready to work.

Jane had barely hung up the phone in the office when a racket from the other room made her heart jump. In the next breath she chided herself. No one was going to burglarize the premises in broad daylight. She left the office and shivered as she realized the cardboard covering the window was gone. Through the empty hole she saw the head and shoulders of a grizzled, heavyset man. He must have been standing on a step ladder, because the window was a good seven feet off the ground.

He looked up and gave a brusque nod. "Tony Caldwell. Chief Oldham sent me. I'm licensed to work on historic buildings. Shame about this window. It was the original glass, probably over a hundred years old."

As she watched, he carefully tugged at the remnants of broken glass that were still stuck in the wooden frame. She bit her lip. "Do you have an estimate for me?" Her business ran on a tight budget, but if she could afford it, she'd rather deal with the repair out of her pocket than bother her landlord.

Tony shook his head. "No charge. I'm doing this for the chief."

She frowned. "It's not the chief's responsibility to get my window fixed."

He kept his head bent to his task. "Don't know about that. Alls I know is that Chief Oldham kept my boy out of jail, and I'm much obliged to him. I do top-notch work. You'll be good as new by closing today." And then he turned away and went down the ladder for another piece of equipment.

Jane wrapped her long, coat-style sweater more tightly around her. Perhaps she should have closed up shop until Monday, but Saturday was her best day in terms of sales, and she hated to lose the much-needed income.

She found the broom and started sweeping up glass. Ethan and the deputy must have righted the display case before they left, because it was in its original position. A few things had been damaged too badly to sell, but they were negligible. She tossed the torn journals and smashed figurines into the trash bin along with four dust pans full of glass fragments. A phone call to her weekly cleaning crew would take care of the rest.

By the time Mrs. Fitzhugh arrived at eleven, the shop looked fairly normal, barring the continuing work on the window. Jane spent a few minutes explaining the situation to her employee and then excused herself to run errands. No need to go into details.

Her first stop was the police station. She owed Ethan a polite thank-you. That was all. She wasn't planning to mention specifics, like how well she had slept with him in touching distance.

Nor how she could swear she smelled his scent in her tiny bath-room. None of that.

The uniformed female clerk at the front desk looked at her curiously, but answered politely, "Chief Oldham is off today, ma'am. And tomorrow. But I'll be happy to take a message."

Jane knew she was blushing. "Um, no, thanks. It's not impor-tant. Thank you." She hightailed it out of there and stood on the sidewalk pondering her options. The midday sun beamed down, and the temperature had climbed into the lower forties. She had a scarf and mittens. The distance to his house wasn't all that far.

Her feet made the decision, and the rest of her followed. She walked briskly, invigorated by the crisp air and the jolt of deter-mination that filled her. She'd sent the first valentine. She was ac-tually going to Ethan's home to thank him for last night. She was being proactive, assertive. A woman in charge of her destiny.

Her courage lasted all the way to his front door. When she rang the bell and stood there with no answer for several minutes, she prepared to slink away. His car was in the driveway. Clearly, he didn't want to see her.

Stubbornly, she rang the bell one more time. She could swear she heard a sound from inside. Cautiously, she twisted the door-knob. It was unlocked. She eased open the door a couple of inches. "Ethan?"

What if he was sleeping? What if he was upstairs having car-nal relations with a strange woman? Her stomach churned, and she backed up slowly, when suddenly, she was sure she heard something from the back of the house . . . a voice.

"Ethan?" This time there was no mistaking it. He was calling for her to come in.

With her heart in her throat, she entered his foyer and shut the door behind her. She stripped off her outer garments and car-ried them over her arm as she walked down the hall.

She found him in the den. It was a toss-up as to which of the two of them was more surprised.

Ethan lay on his back on the carpeted floor, his knees bent with a pillow beneath them, his head unsupported in any way. The position looked monumentally uncomfortable.

He flushed a dark red and mumbled something.

"What did you say?" She hovered in the doorway.

He frowned. "I thought you were Sherry."

She shook her head. "No." Great, just great. Two of the world's most scintillating conversationalists. She leaned against the doorframe. "Why are you on the floor?" A basketball game played on the big-screen TV, and there was a host of comfy seating options. It didn't make sense.

He muttered again, and she became impatient. "Ethan, speak up. What are you doing down there?"

She couldn't decipher the mix of expressions on his face. But agitation and disgruntlement topped the list. "I threw my back out." He spit the words at her between clenched teeth, clearing suffering from this blow to his masculine pride. Men were such babies.

And then it hit her. Oh, God. Her eyes widened, and mortification swamped her, making her knees weak. He'd injured himself carrying her up the stairs. "Humiliation" was a mild word for what she was experiencing.

She stared up at the ceiling, her nose scrunched up, as she felt hot color rush from her throat to her hairline. "I told you I weighed too much for that stunt. Lord, Ethan, I am so sorry."

He shifted and groaned as pain drew his face in sharp lines. "You're not heavy," he insisted with laudable but inaccurate insistence.

She sighed, finally approaching him and perching on the edge of the sofa. "I'm five foot eleven, Ethan. I'm definitely not the soft and cuddly type."

Their eyes met, and suddenly she knew that he knew what they were both thinking. His ex-fiancée was just that kind of woman. One a man could scoop up with ease.

Jane was close enough now to nudge him with her foot, if she'd been inclined. Guilt and embarrassment threatened to choke her.

He reached out carefully and touched her ankle. "You're a very beautiful woman, Jane."

The sincerity in his voice, combined with his fingers on the bare skin where her sock met her pants leg, made her giddy. She didn't know how to respond, so she simply said, "Thank you."

She sat back on the sofa, breaking the connection between them. "Are you taking anything?"

He was wearing jeans and a much-washed green, cotton knit shirt. His big feet were bare, and she wondered if they were cold.

He tried to move again, and groaned. "The doctor has called in a prescription for some muscle relaxers. Sherry's going to pick them up on her way back from Knoxville."

"When will that be?"

"Later this afternoon."

"That's too long," she said. "There's no reason for you to suffer until then. I'll go get them."

It was a measure of his pain that he didn't waste time arguing. He named the pharmacy and pointed her to his billfold on the coffee table.

She paused in the doorway. "Would you like me to get you anything before I go? A drink, maybe?"

"Yeah. A Diet Coke would be great. And there are some straws in the drawer beside the stove."

Jane remembered the kitchen. She'd helped him pick out the navy-and-citrus valances over the windows, along with the set of placemats he was still using. It made her feel strange to see them. But not nearly as much as when she spotted the stack of mail on the bar.

Oh. My. God. His keys lay beside the mail as though he had made it that far and no farther. None of the envelopes were open. He'd simply dropped the stack when he came in and left it alone. It wasn't hard to spot her valentine. All the rest of the envelopes were white except for one neon orange flyer for a pizza parlor, and the lavender one that held Jane's naughty verse.

All the while she was opening the fridge, pulling out the canned drink, and retrieving the straw, her mind raced feverishly. Should she take the card back? Now that she and Ethan were on speaking terms once more, wouldn't it be smarter simply to build on that connection?

Erotic valentines suddenly seemed like the stupidest idea on the planet.

But what if he remembered seeing her lavender envelope? Wouldn't he get suspicious if it disappeared? And besides, tampering with the U.S. mail was a felony. Forgetting a return address was child's play compared to that.

She left the pile of mail untouched and took Ethan his drink. He struggled up on one elbow far enough to take one long swig of liquid. Then, his face taut with discomfort, he eased back to a supine position.

She hovered anxiously, feeling totally helpless and completely responsible. "Can I do anything for you? Rub something . . . ?"

His bark of laughter sent another wave of heat over her face. He managed a tight grin. "Just the pills, honey. Just the pills."

She escaped then, grabbing up the keys he had given her permission to use and heading outside for his car. The whole trip took her less than thirty minutes, including the quick stop at Paper Pleasures to check and make sure things were under control.

The man Ethan had sent was making good progress with the window replacement, and Mrs. Fitzhugh reported a steady stream of customers. Jane had created a Valentine's Day display in the front window on the afternoon of January first, so perhaps the early birds were already scooping up all sorts of romantic gifts and supplies.

She stayed barely five minutes at her shop, anxious to get back to Ethan. When she let herself in his front door, the silence resonated. She tiptoed back to the den and found him sleeping. Quietly she placed the pharmacy bag in his reach and straightened up.

Her heart turned over in her chest. In his reclining position and with his eyes closed—long, thick lashes brushing his cheeks—he looked softer, more approachable. She had to admit that she was a little in awe of his job and the responsibility he bore.

Ethan made a difference in this community. Everyone knew it was only a matter of time until he was in charge of the station. And Jane had a suspicion that even though he showed his boss the utmost respect, there would be positive changes when the chief finally stepped down.

She gnawed her bottom lip, hating to leave the medicine on the floor beside Ethan and disappear. But she also didn't want to wake him. Neither of them had slept enough the night before.

Carefully, making hardly any sound at all, she removed her outer garments, kicked off her shoes, and eased onto the sofa. She pulled the afghan over her, intending to rest for a few minutes until he stirred.

*Ethan came to her in a dream. He knelt beside the sofa where she reclined and leaned over to kiss her. His lips were firm and warm. They moved against her mouth with wicked skill, coaxing her to open for him.*

*When his tongue played with hers, she moaned. Something hot and sweet bloomed between her legs, deep in the heart of her sex. She moved restlessly.*

*He eased her into a sitting position and removed her pants. She should have been embarrassed. But all she felt was arousal . . . insistent, irresistible, deliciously naughty. Ethan's hands were on her thighs, gently pushing them apart. He smiled, a knowing male smile that promised all sorts of delights.*

*When he separated the lips of her sex with his thumbs, she squirmed restlessly. "Ethan." She breathed his name on a sigh.*

*He bent his head and put his mouth at her center. His warm breath against her damp flesh fanned her arousal. When the tip of his tongue brushed her clitoris, she shivered and trembled. She felt both helpless and powerful, torn between the aching need for release and the triumphant knowledge that Ethan was finally hers.*

*She moved her legs wider, cradling his head, her fingers in his hair. He thrust his tongue inside her, and she cried out as her climax ripped through her. She was still lost in the aftermath when he drew her to the floor and thrust hard between her legs.*

*His penis was thick and heavily aroused. She was caught between the hard floor at her back and the heavy male pressing her down into the rug. His eyes flashed with determination, his mouth sharp-drawn, his skin flushed.*

*Again and again he took her. She felt a second orgasm swell and torment her. Her throat was dry, her eyes burning with tears. So long . . . she had waited so long.*

*With one last series of pistonlike moves, he pounded into her. Her strangled cry mingled with his hoarse shout as they tumbled together into a clinging, simultaneous release.*

Ethan opened his eyes and thought he was still dreaming. Jane was on his sofa, sound asleep. For one unguarded moment, he fantasized about standing over her, undressing them both, and joining her on the couch for a long, wonderful afternoon of lovemaking.

He shook his head to clear the disturbing images and paid dearly for his unwitting movement. Sharp pain shot from his neck to his hips, gripping him in a vise of unrelenting tension.

Damn it all to hell. He reached for the medicine Jane had thoughtfully placed in his reach and took the small orange bottle out of the sack. Moving as few muscles as possible, he shook two tablets into his palm, put them in his mouth, and swallowed them with the last of his soft drink.

His shaky groan disturbed Jane when he subsided once again onto the floor.

She shoved her hair back as she sat up and tossed the afghan aside. "You should have let me help you," she said, frowning slightly. "And are you sure you should even be on the floor? You look really uncomfortable."

He clenched his jaw, willing the muscle relaxers to work quickly. "I've done this a couple of times before, and the doc says this is the smartest thing to do. It keeps my back perfectly straight."

She grinned at him, a lovely, uncomplicated smile that went straight to his gut and took his breath away even more than the pain had. "So you've been carrying around other hefty females?"

He grimaced. "Quit fishing for compliments. You know you look like a model. And no, you're the only woman I've carried up stairs."

*A model?* She tucked that amazing, matter-of-fact compliment away to savor later. "Then how did it happen those other times?"

"Doc says stress is the culprit. Tenses up the muscles all over the body, and then one wrong movement and pow—out goes the back."

"You do work awfully hard."

He seemed uncomfortable with her implied praise. "I need to spend more time at the gym. I want to institute some fitness routines with the men once the chief is gone. They'll laugh in my face if I can't even straighten up. Which reminds me . . . " He looked at her cajolingly. "You'll keep this between us . . . right?"

She stood up and fussed with the afghan, folding it in perfect ninety-degree angles. "Your secret's safe with me." Then she stepped into her shoes. "I need to go. Mrs. Fitzhugh leaves at three. But I'll be back to bring you some supper."

His face was oddly blank. "You don't have to do that, Jane."

She shrugged. "I know. But after last night, I'd like a chance to show my appreciation. That was why I came by originally. To say thank you."

She glanced around the room. "Do you need anything else?"

He twisted his lips, clearly hating to ask for help of any kind. "Would you please put the afghan over my feet and legs?"

She swallowed hard. "Sure." Piece of cake. First, approach large, hard-bodied male . . . then cover him. No problem.

Or it shouldn't have been. But in the aftermath of an extremely vivid carnal dream, her hands were clumsy, and her feet even more so. She ended up with the woven fabric tangled around one leg. As she hopped on the other foot, trying to unwrap herself, she lost her balance and tumbled forward with a gasp of surprise.

She tried so hard not to fall on Ethan and injure him more that she landed on her hands and knees, straddling his big, helpless body, her wide blue eyes staring down into his shocked gray ones.

Her klutziness was nothing new. All through school she'd been self-conscious about her height. And teasing from preadolescent male classmates hadn't helped. *Help us out, Stretch. The Frisbee went on the roof.* She'd been awkward and uncoordinated, kind of like a baby giraffe.

In time, the boys grew taller, and she eventually came to terms with her body. But she never entirely outgrew the clumsiness, though it rarely afflicted her with such devastating consequences.

Her boobs were two inches away from smothering him. She licked her lips. "Um, sorry. Did I hurt you?"

He seemed dazed, his pupils dilated, his chest heaving with uneven breaths. "No."

She scooted carefully down his legs and backed onto her heels. From this vantage point, he looked even bigger and more wonderfully male. She deliberately avoided staring at his crotch. The temptation was enormous (ha! pun intended), but she wasn't about to be caught leering at him like a frustrated old maid.

In a matter of minutes, she managed to unfurl the knotted afghan and smooth it over Ethan's legs. In the process, she accidentally stroked his bare foot, but she kept right on, pretending nothing had happened.

When she stood up to leave, a thought occurred to her. She bit her lip, her gaze focused carefully on the far wall. "Do you need help going to the . . . ah . . . you know . . . ?"

She couldn't finish the sentence, but Ethan got the gist. He rolled his eyes. "I'm not paralyzed, Jane. It hurts, that's all. And no . . . I don't think my pride can handle you or anyone else witnessing my contortions while I get on my feet."

She picked up her coat and slipped her arms into the sleeves. "All righty then." Her voice was painfully breezy. "I've got to run. But I'll be back between five and six . . . if you're sure that's okay. It won't be anything fancy."

An odd look crossed his face. For a long moment she thought he was going to turn down her offer. "Yes," he said slowly, "please do. That would be nice."

With a sigh of relief—she'd thought for sure he was going to refuse—she picked up her gloves and slung her purse over her shoulder. "Any other last requests before I go?"

He looked toward the kitchen. "Actually, yes. Can you bring me the stack of mail? I'll go through it while I'm lying here. Might help pass the time."

Her whole body went cold. "Are you sure that's wise? There are bound to be bills in there, and all that financial stuff won't be good for your stress level."

She knew her voice was too high, her words a babble of nonsense.

Suddenly, he wore his cop face—the one that said he knew something was going on and he was determined to find out what. But when he spoke, his words were mild. "I think I can manage to open a few envelopes without having a coronary or needing traction."

She nudged the remote closer to him with her foot. "*Gilligan's Island* comes on in a few minutes. I remember you always used to love that show."

His eyes narrowed. "I still like it. But surprise, surprise. I'm pretty sure I can manage to do two things at once."

Jane had a few ideas in mind she'd like him to try on her. But instead of suggesting them, she turned away and walked from the room with all the enthusiasm of an outlaw going to the gallows.

In the kitchen she picked up the stack of mail and swallowed hard. This was her last chance. All she had to do was slip the damn envelope into her purse. But she couldn't be sure he hadn't seen it. Couldn't be positive that he wouldn't notice if it disappeared.

She glanced at the clock over the stove. Oh, hell. She had fifteen minutes left to walk back to the shop. If she departed right now.

With a sense of fatalism, she tucked the lavender envelope between an outdoorsman catalog and a credit card offer. She went back into the other room and crouched beside him only long enough to drop the mail within his reach. She would have stood again immediately, but Ethan grabbed her hand, nearly tugging her off balance.

He stared at her intently, his gray eyes piercing. "Thank you, Jane."

She stood up, breaking his hold, more flustered than she should have been by his touch and his words. "Don't mention it. It's the least I could do. I'll see you later."

The whole time she crossed the room, maybe thirty seconds total, she was aware of his gaze boring into her back. And she was even more in tune to the fact that her wicked little valentine verse was soon to be discovered.

She wanted to stay and hide behind the wall and gauge his reaction when he read the card. But clearly, she couldn't. Not if she wanted to stay far away from the dangerous-stalker category.

She paused in the doorway and turned around for one last look at the source of her temptation and frustration. "Goodbye, Ethan. Take care of yourself. Don't do anything stupid."

# Four

*Don't do anything stupid.* Jane's parting words rang in Ethan's ears. Did she mean something like him pulling her into his arms and kissing those lush pink lips?

He moved restlessly and caught his breath as the familiar stabbing pain reminded him he was momentarily incapacitated. The medicine had taken the edge off, but he knew from experience that it would take at least forty-eight hours before the tightly clenched muscles in his back eased and let him stand upright.

God, it was humiliating. He was supposed to be such a hardass . . . all fit and tough . . .an example to his men. And instead, he couldn't even carry out a romantic gesture without crippling himself.

Not that last night had been about romance—far from it. But what if it had? How likely was a woman—any woman—to look at him with lust in her eyes if he was incapable of sweeping her off her feet?

He clasped his hands across his abdomen and stared at the ceiling. It touched him that Jane had come by today. And it gave him hope. He'd missed their friendship . . . terribly. And he didn't know exactly why things had changed between them, though he had a guess.

If he was smart, he would seize this opportunity to get close to her again. And if he were honest, Sherry's prodding made some sense. He *did* enjoy being with Jane. In almost every way.

He'd never seriously looked at her in a romantic light, but he sure as hell was now. All it had taken was one chaste night in her bed and the chance to dredge up a host of memories. Memories that were funny and sweet and deeply satisfying.

It was a miracle that Jane was still available. He couldn't be the only man in town who saw her appeal. But some guys were shallow enough and insecure enough to want the image of a petite woman on their arm. So they could be the big protector.

Jane didn't really need his protection. She was strong and resilient and capable of handling her life without him. But suddenly he felt an urgency to look after her anyway. Staying at her apartment last night had been as much for him as it had been for her.

He'd snatched the chance to get in her good graces again . . . to reclaim the closeness they had once shared. All this sexual subtext was unexpected and new. But perhaps it had been there all along, and he had simply been too blind to notice.

Five years ago he had been intent on his career, determined to make his mark, to be noticed, to gain more responsibility. He and Jane used to talk at length about his dreams for the future.

It struck him with sudden shame that he couldn't remember ever having a single conversation about *Jane's* aspirations. Perhaps that was why she had gradually removed herself from his life. Maybe his self-absorption had been boring in the end. Possibly, he hadn't been the friend she needed.

Relationships didn't work when one person did all the giving. If he'd been so focused on his job that he'd neglected Jane's needs, it served him right that he lost her friendship.

But he missed her. And until last night, he hadn't fully realized how much her absence had left a giant hole in his life. Was it too late to reclaim that connection? God, he hoped not. But he'd be a fool to muddy the waters with these new lustful feelings.

If he wanted Jane back in his life as a friend, he'd have to curb his base instincts. It had been several months since he'd been involved, no matter how briefly, in any kind of a sexual relationship. Despite his horniness born of abstinence, and also how deliciously tempting his lovely Jane was, he'd have to keep his pants zipped.

So he might as well get his mind off his dick.

He reached for the stack of mail and flipped through it. Easy enough to tear up the junk mail and toss it aside. He couldn't quite reach the trash can, but he crumpled up the pizza flyer and tried a shot anyway.

Curious, he picked up a medium-size lavender envelope. His name and address were written in beautiful calligraphy. Who in the hell still knew how to do that?

Something about the delicate paper urged him to open the flap with care. His big fingers felt clumsy as he tried not to tear what was inside. He tossed the envelope aside.

It was a handwritten valentine or, to be more accurate, a poem, all done in the same flowing calligraphy. Hearts and little cupids decorated the edges.

He started reading and his jaw dropped.

*A man such as you,*
*A man strong and true,*
*Makes my woman's heart break,*
*Makes my woman parts ache.*

*I'm writing you now,*
*As a sign of my vow.*
*I'm tired of denying*
*This love I've been hiding.*

*So I'll woo you with words*
*And arouse your suspicions*
*Until that fine day*
*When we lose inhibitions.*

*Tonight when you sleep*
*In dreams hot and deep,*
*See me come to your bed and*
*Then dwell in your head.*

*This note's but the first*
*Of a string of my verse,*
*So read this with care*
*And wait for me there. . . .*

The paper fell from his nerveless fingers, and his face heated. Even though he was alone in the house, he was embarrassed as hell. Someone had sent him a love note. Or a sex note. He didn't know what in the devil it was, but it made him nervous. Intrigued, but wary. The world was full of crazies. And he'd seen *Fatal Attraction*.

Yikes.

For a brief moment, he wondered if Jane had sent him the note. The stationery looked similar to the fancy-schmancy stuff she sold in her shop. But when he snatched the envelope to check the postmark, his bubble of excitement popped. The note had been sent on Thursday, January second—an entire day before he and Jane had spent the night together.

He sighed and reached for the remote. Speculation about who was sending him naughty mail took a backseat to his eagerness to see Jane again. He'd be on his best behavior tonight, and he'd prove to her that he could be a good friend. Then maybe they could pick up where they had left off four years ago.

Jane closed the shop promptly at five o'clock and rushed upstairs to primp a little bit. She brushed her hair and put on some lip gloss. Ethan might think it odd if she changed clothes, so the long raspberry sweater she'd had on all day over khakis and a white shirt would have to do.

By five twenty she was in her car driving to the grocery store. She picked up a premade pizza crust and loaded her cart with the toppings and cheese she remembered Ethan liked. Twenty minutes after that, she was once again in his driveway. He'd left the door open for her, so she let herself in and walked quietly back to the den.

He was sleeping again. Poor thing. In addition to Ethan being tired, the medicine was probably making him drowsy. To her dismay, the stack of opened mail near him was crowned with one very familiar lavender envelope.

Well, that was it. He'd read it. She wondered if he would mention it to her. At one time they had been able to talk to each other about anything.

She slipped into the kitchen and unloaded her bags quietly.

It was an easy task to roll out the crust, layer it with all sorts of goodies, and pop it in the oven. She'd thought about adding a tossed salad, but she wasn't sure if Ethan felt like sitting at the table, and lettuce covered in dressing wasn't the kind of thing you could eat on the floor with one hand.

She dropped a knife when Ethan's voice startled her. She picked it up and dried her hands on a towel. "Be right there."

The first thing she noticed when she walked into the room was that the lavender envelope was gone. Well, shoot. What in the heck did that mean? Did Ethan not want her to know he was getting naughty mail from a mystery woman?

She couldn't very well ask about the letter. Not if she wanted to preserve her anonymity. But she was dying to know what he thought about it.

Ethan's mind was on other matters. He looked wistful and eager as he sniffed the air. "Homemade pizza?"

She nodded. "Yes. At least the shortcut version. I didn't make the dough from scratch."

He smiled at her. "I think I can bear it."

She put her hands on her hips. "Do you feel like coming to the table, or do I need to bring it in here?"

His hair was tousled where he had run his hands through it. His grin was playful. "If I say *in here*, does that mean you'll feed me?"

Her shock must have been reflected on her face. There was no way in hell to misconstrue that question as anything other than flirtatious. She took a step backward. "You might choke eating on the floor like that. You'd best try to make it to the kitchen."

Ethan beat his fist on the rug. Stupid, stupid, stupid. All his self-lectures about friendship and going slow had been for naught when he'd mouthed off a sexual challenge right off the bat. And Jane had responded with a look of horror.

He rolled to his side and gritted his teeth as he got to his hands and knees and finally managed to stand up. He was tired of looking like a weak, helpless invalid in front of Jane. If it killed him, he was going to sit upright long enough to wolf down three or four slices of pizza.

It was culinary heaven. Jane had somehow managed to remember all of his favorite toppings and had included them in perfect proportions.

Trying to talk coherently around a mouthful of anchovies and peppers and two kinds of meat was not only rude, but impossible. He swallowed and wiped his mouth. "This is awesome."

She had been polite enough not to mention the fact that he was more or less hunched over the table like a troll. "I'm glad you like it."

He saw that she had already cleaned up all evidence of food preparation, and his kitchen was as spotless as it had ever been. Still, it caught him off guard when she stood up to leave.

He glanced at the clock. "What's your hurry? You got a big date?"

He said it flippantly, but it *was* Saturday night. His heart sank. Maybe she did.

Jane looked at him steadily. "Not a date, no, but plenty of stuff to do."

He wasn't above begging and playing the sympathy card. "I'm bored out of my skull. Why don't you stay for a while? We can talk. Maybe watch a movie. It will be like old times."

She had already put on her coat, and the reluctance on her face was almost insulting. He rarely had to cajole women into doing anything. Something about the uniform elicited female interest and cooperation . . . on every front. But Jane was made of tougher stuff.

She tucked a strand of hair behind her ear. The overhead

light picked out the gold strands and made them shimmer. As she leaned against the doorway, every line of her body was graceful and feminine. It had been years since he'd seen her in a swimsuit, but he remembered thinking with unbiased male appreciation that she'd measure up well to any of those *Sports Illustrated* models.

At last she spoke. "Ethan . . . " She paused, and an odd look crossed her face.

He hadn't a clue what was going on inside her head, but he pressed his case quickly. "And if you're nervous about staying home alone tonight, you can sleep in my bed."

Her eyes widened, and color flooded her cheeks. He tacked on a hasty explanation. "I'll be sleeping on the floor in the den."

She shook her head. "You've always been able to get your way, haven't you?" The hint of amused affection in her voice kept him from taking offense. And, besides, whoever said it was a crime to be persuasive?

He straightened up another half inch, clamping down on a moan. Shit. He was in serious pain. But he managed a cajoling smile. "Why don't you go home and get a toothbrush? In the meantime, I'll check in at the station and see if there's been any progress in the investigation of last night's break-in at your store."

"Don't you think it was probably a teenager looking for drug money or something he could easily turn into cash? In which case, he's long gone."

He nodded. "Probably. But we'll follow through on it anyway. Even though nothing was taken, the property damage kicks it up a notch. We'd like to track down the culprit before he hits another business."

She nodded. "Makes sense. But honestly, Ethan, I'm not afraid to be at home by myself. The window downstairs has been fixed, so everything is fine. I'll stay and keep you company for a little bit, but after that, I really do need to go. And by the way, thanks for sending Tony over. He did a great job."

He swallowed his disappointment. "You don't have to be brave to prove something to me."

Her eyes narrowed. "I'm not out to impress *anyone*. It's my home. And I'm going to sleep there tonight. Like I do every night."

He shrugged. "Fine. Don't have a hissy fit. Now, if you don't mind, will you please turn your back while I stand up and hobble to the den? This is hell on my ego, and I'd just as soon not have an audience."

She flounced around and faced the wall. "Fine."

He tightened his jaw against the wave of pain that gripped him as he walked out of the kitchen. Walked? Ha! That was a misnomer. He moved like he was a hundred years old. Real smooth. No wonder Jane was reluctant to stay.

She waited at least five minutes before she joined him in the den. After a moment's hesitation, she took a seat on the couch. "Is the medicine helping?"

He grimaced. "I guess. But not fast enough."

"It's a good thing you were off today and tomorrow."

"How did you know that?"

"I stopped by the station to thank you this morning. They told me."

"There's no reason to thank me," he muttered. "I was just doing my job." He didn't deserve her gratitude, not after what he had realized earlier. He'd been a lousy friend in the past. So if he was trying to make up for those sins, it didn't merit her thanks.

She was sitting with her feet flat on the floor, her spine ramrod straight. He didn't need the department shrink to read Jane's body language. She was uneasy.

Even so, he was afraid this might be the last chance he had to get through to her. And he wanted a few answers, even at the risk of making her even more uncomfortable.

He sighed. "Can I ask you a personal question?"

Her eyes flared. And something that looked like alarm filled them. "Um . . . sure."

"What happened between us? Why did we stop being friends?"

The oddest thing happened. Jane was relieved. He could see it written on her face. What in the hell did she *think* he wanted to talk to her about?

She licked her lips and tucked her hands in her lap. "People drift apart, Ethan."

She scored high points for evasion, but she was pitting her wits against a professional interrogator. "Nice try," he said wryly. "You removed yourself from my life. I want to know why."

Sudden fury vibrated like an aura around her, charging the air and turning his guest from merely attractive to downright gorgeous. The transformation hit him in the gut.

She leaned forward, her fists on her knees. "I don't owe you any explanations, Ethan Oldham."

He held up his hands, ignoring the discomfort. "Sorry. That came out wrong."

She sat back, but her gaze was still turbulent with emotion. "The past is in the past. Nobody gets do-overs. We're two different people now."

He smiled placatingly. "You don't seem all that different. Please, Jane. I spent a lot of lonely nights wondering what I had done to offend you."

Now her face was wiped clean of all expression. "Are you really that dense?"

Her tone was deliberately provoking, but he refused to let her rip at his temper. "Clearly I am. Men aren't the brightest creatures on the planet."

Her angry posture deflated suddenly, and once again he saw a flash of vulnerability. "It was four years ago, Ethan. Do you remember anything else that happened four years ago?" Her sarcasm seemed out of character, but he had it coming.

This wasn't going to be fun. He'd suspected as much, but hadn't wanted to admit the truth to himself. "I got engaged," he admitted dully. It was a dark moment in his life. And one that didn't portray him in a good light at all.

She bowed her head, staring at her hands as they twisted at a button on her sweater. "You got engaged," she repeated, "and under other circumstances, I would have tried to be happy for you, but you picked *her.*"

His ears perked up. "Are you telling me you *knew* what she was like?"

She blanched. "Of course I knew, Ethan. Everybody in town knew. At least everybody but you."

Her incredulity nicked his pride, but he deserved it. He'd been blinded by momentary lust, and had allowed himself to be reeled in hook, line, and sinker by a woman who was a con artist, a congenital liar, and a master manipulator. To his credit, it had taken him very little time to discover his monumental mistake.

He'd broken the engagement without any qualms, and thankfully, his disgusted fiancée had cut her losses and moved away. During the same period of time, Jane had slid out of his orbit with barely a ripple to call attention to her absence.

He'd noticed. Of course, he'd noticed. But he was too embarrassed and at too much of a low point to do anything about it. By the time he recovered his equilibrium and got back on his feet emotionally, the damage had already been done.

Something struck him. Something unpleasant. He stared at her. "If you *knew* she was a wacko, why didn't you warn me? You were my friend."

The look she gave him was one reserved for the clueless and the deranged. Her blue eyes were dark with something that looked like pain. "Give me a break, Ethan. It's utterly impossible for one woman to criticize another woman to a man without looking . . . " She trailed off, her gaze fixed on the far wall.

"Without looking what?" He felt as if he was on the verge of a major breakthrough.

Her gaze swung back to his and their eyes locked. She twisted her lips in a faint, self-mocking smile. "I was your best friend, Ethan. Did it ever occur to you that I might have been jealous?"

Her answer felt like a blow to the stomach—the kind that knocked the wind out of you. The kind where you lay on the ground gasping desperately for air until finally you can breathe again.

Jane had been jealous of the psycho woman. In a romantic way? His heart leapt in his chest, but his common sense smacked it down. Not bloody likely. He'd not treated Jane well back then, but it was her pride that he hurt, not her heart.

He closed his eyes, for once not feeling at all like the assistant chief of police. It was a position he had worked hard for. He'd given blood, sweat, and tears to the department, and later this year, his dream would be realized, barring any nasty surprises.

But now that he had made it so close to his goal, he realized with sick certainty that the job, no matter how important to him and the community, was in the end just a job. And there was still a big empty place in his life that he'd somehow never been able to fill.

For a brief moment, he remembered the valentine he had opened earlier. When Jane wasn't looking, he had tucked it out of sight. Did he think she wouldn't understand? Or perhaps that she would think he was bragging?

Friends shared things with each other. Maybe it was time to be more honest than he had been in the past.

He cleared his throat. "I'm sorry for what happened back then. I should have apologized long before now, but I let my pride get in the way."

Her face softened. "You made some mistakes, Ethan. We all do."

"But mine was a doozy."

She bit her lip, probably to keep from laughing at him. "This is true."

He wished he could stand up and give her a hug, but that wasn't going to happen. Not tonight.

Tension gripped him, not at all what he needed at the present moment. "I'm glad we cleared the air," he said slowly, his voice husky.

Her gaze was sober. "Me, too."

He was about to suggest they load the DVD, but Jane stood up. "I think I'll pass on the movie."

He struggled up on his elbows. "Do you really have to go?" He'd been hoping their talk might smooth things out between them. But Jane seemed more fidgety than ever.

She nodded. "I'm sure." She stopped on the way out. "Will Sherry check on you tomorrow?"

He nodded slowly. "Yeah. Apparently I'm going to be her guinea pig for some catering stuff."

She lifted a hand and gave a sort of fluttery wave. "Well, that's good then. Take care of yourself, Ethan." And suddenly, she was gone.

His stomach felt funny, and he didn't think it was the anchovies. Her farewell didn't sound like a woman who was planning on seeing him again. He'd assumed they were back to the old Ethan and Jane, but instead, he had a sneaking suspicion that he was no closer to being Jane's good friend than he had been for the past four years.

Jane closed Ethan's front door and leaned her back against it, feeling the pull from inside the house. More than anything, she wanted to stay. But she couldn't make things too easy for Ethan, or before she knew it, he'd be taking her for granted again.

And it still bothered her that he had hidden the valentine. In the old days, they would have laughed together about such an odd piece of mail.

But that was then and this was now. Maybe he hid it because he didn't want her to know a mystery woman was interested in him. Maybe he thought it would make her jealous. And it would . . . if the mystery woman wasn't her. Oh, Lord, she was so messed up.

She got in her car and drove the short distance back to her home and business. It had been dark for a long time now, but there was a streetlight where she parked her car, so she refused to get all jittery and scared over something that had to be nothing more than an isolated incident.

By the time she made it safely upstairs and bolted her door, her legs were a bit shaky, but she was fine. She didn't need the oh so handsome assistant police chief to hold her hand.

She wanted a lot of things from Ethan Oldham, but babysitting didn't make the list. Let the man have a few days to think about his mystery valentine sender, and then . . . voilà. She'd send the next one, and her erotic seduction would be back on track.

As she performed her nightly routines, she tried not to think about the fact that she would have to compose another naughty ode. Maybe this time she'd go for a limerick. Or a haiku.

She snorted and climbed into bed, looking wistfully at the side where Ethan had lain the night before. It took all she had not to bury her face in the comforter and seek his smell. That would be pathetic.

She closed her eyes, too weary for a self-inflicted pep talk. Her plan *had* to work. She was thirty-two years old. If this thing with Ethan didn't pan out, there would be no more second chances. She'd walk away and not look back.

Ethan might be the man of her dreams, but she wouldn't settle for his lukewarm friendship. She wanted grand passion or nothing at all.

# Five

Sherry sat in her car in the parking lot of the police station and tried to convince herself she wasn't going to throw up. She stared at herself in the rearview mirror. *For God sakes, woman, get a grip.*

Ethan was counting on her, and it was time she started to believe that she had more to give than her mothering skills. Debra's mischievous face popped into her head, but she shoved the image away. Her daughter still loved her. Moving to Tampa had nothing to do with their mother-daughter relationship. It had to do with Debra's dreams and her future.

If Sherry told herself that enough times, she might start to believe it.

Resolutely, she got out of the car and walked toward the building. The bitter cold of the past week had vanished, leaving sunny skies and comfortably warm days. Perhaps the weather was an omen.

She'd barely made it into the building before a nice-looking young policeman stepped into her path with a smile. "Ms. Mc-Camish? Your brother sent me to help with the lunch. Just tell me what you need to have carried inside."

He followed her back out to the car, chatting casually about the weather. Sherry tried to keep up with the conversation, but she was too busy making sure nothing spilled in transit to pay much attention.

He was of medium height and sturdy build, and even beneath his shirtsleeves, she could tell that he was muscular. She'd never really had a thing for blond-headed men—maybe because her own dishwater color had never been all that exciting to her—but Officer Temple was very appealing. His short hair was lighter and brighter than hers.

In the large conference room, he helped her arrange the chafing dishes, outfitting them with long-handled spoons, and lighting the warming flames beneath them. Sherry had baked pork chops with French-style green beans, scalloped potatoes, wheat rolls, and apple cake for dessert. She'd also brought tea and coffee.

The station would be supplying the paperware and utensils each week. Ethan had already warned her that she would need to serve the plates ahead of time, or some of the men would go overboard on portions. In which case, her profits would shrink, and the idea of eating healthy meals would be torpedoed by too many calories.

Judging by the smiles and compliments she received, the first meal was a runaway success. She would figure out her profits later, but if this number of men and women participated each time she cooked, she'd be guaranteed a steady income.

Ethan was one of the last to come through the line. She lowered her voice. "How is your back?" It was Tuesday, and she knew he'd returned to work the day before. Stubborn man refused to take a sick day.

He took his plate and urged her to join him. When they were settled at the empty end of one of the tables, he took a bite and groaned aloud. "God, this is good." Then he leaned in closer. "I'm fine. The muscle relaxers finally did the trick."

"And what about Jane?" Sherry had been thrilled to hear that Jane looked after Ethan on Saturday afternoon.

Ethan swallowed some tea and gave her a warning glance. "How should I know? I told you, she came by to say thanks for helping her out during the break-in. When she found out I was not feeling well, she brought me dinner. End of story."

"Did you talk?"

"About what?" He evaded her eyes this time, scooping up a hefty forkful of potatoes.

She nudged his arm. "You know. The long, cold silence between you two."

Ethan finished off the last of his pork chop and glanced at his watch. "Butt out, sis. And I say that with the utmost affection. Worry about your own love life, and I'll take care of mine."


Jane gleefully bypassed the heavy coat in her closet and pulled out a lightweight jacket. She loved living in Tennessee for many reasons, not the least of which was the sheer unpredictability of the elements. Never a dull moment, as all the forecasters in the area would testify.

She'd decided to take a long lunch break since Mrs. Fitzhugh was back. After enjoying a bowl of soup at the little restaurant on the corner, Jane paid her check and headed out the door. It was rent day, and her genial landlord liked receiving the checks in person.

It was his only eccentricity, and Jane was happy to oblige. Mr.

Benson, who was somewhere between eighty and ninety years old, owned Jane's building and several more in the downtown area. In addition to being an absolute sweetheart, he hadn't raised any of his rents in the last decade, which won him many admirers, not to mention the loyalty and goodwill of all of his tenants.

He didn't need the money. By local standards, he was richer than God. And it was common knowledge that he'd willed his entire estate to charity. His extended family was an unimpressive lot. Without the carrot of a possible inheritance, they'd abandoned the old man to his climbing years, although one or another of them would pop up now and again with a pitiful story to try to con him out of some cash.

Jane had timed her visit for one p.m. Mr. Benson had a soap he liked to watch at two, and Jane knew better than to interrupt then.

He opened the door seconds after she rang the bell.

She greeted him with a hug. "I'm guessing your arthritis is doing okay today."

He nodded his mostly bald, liver-spotted head, his bright but watery blue eyes keen. "Yep. No complaints. This nice, warm day is a gift at my age."

Jane followed him into the house. "At any age." She handed him the check along with a small box of homemade chocolate-chip cookies. He tucked the former away in a bank envelope in the small writing desk beside the window, and then popped the lid off the tin of cookies and gobbled one down, childlike glee on his face.

Then he turned, his gaze eager. He had a cane, but on good days, he didn't use it. "Do you have time for a game of gin rummy?"

She slipped off her jacket. "Wouldn't miss it."

It wasn't disloyal to wonder from time to time what would

happen to her business when Mr. Benson was gone. She assumed his assets would be sold off. Which meant she'd either be evicted, or else the new owner would undoubtedly raise the rents significantly, thus adversely affecting Jane's bottom line.

At one time, she thought she would be married and have kids by now. But it hadn't happened. And truly, she was very happy with her career. It gave her an outlet for her creativity, and she loved being her own boss.

But until she could make Ethan fall in love with her or, conversely, get him out of her heart for good, she was never going to be completely satisfied. Shaking off her unsettling thoughts, she turned her attention to the game.

Mr. Benson was sharp, and he wasn't above cheating if he thought no one would notice. Jane nailed him on it every time, and she was pretty sure it gave him a kick to get caught.

Just before two, they wrapped things up. Jane bade her host goodbye. As she slipped into her jacket, he patted her arm, and she smelled the familiar scents of Old Spice and pipe smoke. His expression was shrewd, as though he saw every thought in her head. "You worry about me too much, little lady. There's a lot of fight left in this old bird, all evidence to the contrary. You should be out living your life, instead of checking up on an old man."

She kissed his cheek. "Maybe I come here for me. Have you ever thought of that?"

He was standing at the door grinning as she waved and went down the walk. She was suddenly eager to get back to the shop. A new shipment of paper had arrived earlier in the day, and she couldn't wait to pick out the perfect one to use for her next erotic valentine.

She and Ethan hadn't seen each other all week. On Tuesday, they'd had a brief phone conversation, in which he had updated her on the break-in. As they had both suspected, the partial prints were no help. And without any other significant physical evidence, it was doubtful the case would ever be solved.

Fortunately, she had gotten over being spooked every time she ventured downstairs at night. She often tidied things up in the shop or looked through catalogs after she had dinner. So it was a relief to know that one frightening incident hadn't turned her into a complete wuss.

Back at the store, she sent Mrs. Fitzhugh on her way and finished out the afternoon dusting shelves and straightening stock. After a quick dinner of an apple and yogurt, she settled in to prepare her second mysterious valentine.

This time, she picked a sheet of whisper pink vellum. She cut apart a lace doily and carefully glued it around the edges of her note-to-be. While that was drying, she grabbed some scrap paper and composed her next verse.

Or tried to . . .

Poetry was not an easy skill to master. She should have remembered that from high school. And besides, back in tenth-grade English class, she hadn't been attempting to use suggestive phrases and sexy come-ons. Dirty poetry was even more difficult. Especially since she was trying to write *classy* dirty poetry.

Was that an oxymoron??

She held her favorite calligraphy pen over the paper and waited for inspiration. Anytime she got close to Ethan, her breath grew shallow, her heart beat faster, and her panties got damp. It had to be a chemical thing. Why else had she been unable to get him out of her head?

She closed her eyes and remembered what he looked like when he laughed. As he'd accumulated more and more responsibility over the years, she was afraid that he smiled less and less. And that was a shame. Because his smile and his dimple were lethal. They made a girl's legs weak, made her resistance turn to the consistency of Jell-O.

Not that she had ever needed to fend him off. Quite the contrary. It had been a close call a number of times when she thought about throwing herself into his arms and kissing *him* senseless.

His lips. Oh, wow. His firm, wonderful lips . . .

Her memories went further, taunting her with last Friday night's events. Ethan smiling at her. Ethan in her bed. Ethan carrying her up the stairs.

Ah, now she was ready. . . .

*Dearest Ethan,*

*Alone at night*
*With nary a light,*
*I imagine you nude,*
*If you don't think it rude. . . .*

*My hands stroke your chest.*
*You nibble my breasts.*
*Romance and lust*
*Might well nigh combust. . . .*

*I long to begin*
*A life with no end.*
*Don't shut me out,*
*And if you have doubts,*

*Rest assured that my love*
*Like a snug velvet glove*
*Will wrap you in heat*
*From your lips to your feet. . . .*

*I'll preserve the charade*
*And the pact that I've made*
*With Cupid's wild dart*
*To pierce your true heart.*

*So fair warning,* mon amour,
*After this one, four more. . . .*

Jane stared at the scrap paper. She'd erased and rewritten so many phrases and words, the whole thing looked like chicken scratch.

She retrieved the decorated sheet of paper and laid it atop a smooth surface. Then carefully, oh so carefully, she copied her newest effort. When it was blotted and checked for mistakes, she put it on a thin sheet of cardboard to protect it and slid it into a large white envelope.

With a computer-generated address label bearing Ethan's name and home address, the whole thing looked like a generic piece of business mail. Perfect.

Tomorrow she'd mail it, and then wait and see what happened.

Friday afternoon, Ethan came home in a foul mood. He had the weekend off again. He should have been riding high. But a number of frustrations had piled on top of one another, and he was ready to kick something, or explode, or both.

He scooped a handful of mail out of the box and juggled it while he unlocked his door. It was Friday night. Every other single man in Statlerville probably had a date tonight. Did Ethan? Hell, no. And it was his own fault. Despite what he might have hinted at to his sister, there was actually any number of very good prospects in his potential dating pool. Nice women. Hot women. Intelligent women.

And a handful who were all three.

But every time he thought about picking up the phone to call one of them, all he could see in his mind's eye was an image of Jane, fast asleep in her soft, comfy bed.

And the more he thought about Jane, the more horny and frustrated he got.

Which totally wigged him out, because regardless of their extended estrangement, Jane was his dear friend. She didn't deserve to be treated like a sex object.

And what about the damn mysterious valentine? He couldn't get that out of his head either. He should have already thrown the stupid thing away. It was probably a hoax, or a joke perpetrated by some local college girls.

But all in all, what with the hot love note, his recent night spent in Jane's bed, and a way too long dry spell in the carnal-arts department, he was a mess.

He opened a can of tuna and thought longingly of his sister's latest offering down at the station. The catering idea had gone over like gangbusters, and it did him good to see the happiness and glowing pride on his sister's face. She deserved every bit of her success. And the men and women under his command were reaping the benefits.

He ate the tuna straight out of the can and flipped on the TV to surf for a sporting event. He was game for anything but golf or deep-sea fishing.

Half an hour later, wondering why he paid for cable when there was nothing but drivel on any of the hundred-plus channels, he stretched out and kicked restlessly at the arm of the sofa. He linked his hands behind his head and let his mind wander to Jane, wondering what she was doing tonight. Now that they were on speaking terms again, was it kosher to call her? He wanted to hear her voice.

A jolt of something hot and sweet stabbed deep in his gut, and he realized he was getting a boner. He closed his eyes and freed his cock from his pants. With his right hand, he encircled his dick and began to stroke lazily.

He felt as guilty as a thirteen-year-old trying to sneak a peek in the girls' locker room, but he couldn't help himself. He thought about Jane.

He imagined what her breasts would look like if he unbuttoned her shirt. Her skin was pale, even in the summertime. Right now it would have the rosy glow of alabaster. He let the fantasy unwind. In moments, he had her bare to the waist, her hair in disarray on the pillow, her eyes gazing at him with dark azure fire.

Carefully, he unzipped her pants and dragged them down her legs. The fantasy Ethan moved slowly, giving the real Ethan plenty of time to stroke his shaft with a firm grip, letting the hunger build.

*Ethan.* She said his name in an aching voice, entreaty in her soft sigh. He could see in her gaze what she craved. Gently, tenderly, he moved over and nudged his hips between her thighs. It would be their first time. He wanted to make her moan and shudder with pleasure.

He was barely inside her when his climax slammed into him. It stole his breath and made him curse the release that was better than nothing, but so much less than he needed or wanted.

He lay there, his chest heaving, and felt a hellish mixture of emotions. Shame. Confusion. Regret for the past . . .

And once he had waded through all that, one other feeling stood out: determination. He had lost Jane once, because he hadn't realized just how valuable that relationship was. He wouldn't let it happen again.

He zipped his pants and stood up, groaning when he spotted

the pile of mail he'd tossed on the coffee table. It had been a busy week, and there were at least half a dozen bills that were due by the middle of the month.

He went in the kitchen for a beer, pulled up the online-bill-pay screen on his computer, and settled down to work. It wasn't the most glamorous way to spend a Friday night, but at least it would be done.

The large white envelope at the bottom of the pile looked like something from his insurance company, but there was no return address to identify it as such. The only other markings on it, besides his address, were the words PLEASE DO NOT BEND in block letters.

He flipped the envelope over and tore the flap loose. Whatever it was, it wasn't much. The envelope weighed nothing at all, almost as if it were empty.

But the envelope wasn't empty.

Holy crap. It was another erotic valentine, this one more beautiful than the last. The same flowing, feminine calligraphy he had admired in the previous note appeared in this one as well.

He read slowly. . . .

*Dearest Ethan,*

*Alone at night*
*With nary a light,*
*I imagine you nude,*
*If you don't think it rude. . . .*

*My hands stroke your chest.*
*You nibble my breasts.*
*Romance and lust*
*Might well nigh combust. . . .*

*I long to begin*
*A life with no end.*
*Don't shut me out,*
*And if you have doubts,*

*Rest assured that my love*
*Like a snug velvet glove*
*Will wrap you in heat*
*From your lips to your feet. . . .*

*I'll preserve the charade*
*And the pact that I've made*
*With Cupid's wild dart*
*To pierce your true heart.*

*So fair warning,* mon amour,
*After this one, four more. . . .*

It wasn't signed, nor had the last one been. But this time the sender called him by name. The investigative cop in him assessed the details even as the man—the recently celibate man—responded instinctively to the words and images. *A snug velvet glove?* Sweet Jesus. That could only mean one thing. In spite of himself, he reacted physically to the provocative note.

Who in the devil was sending him seductive messages? And the final stanza hinted at four more valentines to come. . . . Holy hell. Would they each be hotter than the last?

He jumped to his feet, his forehead damp and his skin tight. Who thought enough of him to write this kind of stuff? The last woman he'd dated more than two times was Wanda, the gal down at the auto-parts store. They'd hit it off and had shared some fun. But that was over six months ago, and recently he'd heard Wanda's old boyfriend was back from Iraq. Word on the street was that they were engaged.

Besides, he couldn't see Wanda composing pretty poetry. She was more of an outdoors female, hunting and skiing and riding her Harley. He honestly wasn't able to think of a single woman he knew who would do such a thing. He turned over the envelope and stared at the postmark. January ninth—exactly a week later than the first one. Which meant that again the mystery woman had mailed her note on a Thursday.

He glanced at the calendar and counted four more Thursdays. As he suspected. The schedule thus far indicated that her final note, if indeed she did send more, would arrive the week before Valentine's Day. Did that mean his mystery admirer had something planned for February fourteenth? Like maybe kidnapping or torturing him or leaving a dead animal on his doorstep or maybe even a voodoo doll?

He studied the envelope again, wishing he had thought to handle it with gloves. But he'd never had to preserve his personal mail as a crime scene. It was too outlandish to even contemplate. And besides, there were bound to be all sorts of prints on the envelope from various mail facilities and postal workers.

Then it struck him. In addition to the date, the postmark very clearly said *Statlerville*, which narrowed his field of study considerably. The only mail to actually be postmarked locally was the mail that people dropped into the "local" slot *inside* the main post office building downtown.

He went into his bedroom and retrieved the original note from his bedside table. He didn't spend time wondering why he had kept it or why it was where it was.

He eyed the lavender envelope intently. Bingo. His mystery lady had mailed both cards from inside the post office—more precisely, in the slot marked "local."

Which probably meant she was someone he knew. He wasn't sure if that was better or worse.

He put both letters back in his drawer and covered them up with a folder from work. Feeling ridiculous, he closed the drawer and sat down on the edge of the bed with a sigh. He was so screwed.

Here he was getting turned on by a female whose face and name were an enigma. And at the same time, he was having romantic, sexual thoughts about a woman who had been his friend for almost twenty years . . . and whom, up until four years ago, he would even have categorized as his *best* friend. Maybe he was losing his mind.

He reached for the phone and then drew back his hand. If he was going to contact Jane at all, it had to look like a friendly gesture. Which meant that tonight and Saturday night were out. Date nights carried too much emotional baggage. Maybe Sunday.

He'd call her up and suggest going out for ice cream. *In January?* His subconscious jeered. Okay, so maybe he'd take her out for a drive so they could talk and catch up. Immediately, his mind went further . . . to parking out on some rural lane, taking Jane in his arms, kissing her slowly, sliding his tongue into her warm, sweet mouth, and mating it with hers.

He stood up and went to the wall, banging his head against it as he ground his teeth together. What was happening to him? He was fantasizing about two women; one of whom might be a deranged stalker, and the other who was not an appropriate object of his lust.

Why couldn't he find a nice uncomplicated female and get laid, no strings attached, no baggage, emotional or otherwise?

With a mild curse for his own pathetic state, he rummaged in the floor of the closet for his gym bag, scooped up his keys, and headed for the gym. If he couldn't relieve his sexual tension the old-fashioned way, at least he could punish his body enough that he might actually be able to sleep.

Two hours later, he stumbled back into the house. He'd come perilously close to throwing his back out again, and he'd sweated through his shirt and shorts.

But even as he stood in a tepid shower and scrubbed his body, he couldn't resist reliving his Jane fantasy, enduring the predictable results, and later rolling restlessly, his hunger unfulfilled, in his cold, lonely bed.

# Six

Jane was going nuts. She'd discovered a serious flaw in her "seduce Ethan with erotic valentines" plan. The problem was simple. She had no way of gauging Ethan's response. Even though she planned to reveal herself as the authoress of the notes at a "ta-da" moment, in the meantime, it sure as heck would be helpful to know if they were working.

The fact that she'd actually been in his house the day he opened the first one should have given her an inside track. But Ethan had hidden not only the valentine, but also his reactions.

She was so agitated all day Saturday that an hour before Mrs. Fitzhugh was scheduled to leave, Jane excused herself, put on her running shoes, and hit the pavement. She had to do something to get this nervous energy under control.

Last night she hadn't slept a wink. Every time she had dozed off, visions of Ethan's gray eyes, his thick, dark hair, and his broad, wonderful chest rocketed around in her brain. His smile, his big gentle hands, his narrow waist and lean hips . . .

She ended up helplessly aroused and seriously frustrated, her body one big, aching, needy void.

Today had seemed endless, and it was only early afternoon. She wanted to go over to Ethan's house, pound on his door, and ask him if he had received any suspicious mail. But that was out of the question. So she needed to cultivate patience . . . right now.

The irony was not lost on her.

In an effort to stay far away from Ethan's street, she ran in the opposite direction. As she passed Mr. Benson's home she saw a young man perched on a ladder, painting his heart out. The boy had already finished one entire side of the house and was doing some work up under the eaves. The old man had a habit of hiring kids in the community to do odd jobs. He believed it kept them out of mischief. In Jane's eyes it was simply another example of her landlord's generous spirit.

She barely had time to take a quick shower when she got back. Mrs. Fitzhugh was a model employee, but she liked to leave at three on the dot.

The rest of the afternoon dragged even more than the morning. Jane waited on five or six customers the whole time. And they each spent less than ten dollars, mostly on items from the Christmas clearance table.

Sometimes she wondered if she would be doing this forever. It wasn't that she didn't enjoy being a businesswoman. She was proud of the fact that she was able to turn a decent profit year after year, and during the summer and fall, there was never a dull moment.

She had fun decorating the front windows for the chamber of commerce's seasonal contests. And she'd even volunteered at the high school the past two autumns, helping the cheerleaders create signs and banners for all the home football games.

She was part of the community. This was home. Her parents had moved to Knoxville a few years ago, but they were close enough for her to visit them on a regular basis. All in all, she had a very satisfactory life.

But sometimes at night when she was contemplating the great mysteries of life, it occurred to her that the only thing better than running Paper Pleasures would be the chance to be doing her own scrapbooking at home, creating volumes like *Our Wedding Day, Baby's First Christmas, Summer Trip to Magic Kingdom*.

Both of her best friends from high school had married several years back. One was the mother of toddler twins, lived in Dallas, and still managed to run an online parenting newsletter for more than two hundred thousand subscribers. The other friend had just been named a junior partner in a prestigious law practice in Knoxville, and was married to a brilliant man with a political career in his future.

Jane felt like a slacker occasionally when she got a glimpse of their busy lives. Her two-year community college degree didn't qualify her to do a whole heck of a lot. But she was happy for the most part. And she loved the quiet pace of Statlerville. She could think of nothing more wonderful than raising a family with Ethan here in the shadow of the Great Smoky Mountains.

But she was beginning to think that her dream was nothing more than a wistful fantasy. And why had it taken her four years after Ethan's aborted engagement to finally make a play for him?

Because she was a coward—that's why. She would rather live with the *possibility* of happiness than risk losing even that ephemeral dream to reality.

Well, those days were over. She had set her plan in motion. If it failed, she would give herself the opportunity to grieve, and then she would probably relocate. She refused to spend the best years of her life pining for a man who was too dumb to see what was right beneath his nose.

It was sometime after midnight when the smoke alarm woke her up. Not the one upstairs. The shrill beep was farther away . . . downstairs . . . in the shop.

Her heart slammed against her ribs as she dragged on her robe and slippers and stumbled to the door at the top of the stairs. It was cool to the touch, so she opened it a crack. Immediately, noxious black smoke curled into her apartment. She didn't spot any flames, but she slammed the door and reached for the phone to call 911.

This time Ethan heard the news on the police scanner at his home. For long seconds, he was in shock. Not again. No way. But the location was unmistakable. Jane was in danger for the second time in barely a week.

Thank God he was still mostly dressed. He snatched up his badge, slid his feet into his shoes, and picked up his service revolver and shoulder holster. He had a bad feeling about this.

He was fast, but the fire department was faster. By the time he took the corner on two wheels and jerked his car to a stop, half a dozen men in heavy yellow-and-silver fire gear were already entering the building.

Ethan knew the fire chief on sight. They had been a year apart in school. Ethan grabbed the man's arm. "A woman lives upstairs." The chief's eyes widened, perhaps shocked by Ethan's panic.

Ethan tried to pull it together. He'd be no help to Jane if he lost his cool. It was some small comfort that he saw no flames, despite the heavy smell of smoke in the air. The crew must have contained the blaze rapidly.

It was like taking a brick to the chest when he saw Jane come around the corner of the building, supported by a tall, grime-covered fireman. Jane's face was etched in pain, and she was leaning heavily on her escort.

Afterward, Ethan never remembered crossing the street and going to her. He clutched her close, his pulse racing like a freight train. "You're hurt. Where?" The words were like sharp gravel in his throat.

She leaned into him, and he tightened his grip, feeling gut-wrenching emotions he'd have to sort out later. The fireman spoke up. "We found her at the foot of the fire escape. She made it out of the building, but when she jumped down from the end of the ladder, she hit a patch of gravel and fell pretty hard."

Ethan urged her toward the ambulance that had just arrived on the scene. "Over here, Jane." She allowed him to support her as they limped along, and her weary compliance made him want to curse. Who in the hell would want to hurt such a strong but gentle woman? The knot in his gut eased a fraction when the paramedics checked her out and pronounced her ankle sprained, not broken.

He could hardly bear to leave her, even for a second, but he wanted to consult with his men on duty. The information was shocking and disturbing. The exact same window had been broken out a second time. The fire appeared to have been malicious in nature rather than outright destructive. Three aluminum mop buckets, each containing more than two dozen smoke bombs, had been lighted simultaneously.

The dense smoke was sufficient to set off all the sprinklers in Jane's shop. With an inventory that was upward of eighty percent paper products, the damage was extensive and would take time to replace. The loss of business in the interim would be inescapable. As bizarre as it seemed, someone was out to get Jane.

He strode back to the ambulance. The paramedics had finished taping Jane's ankle and were now cleaning some of the worst of the cuts and scrapes she had sustained when she fell. Her thin cotton pajama pants were ruined. Large rips at both knees revealed flesh that was scraped raw.

He winced in sympathy when the EMT rubbed antibiotic ointment on Jane's abraded skin. And in a dark, caveman corner of his brain, he managed to be pissed that another man was stroking Jane's leg.

He choked back his inappropriate urge to shove the guy aside and, instead, crouched by Jane and took her hand. Her pretty blue robe was probably a loss, in addition to her pants. It had been torn as well, and the hem was damp where she had walked through puddles on the street. The thin T-shirt beneath the robe clung to her braless curves, making him want to snatch the lapels together.

"Jane? How are you doing, honey?"

She lifted dazed eyes to his. "I've been better." Her eyes were dark with grief and confusion. "Who would want to do this to me?"

He measured his words. "I was hoping you could help us out with that. Last week seemed like random mischief. In light of tonight, obviously not. Can you think of anyone who has a beef with you?"

Even as he asked the question, he knew it was ludicrous. Jane was the poster child for nice women everywhere. As he recalled, she had been known to use live traps for the mice that inhabited her old building. Once they were corralled, she took them out to the country to release them. It was hard to imagine anyone who might want to get back at her for some perceived slight or offense.

But now was not the time to grill her. She was pale, and even though she was calm, he knew full well that the aftermath of adrenaline left a person shaky.

He exchanged glances with the paramedic. "She checks out okay?"

The man nodded. "Her BP's up a little, but that's to be expected. And the cuts are superficial for the most part. She might want to call her doctor for some pain meds if she has a hard time sleeping for a few days."

Jane shook her head vehemently. "I'm fine. May I go now?"

Ethan saw her face change the moment she heard her own words . . . witnessed her quiet misery as she realized she had nowhere to go. Before Ethan could stop her, she had risen to her feet and was hobbling over to where the fire chief stood, talking into his radio.

She faced him resolutely. "When may I go back in?"

The man glanced back at Ethan. "Um, well . . ."

She went toe-to-toe with him. And since the guy was fairly short, Jane looked the poor man straight in the eyes. "It wasn't really a fire, right?" She'd apparently picked up the gist of the conversation around her.

He shook his head. "No, ma'am."

"Then there's no reason I can't go back up to my apartment."

Her fierce scowl might have amused Ethan in less volatile circumstances. And he actually felt a measure of pity for his comrade on the front lines.

The fire chief winced and hung his head. "Sorry, miss. The smoke damage will have affected the upstairs as well. And until we finish our investigation, you won't be allowed to go back inside."

Jane stared at him in silence. "Well, that's just bloody lovely." And then she burst into tears.

Ethan urged her away, steering her toward his car. "Take it

easy, honey. You can crash at my place tonight or for what's left of it. I've got a spare room, and I'm sure I can round up a toothbrush somewhere."

She dashed at the tears on her cheeks with an angry hand. "I don't need you to take care of me, and I'm not falling apart. I'm just upset."

He tucked her hair behind her ear. "Of course you're upset. You deserve to be. But even Lois Lane let Superman help her out occasionally."

As he had hoped, that comment drew a small grin. The tension in her frame relaxed visibly, and she sighed. "Since when did you become a superhero?" She allowed him to help her into the car, and then he ran around to the driver's side and hopped in.

He checked his rearview mirror and pulled out. "I know you don't *need* my help, Jane. I know you're able to take care of yourself. But humor me. All of us police types get off on rescuing people. You should know that by now. It's in our DNA."

She leaned back in the seat, her long, slender neck seeming barely able to hold up her head. And then she surprised the hell out of him. In the dark intimacy of the car, with the heater running full-blast and a country song playing softly on the radio in the background, she laid a hand on his thigh. "Thank you, Ethan. I don't mean to seem ungrateful. When you showed up tonight, I was so glad to see you."

He swallowed hard, gripping the steering wheel. "You're welcome," he said gruffly.

She stroked his thigh, and as much as he wanted to believe she was flirting, he realized that she was probably doing it without thinking. She'd been awakened out of a deep sleep, and forced to evacuate her home, and then she had taken a hard fall. It was a wonder she was coping as well as she was. And maybe it was one of those situations where she craved human contact.

Any man would do.

That thought didn't sit well. Hell, no. He had been Jane's good friend at one time—probably her best friend. And that gave him certain privileges. Such as being the hero when life threw her curve balls. If he played his cards right, perhaps he'd be able to reclaim the relationship he'd torpedoed through his sheer stupidity.

For a long time, he'd simply refused to think about his short-lived and quickly aborted engagement. It was too damn embarrassing. Looking back, he was appalled at how easily the woman had manipulated him with sweet words and lots of sex. At the time, he'd had some stupid notion that being married would give him a leg up in getting the promotion to chief of police.

Despite the fact that back then his slacker boss still had a few years to go before retiring, Ethan had decided that tying the knot made sense. And the bonus of getting laid every night with a woman who was spontaneous and wild and crazy was icing on the cake.

But once he had the engagement ring on her finger, he quickly found out that "wild and crazy" was synonymous with "girl most likely to max out your credit cards and move all your ready cash to a Swiss bank account." In retrospect, he suspected that the woman had some serious narcissism and abandonment issues. And that made it even worse. He was a trained professional, for God's sake. He should have spotted the signs.

His brief traipse down memory lane ended suddenly as he focused on the quiet woman beside him. He couldn't help but notice her long, long legs. And after that, it was only a half step to imagining those same slender, shapely limbs wrapped around his waist.

He actually blinked his eyes to clear his vision. What kind of pervert fantasized about his best friend when she had recently undergone a traumatic experience? Something must be seriously wrong with his moral compass. He owed Jane his utmost respect and consideration. Not his horny, base attentions.

But when he helped her from the car, her lanky frame leaning trustingly against him, it took all he had to slam the lid on a rush of arousal so potent it stunned him. The feel of her slender body shoulder to shoulder, hip to hip with his was heady stuff. He had to force his hands to stay out of trouble.

Once they made it inside, she was practically swaying on her feet, her cheeks totally devoid of color. He steered her to the bathroom. "Get in the shower, and I'll grab something of mine for you to wear. There should be a toothbrush in the drawer beside the sink." He was trying his utmost to respect her privacy, but he was not at all sure she was in any shape to be standing on her own.

He left her long enough to round up a pair of elastic-waist sweatpants, a soft cotton shirt, and some thick wool socks. When he opened the bathroom door a crack to lay the clothes on the counter, steam wafted out, carrying the scent of his soap.

Imagining Jane's nude body glistening wet, covered in clingy suds, made something inside his brain short-circuit. He leaned against the wall in the hall, his heart lodged in his throat. He couldn't ignore it any longer. He was seriously attracted to Jane.

Lord knew why he hadn't seen it before now. Looking back, he must have been a fool to think that the significant amount of time he had spent in her company was motivated by nothing more than platonic friendship.

Somewhere beneath the surface, his libido had clearly recognized what his not so bright brain had refused to accept. Jane was the kind of woman a man took to his bed and his heart. She was a keeper.

By the time he heard the water shut off, he had managed

to get rid of his boner. Thinking about Jane in danger did the trick. Knowing she had been vulnerable to some psycho . . . twice . . . made his stomach turn. Even though the events of to-night were not life-threatening, anything could have gone wrong. What if Jane had hurt herself seriously when she fell from the fire escape?

He would have felt directly responsible.

The break-in last weekend should have been a tip-off. He and his detectives should have tried harder to find any shred of evidence. They had all assumed it was a simple burglary attempt, a punk looking for ready cash.

But tonight's chain of events made it clear that money wasn't the motive. Whoever lit fire to those buckets of smoke bombs wanted to cause Jane heartache and financial difficulty. And Ethan was not going to rest until he'd nailed the bastard's ass to the wall.

She found him in the kitchen. The clothes didn't come close to fitting her. He outweighed her by at least forty pounds. But she had made do.

He motioned toward the stove. "I warmed some milk. Do you want anything to eat before you go back to bed?" It was almost three a.m., and she looked dead on her feet.

She wrinkled her nose. "I'm allergic to milk."

He swallowed hard. "Of course you are. I should have re-membered." It embarrassed him that he hadn't. Just once he would like to impress her. But at this rate, it wasn't likely to hap-pen anytime soon.

He opened the fridge. "How about a caffeine-free Coke? Or some orange juice?"

She yawned suddenly, her eyelids drooping. "I think I'll sleep just fine. But you stay up and eat a snack if you want to. I can stretch out on the sofa."

"Nonsense." He took her arm and steered her down the hall. "Sit on my bed for a minute and give me a chance to make sure the sheets are clean in the guest room."

He was back in no time, but Jane had already fallen asleep. She lay in an awkward position, one arm curled around his pillow. Her damp hair clung to her cheek, and his too-big sweatpants had slid down her hip on one side.

She wasn't wearing any panties.

It shouldn't have shocked him. If she'd had underwear on earlier (and perhaps she hadn't), she surely wouldn't have wanted to put it back on after her shower. All of her clothes smelled like smoke.

He eased the pants to a safer latitude, and stood irresolute. Carrying her to the guest room might sound tender, but it hadn't gone so well the last time he tried such a maneuver.

He tugged the covers back and eased her between them. She never even blinked. By the even tenor of her breathing, he suspected that she was deeply asleep, unlikely to be aware of anything until morning.

He could go to the sofa. It would be the gentlemanly thing to do. But the living room was the coldest room in the house, and what he really wanted to do was sleep with Jane. He would stay on top of the covers, he told himself, eager to rationalize his behavior. With a couple of blankets to keep him warm, he'd be fine. And besides, last weekend she had *asked* him to keep her company.

He carried out his preparations, which included a quick shower of his own, and then climbed onto the end of the king-size mattress opposite his houseguest. Fatigue rolled over him the minute his head hit the pillow, and he barely had the energy to turn out the light.

\*     \*     \*

It was sometime before dawn when a noise wakened him. The distress in the quiet whimpers sent his heart racing until he realized Jane was having a nightmare.

He scooted closer, frustrated by the bedding that kept him from pulling her into his arms. He touched her cheek. "Wake up, honey. Jane . . . you're dreaming." He stroked her hair, trying to bring her to consciousness without further trauma.

She opened her eyes with a choked gasp, her chest heaving with the tenor of her rapid breathing.

He cupped her face with his hand. "It's okay, Jane. No one is going to hurt you."

He kept his voice low and soothing, not quite convinced she was fully awake. The room was dark, but he was loath to turn on a light. It was probably better for her to slip back into sleep naturally.

He felt her shiver, and he tucked the comforter more securely around her shoulders. That action had the added benefit of keeping his hands away from dangerous territory. It startled him when she spoke.

Her words were almost inaudible. "There were flames everywhere. I couldn't find the door."

He continued playing with her silky hair, keeping his touch light. "It was a nightmare. You're safe here with me. Go back to sleep."

For long, silent seconds he thought she had done just that. Her breathing was regular again, and the tension in her body relaxed.

But then she stirred restlessly, shoving back the covers and turning on her side. His hand fell away from her hair, and he wondered if that had been her intent. He couldn't make out her features in the darkness, but he could detect her feminine scent. Even with his soap, she smelled like Jane. He wanted to bury his face in the curve of her neck and inhale her warm, soft skin.

Instead, he eased back to give her room. "Is there anything I can do for you? Are you thirsty? Cold?"

She must have suddenly realized that she wasn't in the guest room. Her voice held a note of humor. "I see that I conked out on you in your bed. My apologies."

He yawned. "Not to worry. This mattress could sleep an army."

"What time is it?"

He glanced at the digital clock on his side of the bed. "Almost five."

He heard her exhale in a long sigh, but she didn't say anything.

He reached out to touch her arm and made contact with a soft breast. Shit. His reflexes were lightning-fast. He jerked back his hand like he'd been burned. He swallowed hard. "I'm serious, Jane. It's way too early for either of us to get up on a Sunday morning. What do you need to make you go back to sleep?"

He could barely hear her breathe.

Then she found his ear in the darkness and traced it with a fingertip. "You could make love to me."

# Seven

The silence in Ethan's bedroom was deafening. And it lasted for about a millennium. Jane couldn't decide if it was good or bad that she couldn't see his face. Abject horror . . . or uncomfortable embarrassment. Either reaction would be unacceptable.

He startled her when he finally choked out, "Well . . . uh . . ."

She punched his arm, trying to speak lightly even with a boulder of mortification crushing her stomach. "Oh, good grief. I was joking, Ethan. Go back to sleep."

She rolled over and stared dry-eyed into the darkness. Well, that was productive. She bit her lip. What had possessed her? It was always a mistake to deviate from the plan. She needed the erotic valentines to soften him up. Then and only then would she a take a chance on revealing her "mystery poet" identity. She was banking on the fact that he had some level of affection for her, as well as the fact that he was a guy and therefore predisposed to being seduced.

She hadn't gotten past that point in her imagination. If she seduced him and he still didn't want to fall in love with her, well . . . it was just too damn bad. In that scenario, he deserved to die alone and miserable. Ha.

She ignored the ache of hurt in her stomach. Offering herself to a man while ensconced in his bed seemed foolproof. But clearly, Assistant Chief of Police Ethan Oldham was made of sterner stuff.

*What if he doesn't want you at all, Jane? What if he's never been attracted to you? What if he thinks way-too-tall women with not an ounce of feminine wiles are just plain boring?*

She buried her head in the pillow and swallowed a groan. She ached to feel him slide between her thighs and bury his thick, warm flesh inside her. The yearning was so strong, it brought tears of frustration to her eyes.

She blinked them back angrily and listened intently to see if Ethan was snoring. Was he still awake? Had she shocked the crap out of him? Had he believed her when she'd said she was kidding?

Even from three feet away, she couldn't tell. Her eyelids drooped, and she yawned twice in a row, practically popping her jaw in the process. The last thing she remembered before slumber claimed her was hearing her name whispered in the darkness.

Ethan knew the moment Jane's breathing settled into a regular cadence. He'd give his right arm to fall asleep as well, but her ingenuous invitation had put an end to any chance he had of sleeping this night.

He eased from the bed, extracted some clothes from a drawer, and exited the room, pulling the door closed behind him. He felt punchy, not only from lack of sleep, but from what she had said. *You could make love to me.*

Holy hell. What if he'd barked out an affirmative before she had a chance to rescind her invitation? If he'd been quicker to respond, not so paralyzed by shock and indecision, he might at this very moment be buried inside her, thrusting wildly, giving them both pleasure beyond their wildest dreams. Thinking about it made his hands shaky, his mouth dry, and his dick hard.

He groaned softly and headed for the kitchen. The headache he had was one that caffeine probably wouldn't cure, but it sure as heck couldn't hurt.

Three cups of coffee later, the first pale hint of dawn was lightening the sky outside his window, and he decided it was late enough to check in at the station. After a half hour on the phone, first with his own guys and then with the ladder and hose boys, he had more questions than answers. But in the meantime, he'd secured permission to take Jane back to her apartment to pack a suitcase and recover her valuables.

Her building had been under surveillance all night. In many situations, an arsonist returned to the scene of the crime. Not that this was arson in the truest sense of the word. More like serious vandalism.

At nine o'clock, Jane was still sleeping. He tiptoed into the bedroom, unable to resist the temptation of studying her unobserved. She had thrown back the covers. His oversize, shapeless clothing should have made her look unattractive. But he couldn't see a thing to criticize. She was beautiful.

Her hair, now dry, fanned across his pillow, the mix of colors from vibrant gold to warm brown to pale honey far more interesting than plain blond. Her features were delicate: high cheekbones, a narrow chin, and a small, straight nose. She'd worn braces in middle school, and now her lovely smile had the knack of leaving him breathless.

He must have made a noise, because she stretched and blinked sleepily and sat up. "What time is it?" Her voice was husky, her fair skin flushed.

He shoved his hands in his pockets. "After nine."

Her mouth dropped. "Ethan! Why did you let me sleep so late?"

He shrugged, unrepentant. "You needed the rest."

She tossed back the covers, swung her legs over the side of the bed, and snatched hastily at the waistband of the pants as they threatened to come off. Ethan had one quick glimpse of a creamy hip.

He cleared his throat. "I talked to the fire chief. He's giving the okay for you to go in and get clothes, your purse, whatever else you need."

She frowned. "And when can I start the cleanup?"

"Maybe later today. He'll let you know. I couldn't remember your cell number, so I gave him mine."

She stood and faced him, shoving her hair out of her face. "Thank you. If you'll give me a ride over there, I'll get out of your way."

He took a step closer and was intrigued when she backed up a half step. Though she projected an air of calm, in her eyes he saw confusion and wariness. Did she feel a fraction of the pull that was tormenting him?

He cleared his throat. "It's no trouble, Jane. I'm supposed to be off today, but once you're settled, I want to take a look at the evidence that was gathered last night and this morning. I trust my guys, but this punk has made it personal."

He gave up the fight to keep his distance. He took her face in his hands and dropped a teasing kiss on her nose. She was trembling, and since he had turned the heat up several degrees, he had to assume her condition was caused by something else. Him? He'd like to think so.

She had her arms wrapped around her waist. "I'll feel better when we know who did it."

He rubbed his hands up and down her arms. "We'll get him. Don't you worry."

Jane was moments away from jumping Ethan's bones when the phone rang.

It took him a full three seconds to release her and reach for the receiver on the bedside table. His movements were slow and jerky. She used his momentary distraction to escape to the bathroom.

Staring in the mirror was a mistake. She looked like a bag lady on a three-day bender. Her hair was fluffy, for lack of a better word, clearly the result of falling asleep when it was still damp. And her pale face, devoid of makeup, was in bad need of some lip gloss, which was one thing Ethan's well-stocked bathroom couldn't supply.

She slid her feet into her ruined slippers and grimaced. The sooner she got home the better.

Ethan was not happy when she bade him goodbye at the back door to her building. He'd fed her breakfast and chauffeured her home. But that was the extent to which she was willing to impose on his good graces.

She was wearing one of his coats, and she felt awkward and in serious need of some privacy to regroup. "Thank you for all your help, Ethan."

He got out of the car despite her protests. "You shouldn't go in alone."

She grinned wryly. "There's no structural damage. I'm going

to change clothes, get what I need for the short term, and then probably go over to Mr. Benson's and talk to him about how to proceed." Last week she hadn't bothered him. But this cleanup would be far more costly and complicated, and she wasn't familiar with her landlord's insurance coverage.

Ethan folded his arms across his chest, leaned a hip against his car, and pinned her with a narrow gaze. "You shouldn't plan on sleeping here tonight."

She lifted her chin. "If they give me the all clear, I certainly will. I've got a big job ahead of me and no time to waste."

"The place stinks," he said bluntly.

"Bad smells never killed anyone."

She saw him grind his jaw. "You could still work all you want and at the end of the day sleep at my place."

She gave him a sweet smile. "People might talk, Ethan. We don't want to give them the wrong impression . . . you know, since we're just good friends."

Ethan stewed about her parting shot for the rest of the day. If he hadn't known better, he'd think her words were a challenge. Almost as if she was pissed he hadn't made love to her. But that didn't make sense. She had been joking about the sex thing. She'd told him so.

Or had she been trying to backpedal last night when his stunned astonishment made him slow to respond? Oh, hell, women were impossible to understand.

No one raised an eyebrow when he showed up at work. He'd been known to come in on his days off—perhaps not the best idea in the world, but when you're bucking for a promotion, it had made sense to him to put in some extra hours here and there.

The job was as good as his—nobody disputed that. But his workaholic ways had become a habit.

He had gone over all the evidence from last night's fire and was entering some stuff in the computer when a knock sounded at his door. Ordinarily, the door stayed open. He thought it was a good policy. But today, off the clock, he'd opted for privacy.

Grimacing at the interruption, he sighed and swiveled his chair. "Come in."

The young officer hovered in the doorway until Ethan waved a hand. "Have a seat." Randy Temple was a fine young officer. He'd come to them from somewhere like Kansas or Nebraska. After a vacation in the Smoky Mountains, Temple had decided he wanted to relocate.

His fellow officers liked him. He was confident but not cocky, and he was rock-solid both in ability and in gut instincts. Ethan considered him one of the best—the kind of man you could rely on in a crisis and know he had your back.

Ethan leaned back in his chair, keeping his posture deliberately casual. Temple seemed . . . odd. Not agitated—that was too strong a word—but something. And he had yet to be seated.

Ethan was puzzled. "What can I do for you?"

Temple glanced into the hall. "May I close the door, sir? This is a private matter."

Ethan's stomach tightened. "Of course."

Finally, the younger man sat down.

Ethan schooled his face to impassivity. "What's up?"

Randy Temple took a deep breath. "I wanted to ask your permission to date your sister."

Ethan blinked. In a million possible scenarios he might have invented, this didn't make the list. "Date my sister . . . ?" He heard the incredulous question in his own voice.

Randy nodded gravely. "I want you to know that I respect her and that I would never do anything to hurt her. You're my superior officer. I didn't want this to be any kind of *thing* between us."

The sheer earnestness on the younger man's face poked Ethan's funny bone, but he dared not let any amusement show. "I appreciate that, Temple." That was as far as he got. What was he supposed to say?

Randy's posture relaxed a millimeter. "I've gotten to know your sister a little bit . . . you know, when she's been bringing the meals. She's a very special woman."

Ethan nodded absently, wondering how in the hell he had gotten trapped in this awkward conversation. "Um, Temple . . . you do realize that my sister is considerably older than you?" He felt honor bound to point that out, though he would never divulge Sherry's exact age.

Randy shrugged. "Yeah. I figured as much. But it doesn't matter to me at all."

From the fervent note in Temple's voice, Ethan surmised that a serious crush held his junior officer in thrall. Well, hell, it would do Sherry good to know that a man saw her as appealing and available. She lived like a nun.

He gave the other man a terse nod. "It's not for me to say. Sherry's her own woman. She makes her own decisions. But I have no objection."

Randy's tense expression finally lightened. "Thank you, sir. I won't let you down."

On Monday, Sherry pulled up into the parking lot at the police station and gave herself the usual pep talk. She was gaining confidence, but it was still difficult to walk in there and be chatty and friendly. She was a very private person. It was a habit she'd developed in the devastating days when she'd found out she was pregnant at seventeen.

Everywhere she went, people had whispered behind her back. Some of the chatter was merely curious and interested, not cruel. But she hated knowing that her every move was being watched. And she began withdrawing in order to protect her out-of-control emotions and her tiny unborn baby.

Early in high school she'd been one of the popular girls. But that had fallen by the wayside as soon as she and Barry got pregnant. After that, school had become a prison sentence rife with whispered gossip and pitying looks.

It had been easier to stay inside her head, as it were. She communed with the infant growing inside her, bonding long before the moment of birth.

Barry had been on the periphery of her life. He was a typical awkward adolescent, ruled by his hormones and sports. His parents saw Sherry as the bad-girl seducer, and though they finally consented to allow their wonderful Barry to marry the mother of his child, they'd made no secret of their distrust of Sherry.

It was a hell of a way to grow up fast.

A horn honked nearby, startling her, and she jumped out of the car. Here she was daydreaming while the food in the back was getting cold.

Last week she had served meals on Tuesday and Thursday. The food was such a success that everyone, Ethan included, begged her to make it a Monday-Wednesday-Friday affair. So here she was, wondering if she was biting off too much to chew.

Officer Temple seemed to have knack for knowing when she would arrive. Already, he was striding across the parking lot, his handsome face wreathed in a smile. He greeted her and waited patiently until she loaded him up with several large containers.

In the conference room, they worked together side by side. He was helpful and courteous, and he had a sly sense of humor. They had everything ready ten minutes early, so she poured him a glass of tea.

As she handed it to him, their fingers brushed, and she felt an odd sensation of warmth. She smiled and picked up her own glass. "I have to thank you again, Officer Temple. You've been a huge help. But I don't want to keep you from your important work."

He took a sip of tea. "I'm happy to do it. It puts me near the front of the line."

His gentle teasing and the warmth in his eyes made her flush. "It's nothing special," she insisted. Today she had prepared turkey tacos with all the fixings. It was a healthy alternative, and once the guys and gals loaded up their tacos with plenty of extras, they would never miss the ground beef.

He tipped back his head to drain the disposable cup, and Sherry saw the muscles in his throat contract. She looked away quickly. So it startled her when she felt his hand on her forearm.

His expression was intent. "Ms. McCamish, do you think we could call each other by our first names?"

She bit her lip. "Well, sure."

His smile made her want to squirm. "Sherry," he said softly. The way his tongue wrapped around the two syllables left her unsettled.

She lifted her shoulders. "Kind of an old-fashioned name. No one uses it anymore."

He cocked his head, and she could swear he was staring at her mouth. "I like it," he murmured. "Why don't you give mine a shot?"

"Hmmm?" She was admiring the tiny flecks of amber in his brown eyes.

"Call me Randy," he said patiently.

She licked her lips. Where in the heck were her customers? She started to speak, and her dry throat almost choked her. After another quick sip of tea, she spit the single word out hastily, her voice a mere whisper, "Randy."

His beaming smile was a bit over the top. But it warmed her nevertheless.

At that moment, a crowd of uniformed men and women jostled good-naturedly through the door, putting an end to the odd interlude. For the next hour, Sherry scooped and served and cleaned up, overconscious of the man at her elbow making her job easier, anticipating her every move.

By one o'clock, the rush was over. She retrieved her containers and stored the small remaining amounts of meat, cheese, etc. Despite the boredom of eating the same meal twice in one day, she would polish off the leftovers this evening. Being thrifty was too deeply ingrained a habit for her to do otherwise.

She glanced at her companion. "These aren't heavy now that they're empty. I know you have work to do, and I can handle this."

He ignored her and helped carry everything out to her car. When it was all stored in the back, he opened her door and waited until she was seated. Then he leaned down, one arm resting across the top of the doorframe, the other propped on the open door.

His smile had disappeared, replaced by the serious, intense gaze she'd noticed earlier. "Will you go out to dinner with me tonight?"

Her mind went fuzzy and her stomach pitched. She couldn't quite wrap her brain around what he had said. "Excuse me?"

Still he didn't smile. "I'm asking you out on a date," he said quietly, utterly patient.

The saliva in her mouth had mysteriously dried up, and her tongue had lost the ability to form even simple words. "I, ah . . ."

His eyes narrowed. "Do you already have plans?"

"No." Well, heck, that was not what she'd meant to say, not at all.

A small smile bloomed in his eyes, but the line of his mouth remained stoic. "So will you? Go out with me?"

She was pretty sure his gaze had strayed ever so briefly to her breasts. "Do you know how old I am?"

He shook his head. "Do you want to tell me?"

She didn't. Not really. "Thirty-eight. And what are you . . . about twelve?" She winced. That was rude and uncalled-for. But he had really rattled her.

He didn't take offense. "I'm twenty-nine. Is that a problem?"

She couldn't believe she was having this conversation. "I have a grown child," she blurted out, expecting to see shock or disapproval on his face.

His shrug held neither. "I know. I've seen a picture of the two of you on Chief Oldham's desk."

Her hands gripped the steering wheel. In the ten years since her divorce, she hadn't dated. Period. She'd been a full-time mom, her entire focus on Debra. Even when her daughter had ceased to need her as much, Sherry had always been available. She'd worked a part-time job at the animal shelter to bring in some extra cash, but the vet knew that in any kind of crisis, Sherry's daughter came first.

She'd lived the life of a nun, still paying penance for an adolescent mistake. If there had been men interested in her, she hadn't noticed.

Randy crouched beside the car. Now his face was even with her breasts. Slowly, perhaps waiting for her to reject his overture, he reached out and pulled her left hand from where it had a death grip on the steering wheel.

His thumb stroked the back of her hand. *Sweet glory*. Her skin was on fire.

He watched her face as he toyed with her fingers. "You haven't answered me," he said, his voice husky.

The uneven timbre made her shiver. "I don't think this is a very good idea." Her lips formed the correct words, but some long-buried part of her was shouting out, trying to be heard, *Give him a chance.*

Now his brash grin was lopsided. "I think it's a damn good idea, Sherry."

The way he said her name made something deep inside her unfurl and awaken. She struggled with her conscience. It would be wrong to go out with him. Wouldn't it?

While she was still trying to make up her mind, he leaned in, one hand on her thigh for balance, and kissed her. It was a brief, rather chaste brush of the lips. But it rocked her world. How sad was it that she hadn't been kissed romantically in a decade?

She felt like a dried-up old woman. Near tears at the beauty of what one brief kiss had brought back. Tenderness. Sexual awareness. Exploration. Hope.

He backed away and stood up. Had she responded? She wasn't even sure. Without thinking, she raised her hand to her lips, trying to feel the heat that tingled there. He must think she was mentally challenged.

Randy smiled down at her. Not a cocky "I know you want me" smile. But something sweeter. Something more real. Something profound.

He persisted, even in the face of her stunned silence. "Will you go out with me tonight?"

She bit her bottom lip, excitement and fear battling for supremacy. "Where would we go?"

Her naive question coaxed another smile from him. "Somewhere nice . . . maybe in Knoxville."

His answer settled her nerves. It was unlikely that they would run into anyone she knew if they were forty-five minutes away from home.

Still she dithered. "Why?" she asked baldly. She knew she was being socially clumsy, but everything about this was new to her, and clearly, his age worried her.

He took a deep breath. "You're a beautiful woman. I'd like to get to know you."

"Ethan might not approve of me getting involved with someone at the station."

His lips quirked. "I've already asked him. He gave his blessing."

She felt her face heat. Her baby brother *knew* about this. God, it was mortifying. Was Ethan amused by the odd pair she and Randy would make?

She tried one last time to dissuade him. "I don't really date."

"Good," he said, his tone smug. "I won't have to worry about fending off the competition."

She rolled her eyes. "Believe me, you're safe on that score."

He stepped back and closed her door. The window was still down, and when he leaned in this time, their faces were close enough for another kiss.

But Randy Temple was a strategist. He left her yearning for more. Instead, he brushed her cheek with a finger. "I'll pick you up at six o'clock."

And then he turned around and walked back into the building.

# Eight

Sherry stood in front of the full-length mirror on the back of her closet door and fought back semihysterical laughter. She had no date clothes.

She had mom clothes . . . and church clothes . . . and even a few outfits that were suitable for dealing with sick animals. But she had nothing remotely appropriate for a date with a handsome man like Randy Temple.

She glanced at her watch. It was already four thirty, so making a dash to buy something new was out of the question, even if she'd wanted to spend the money.

There was only one other option.

In the last two weeks, she had avoided going into Debra's bedroom, because of the panic it invoked. If she faced the fact that Debra was moving out for good, she had to admit that her life was in a tailspin.

If she wasn't a mom, what was she?

It took courage to open the door. The instant she crossed the threshold, Deb's signature apple scent filled her nostrils. Sherry's lips trembled, but she clamped her jaw. This was no time for a meltdown. Randy would be on her doorstep in a little over an hour. She had to be ready, because she sure as heck wasn't the kind of sophisticated woman who would invite him in for a drink before they left. She wouldn't know what to say or do.

It would probably be several weeks before Debra could get away from her new school long enough to come back to Statlerville to pack up her stuff. In the meantime, her closets were still bulging . . . particularly with winter clothes. After all, there wasn't much need in Tampa for wool sweaters and heavy coats.

Which meant Sherry had a lot to choose from.

After ten minutes of paralysis as she rifled through neon pinks and blinding lime greens and gaudy turquoise prints, she finally gave a sigh of relief. On a padded hanger near the back of the closet was a simple black cashmere turtleneck. The tags were still attached.

Barry's wife had picked it out for Debra for Christmas a year ago. It was a thoughtful gift, expensive and classic, but Sherry's extrovert daughter had never been one to blend into the background. So the sweater hung, unworn.

Sherry was pretty sure Debra would never miss it.

She took the sweater back to her bedroom and put it on over a seamless bra. Then she stood there shivering in her panties as she dithered over what to pair the sweater with. A dark khaki corduroy skirt, seldom worn, caught her eye. The fitted waist was flattering, and the hemline would look good with the black boots Deb had given her for Christmas.

They had opened their gifts early, since Deb was going south for the holidays. Sherry had *oooh*ed and *ahhh*ed over the butter-soft knee-high leather boots, but in her mind, she couldn't ever imagine wearing them.

They were sexy. There. She said it out loud. And the last thing she felt these days was sexy.

She stepped into the skirt and zipped it up. Then she wriggled her legs into silky panty hose and put on the boots. The woman in the mirror was a stranger. Although the sweater was a turtleneck—no provocative neckline—it hugged her breasts far more than anything she normally wore out in public. The skirt showed off her narrow waist and curvy hips, and in the boots, her legs looked long and feminine.

Before she could change her mind and her clothes, she raced to the bathroom and started applying makeup. She rarely bothered with her looks, so adding eyeshadow, mascara, and lip gloss felt over the top.

But when her shaking hands completed the task and she looked in the mirror, she was reassured by her reflection. Her green eyes looked big and mysterious, her lips soft and sensual.

She felt near tears suddenly. How long had it been since she deliberately made herself look pretty?

Biting back the unwelcome emotion, she returned to her bedroom and picked out a handbag that matched the boots. With her black wool coat, she was ready.

She left the coat on the chair by the front door and paced nervously. What did women do while waiting to be picked up for a date?

The small house was clean from top to bottom. She was a meticulous housekeeper. And she had burned a candle earlier, so the air smelled of jasmine and lemon. But she wasn't going to ask Randy to come in. Was she?

By the time he actually rang the bell, she was a mess. She opened the door, half inclined to tell him she had to stay home.

The cat was having kittens. The cable guy was on the way to fix a faulty wire. Her checkbook was out of balance. She couldn't miss *American Idol*. Any one of a number of excuses came to mind.

But all she managed to say was a weak hello.

Randy's eyes widened when he saw her, and the smile faded from his face. "Wow . . . Sherry . . . you look . . . amazing." He seemed to be having trouble stringing words together.

His lack of composure comforted her. Perhaps she wasn't the only one feeling off balance.

On the drive into Knoxville, they chatted about innocuous topics. There were plenty of places to eat in Statlerville, but Sherry was glad Randy had opted to take her a little farther afield, where they weren't likely to run into anyone they knew. She was very self-conscious about his age . . . and hers.

Not that she was old enough to be his mother, or even close. But in terms of life experience, she felt terribly ancient.

She'd expected him to take her to one of the well-known upscale restaurants for a fancy dinner. But instead, they took an unfamiliar road that led down to the banks of the Tennessee River. The riverfront was lit up with lights along a walking path, and the water reflected the illuminated signs for a couple of small restaurants.

Even then, she still didn't get it.

Randy parked and helped her out of the car. He led her to the dock, where a small riverboat was tied up. It was a two-story affair very popular in the spring and summer for hosting weddings and proms.

On a dark, cold January night, it rocked slowly in the frigid water, a bit forlorn.

Randy took her hand. "I wanted to have a chance for us to get to know each other," he said solemnly. "And a noisy restaurant didn't sound appealing. So I rented the riverboat for a few hours."

Her eyebrows rose. "The whole boat?"

He shrugged. "It's not exactly peak season. The guy cut me a deal."

As they boarded, the captain and copilot introduced themselves. No other staff members were on board. Randy led her down two steps into the main cabin. In nice weather, the large windows would be open wide. But tonight, the medium-size room was snug and warm.

On the far wall, a table and two chairs had been set up beside the largest window, giving a view of the water and the bridges in the distance. Randy hadn't gone overboard with anything that could be construed as inappropriate for a first date. But their meal, warming beneath metal covers, was already in place.

Sherry was startled when the engines kicked in. Soon she felt the steady thrum as the boat moved slowly away from the dock.

Randy held out a hand. "Are you hungry?"

She was—starving, in fact. She took off her coat and put it and her purse on a nearby bench. Randy helped seat her, and she shook out her heavy cloth napkin and spread it on her lap. "I'm impressed."

He grinned at her, taking the chair opposite her at the small round table. "Well, the food won't compare to what you can do. You cook like a professional chef. But I was hoping to make up for it with the ambience."

She laughed softly, charmed in spite of herself. It was immensely flattering that he had gone to so much trouble. As they ate, she really didn't pay much attention to the meal at all. The chicken dish was good, but she was too nervous to enjoy much of it.

Little by little, watching the inky, slumberous river as they drifted along, Sherry forgot to be self-conscious. Randy was easy to be with.

By the time they reached dessert, Sherry was wondering

why she had felt so reluctant to accept this date. This was nice. Two adults sharing a meal and conversation. Nothing to get all worked up over.

Randy took a sip of his beer. They had a bottle of white wine, but Sherry wasn't much of a drinker and had stuck mostly to ice water. He was studying her face with an intensity that made her feel self-conscious.

She shoved her hair behind her ear. It was loose tonight, and she had taken the time to curl it. Which was a lot more work than throwing it up in her customary ponytail, but she was glad she had gone to the trouble. The appreciation in Randy's eyes made it all worthwhile. "What?" she asked with a little laugh. "Do I have spinach in my teeth?"

He leaned back in his chair. "Tell me about your daughter." The gentle sincerity in his gaze surprised her. In past experience, most men were not at all interested in hearing about a woman's excess baggage. Which was why she basically hadn't dated for ten years.

She smiled slightly. "Debra recently turned twenty. After finishing up at the community college, she decided to complete her four-year degree in Tampa and then stay there for graduate work in marine biology. She'll be living with her dad."

"You miss her." He cut to the heart of the matter with surprising ease.

She nodded, relieved to know she could talk about it without tears. "It's been just the two of us ever since my husband and I divorced when she was ten. I guess you can do the math. I got pregnant at seventeen, became a mom at eighteen. It was difficult, of course. And Barry and I tried to make it work. But rarely can you base a marriage on teenage hormones and expect it to last. He's happy now. His new wife is a nice woman. She's been good to Debra. That's my story, I guess."

"Did you ever think of giving her up for adoption? When you first found out, I mean."

"Never. It was a difficult period of my life—one I never really stopped paying for, I guess. But I've never once regretted Debra. She's been my life."

"I admire you," he said quietly. "Small-town gossip can be cruel."

How did he know? She rarely thought about those early days. It was a rough time, one she didn't care to dwell on. "Yes, it can," she said slowly. "I thought I'd never get past the whispers, the pointed stares."

She clenched her hands in her lap to stop them from shaking. "What about you? I heard you moved here because you loved the mountains."

His half smile was shadowed by some unnamed emotion. "That's true as far as it goes," he said slowly. "But the real reason was to get away from my dad."

Her stomach clenched. "Abuse?"

His eyes were bleak. "Not the way you mean. I had just graduated from the police academy when it came out that my father, a local judge, had been taking bribes and kickbacks. Here I was, practically shining my pretty new badge every morning, ready to take on all the bad guys in the town. . . ." His throat worked, and he fell silent.

She winced inwardly. "And he was one of them."

"Yeah." He stared at his plate. "I hated him for a while. He humiliated my whole family. And I don't think he ever really thought he was doing anything wrong."

She bit her lip. "I'm sorry, Randy. That must have been agonizing."

"I couldn't stay. He served a few months of a sentence, and once he was back home, I took off. Ended up in Statlerville." His lips crooked. "Your brother has gone a long way toward restoring my faith in the process."

"Ethan is a wonderful man, but he works too hard."

"It must run in the family. I've never seen you slow down yet." His teasing lightened the mood. He held out a hand. "Do you feel like dancing?"

"Dancing?" She stared at him blankly. It might as well have been a foreign word.

He tugged her to her feet. "It will come back to you." He flipped a switch on something that looked like an intercom, and suddenly, slow, romantic music filled the room.

She stood stiffly in his embrace. God, how long had it been since she danced? Probably her junior prom. She'd missed her senior prom because her baby was suffering from colic.

She pushed away the memories. Concentrated instead on the feel of Randy's warm, hard body aligned with hers. He held her close, but not too tightly. After a few awkward steps, she exhaled and let her spine relax a fraction. The sensation of being enfolded in a man's arms was something she hadn't experienced in a very long time.

They danced forever, it seemed, lost in a private bubble engendered by the empty boat, the lovely meal, and the evocative music.

They talked now and then, but the silences were comfortable. She learned the way his smile felt against her cheek, registered the appealing rasp of his slight stubble. He'd barely had time to get home and change clothes, much less shave. But she liked it. It suited his masculinity. And the differences between them made her breathless.

She noticed his erection early on. He didn't make a big deal about it, and neither did she. The connection between them was new but very real.

And the fact that he wanted her made her feel . . . well, something. She couldn't pin it down. There was caution, of course. That was ingrained in her nature. But there was also something very tenuous and fragile—a gentle curl of anticipation.

Everything inside her melted and went soft in response to his obvious need. He was every inch the gentleman, but in his ragged breathing and the steady thump of his heartbeat, she felt his hunger.

Laying her head on his shoulder, she closed her eyes and floated. It was lovely to be wooed, to feel the endless possibilities. She'd lost out on all of that because of one immature mistake.

One for which she had paid dearly. Despite the joy she'd had in being a mom, she'd never really experienced being any man's one and only. Barry had tried. So had she. But the love wasn't there. Affection, yes. At least in the beginning. And a certain amount of physical compatibility . . . when they weren't too tired from going to school and caring for a baby. But never any of the emotions the songwriters touted. No romance.

Sherry was not naive. This thing Randy felt for her would burn itself out. She was nine years older than he was. He deserved to find love with a woman his own age, get married, travel, start a family.

Even if she allowed herself to fall for him, she couldn't cheat him out of a normal life. Following complications after Deb's birth, Sherry had been forced to have a hysterectomy. It had broken her heart, but she had made peace with it, particularly when it became clear that she and Barry wouldn't be staying together.

Instead of dreaming of a future with a man who adored her and a house full of babies, she'd turned all the love in her heart to raising her daughter. The temptation was there to spoil Debra, even on a limited income. But somehow she had managed to rein in her unhealthy impulses, and had been a fairly strict mom.

She'd done the job of parenting the best she knew how, and she was proud of her daughter.

Randy's lips brushed her cheek, and she made a little sound of surprise. He touched a spot below her ear with the tip of his tongue. Her knees threatened to buckle. Arousal, unexpected but heady and sharp, filled her bloodstream. His hands moved over her back, warm and firm.

"You are so beautiful and so sweet." His whisper in her ear made her choke back a moan. She had forgotten the twist of sexual desire, or maybe she had tried to. But nothing she experienced alone in her barren bed came close to this.

He found her mouth. The kiss was hot and passionate. But it was too much. Too soon. She panicked and pushed out of his arms.

"I'm sorry, Randy. Please take me home."

Ethan cursed softly under his breath. All hell was breaking loose at the station. Apparently, several lots of this year's flu vaccine had been duds. The strain going around had hit his ranks with a vengeance, and he was scrambling to cover shifts.

He'd been less than useless to Jane. If he had his way, he'd be over there right now, helping her deal with the mess that was still surrounding her. But duty had to come before his personal life, no matter how much it chafed.

The investigation into the so-called "fire" at Jane's was ongoing. The initial investigators had recovered a number of viable fingerprints at the scene, but when they ran the prints through several databases, no matches showed up. Which meant the perp was a first-time offender.

On the one hand it reassured Ethan that Jane wasn't in danger from a career criminal. But in another way, it worried him. Which law-abiding citizen in Statlerville was so angry with Jane that he or she wanted revenge?

The other thing pissing Ethan off was more aggravating than important. Since last week, he'd been planning on staking out the main post office tomorrow, Thursday, in hopes of determining the identity of his mystery admirer. Even in the midst of chaos, the naughty verses stayed in the back of his mind.

He was intrigued. He admitted it. And more than once, he'd almost told Jane about the two erotic valentines he had received so far. But he remembered what she said about being jealous of his fiancée four years ago, and he finally decided to keep his mouth shut.

He hadn't been sleeping well. He'd dreamed about the sexually explicit notes again and again. And the last few nights, Jane had played a starring role as the author of his titillating mail. Which made no sense at all, except for the fact that the two women were getting mixed up in his head, in his subconscious. Jane. The phantom seductress. One a friend. The other an intriguing stranger whose secret he was determined to expose.

But he was out of luck this week. He'd be lucky to find time to check on Jane, much less spend several hours hanging out at the post office.

He ground his teeth together and strode toward the command center. He was the assistant chief of police. He had a job to do.

Jane was sick to death of seeing and touching wet, crumpled stationery. The stench of the decomposing paper, combined as it was with the lingering smell of the noxious smoke, gave her a headache that wouldn't go away.

Mr. Benson had been over each day to check on her. He'd contracted with a professional cleaning service that specialized in smoke damage and related problems to come in and attack the building from top to bottom. They were to start Friday evening and work straight through the weekend. But in the meantime, it was up to Jane to sift through the mess of inventory and decide what, if anything, could be salvaged.

Her renter's insurance would cover some but not all of the replacement costs. It would be perhaps a year before her budget would recover from the loss. And she wasn't entirely sure it was worthwhile keeping the shop open.

Her personal belongings upstairs were another worry. Even though she had a washer and dryer, it had seemed far simpler to empty her closets and go to the Laundromat so she could wash everything at once. And she had already discovered, much to her dismay, that some fabrics required a second cleaning to eradicate the smell.

It was slow, exhausting work.

Ethan had come by in the evenings, offering his help. But it had been after nine each time, and she could see the exhaustion in his face. The flu epidemic was making his job hellishly complicated. And as wonderful as it would have been to lean on him, her concerns were not nearly as important as the responsibilities he bore.

Still, she missed him. At first she wondered if her impulsive invitation to have sex had spooked him. She'd barely spoken to him since they parted company on Sunday. But then she'd read in the newspaper about the unprecedented number of officers who were stricken with the flu, and she had breathed a sigh of relief.

Ethan wasn't avoiding her. He was working his ass off.

She could relate.

Thursday she took a few minutes midmorning to drink some coffee and have a snack. She hadn't been eating or sleeping well—the inevitable result of stress. She sat at her kitchen table for a half hour and jotted an attempt at a sex poem. She really didn't have the time, but she was reluctant to let her erotic-mail campaign lapse, and besides, she needed a break.

She'd brought a few sheets of thick handmade paper upstairs with her, enough to do four more notes. Pockets of undamaged material remained here and there in the store. The items were too few and too scattered to sell, so she would keep them for her personal use.

When the last of her coffee was gone, she read through her third verse one more time. It was her most earthy, in-your-face attempt yet. Would Ethan be aroused by it? Would he read it again and again and wonder whose hand had written it? Would the words lodge in his psyche?

She didn't have time to rifle through the boxes of junk down-stairs and find decorations. This note would have to fly on its own. Still, the paper was nice. It was lemon-colored, lightly speckled with orange and gold dots. Sort of like the freckles that appeared on her nose and cheeks the first time she courted the summer sun each year.

It was a good five hours later before she finally made it to the post office. She'd had to take a shower before she could leave the building. Not only had she smelled like smoke, but her clothes had been filthy. All that wet paper left little gluelike blobs that stuck to anything they touched and turned into concrete if she didn't remove them before they hardened.

This time she didn't feel as self-conscious about mailing her letter. Was this how criminals reacted? Did they get so accus-tomed to the rush of adrenaline that it ceased to make them ner-vous when they perpetrated a crime?

She strolled up to the "local" slot, took one last look at her letter, and boldly slid it into the opening. Immediately, her heart felt lighter. She had a good feeling about these notes.

In her imagination, she saw Ethan's face when she finally

came clean about her secret. His dark eyes would flare with passion. He'd sweep her off her feet. . . . Oh, poop. Maybe not that. She sighed, catching sight of her reflection in the plate-glass window as she exited. She towered over the white-haired senior citizen who smiled and walked ahead of her down the steps to the parking lot.

It all boiled down to one simple truth. No matter how intrigued Ethan became with her string of notes . . . no matter how long a history she and Ethan shared as friends . . . it was all for naught unless he was attracted to her. And when it came down to the end, he might prefer cute and cuddly to a reasonably attractive beanpole.

Maybe if she could wear couture clothes and go to fancy parties and wear slinky dresses cut to her navel . . . maybe then she would appreciate her height and be confident enough to hold her head high.

But it was hard to give up a fantasy. Men liked to be protectors. Ethan had told her that himself. And what better way to prove a man's masculinity than for him to change lightbulbs, carry packages, reach for things on the top shelf, and coddle his smaller, weaker mate.

Well, hell, she wasn't small. And she surely wasn't weak. So if that was what Ethan wanted in a woman, she was out of luck.

On the other hand, if she could convince him that they would be far more exciting as lovers than as friends, the consequences might be unprecedented. And really, really exciting.

# Nine

Ethan knew he was a stubborn man. It was a trait that had served him well in many situations. That and his insistence on studying every aspect of a case before making any strategic moves.

So he covered all his bases before he confronted Jane at her shop Friday afternoon. He had chatted with Mr. Benson and ascertained the cleaning crew's schedule. Jane had to be out by five p.m. Ethan was waiting by her car at four forty-five. Given the flu situation, he still had to work the weekend, but tonight was all his . . . and Jane's.

She stopped dead in her tracks when she saw him. "What are you doing here, Ethan?"

He shoved his hands in his pockets and leaned a hip against the hood of her light green Hyundai. "Waiting for you." He reached out and took her suitcase and a carry-on from her hands. "We'll take my car."

She dug in her heels literally and metaphorically. "You're not making sense."

He grinned, feeling lighthearted and in an unexpectedly good mood. After the week he'd had, it was a miracle. But Jane had that effect on him. Like always.

He tossed her luggage in the back of his Jeep. "Mr. Benson told me you were going to a motel this evening. So I'm taking you home, beautiful. Consider it my civic duty. If it will soothe your conscience, feel free to dust my junk, alphabetize my spices, or iron a few shirts so you won't feel beholden to me."

Her lips twitched. "Is that what you think we women do for the men in our lives?"

"Am I?"

"Are you what?" She was looking down, fastening her seat belt, so he couldn't see her face.

He resisted the urge to touch her. Instead he turned the key in the ignition. "The man in your life."

He recognized the exchange for what it was. They were flirting. It felt weird but good. Jane didn't bother to respond to his last sally. But she stared out the front windshield with a small smile on her face.

For once, he was sorry they lived so close to each other. He'd have liked an excuse to drive for hours with Jane as his captive. An uninterrupted block of time.

But he'd make do with what he had.

Jane gave him a funny look when he insisted on carrying her bags into the house. She glanced at the mailbox. "Do you want me to get your mail?"

He froze midstep and nearly stumbled. Unbelievable. He'd forgotten it was Friday. "Um, don't worry about it. It's probably catalogs and bills. No rush."

He strode to the door and unlocked it, hoping like hell she

would follow. He exhaled a sigh of relief when he realized she was on his heels.

Inside, she hovered in the hallway as he took her stuff to the guest room. When he returned ten seconds later, she was still where he had left her.

He waved a hand. "Make yourself at home. I'll order us some pizza if that's okay."

She ignored his directive and followed him into the kitchen. He refused to admit, even to himself, that it made him nervous when she watched him dial the phone.

He rattled off their order without asking for her input. And then he blinked when he realized he had requested their old standard duo: one medium Hawaiian and one large supreme. He hung up the phone and felt his tongue swell with sudden nerves. He'd planned things out to get Jane here. And it had worked.

But what the hell was he going to do with her now?

She was standing in the doorway with her arms wrapped around her waist. Her long legs were encased in soft, well-worn denim that did great things to her ass. The brown fleecy jacket she wore was unzipped, revealing the cinnamon tank top beneath.

Everything about her stance and her clothing was casual. But the whole package was dynamite. She was beautiful in a bone-deep, completely natural way. It made him restless and unsettled and horny.

And since he hadn't quite yet decided how he felt about lusting after Jane, he deliberately turned his mind to safer avenues. "You want to watch the game?"

He didn't have to elaborate. Everyone in town knew that the University of Tennessee men's team was playing North Carolina tonight.

Her face lit up. "Sure."

She teased him about his brand-new big-screen TV. He

adjusted the volume and joined her on the sofa. "You're just jealous."

She snorted and curled into her corner with an afghan. "Men and their toys. Why is it that bigger is always better?" Even her laughter made him horny. And he wasn't going to let that one pass.

He propped his feet on the coffee table. "It is, trust me. And I'm surprised you don't agree."

It was the most sexually provocative thing he'd ever said to her. She blinked, and he saw her lips open and close as if she couldn't quite come up with a snappy response.

He let the silence build, wondering if she would finally make a comeback. But Jane was mute, her eyes glued to the television screen. It wasn't until the food arrived that she spoke again, and then it was only something mundane about drinks from the kitchen.

They ate the warm, gooey pizza sitting side by side. Jane abandoned her afghan and joined him in the middle of his big leather couch, their hips almost touching. He could smell her light perfume, and honest to God, he lost his appetite . . . for pizza.

He knew, in some analytical corner of his brain, that something was going to happen tonight. It might be good and it might be bad. But it would definitely be a watershed moment.

He brooded all during the ball game, watching Jane squeal and bounce and cheer as the Vols whittled away at the other team's early lead. He must have acted normally on the outside, because she didn't appear to notice anything odd about him.

His chest was tight and his throat was dry. After all this time, was he really going to take a chance on ruining the relationship that had so recently been resurrected? What were the chances this would play out the way he wanted it to? One in a hundred?

Jane stripped off her jacket. He'd turned up the heat when they came home, and with the excitement generated by the game, she was flushed, her skin luminous.

He had one eye on the television and one eye on the way her thin tank top outlined her full, perfect breasts. Not too big. Not too small. Perfect. The kind of curves a man fantasized about holding, licking, burying his face between. He coughed and took a long slug of his beer.

The game went into overtime.

Ethan cursed inwardly.

At the beginning of the second overtime, he realized that someone up there had a warped sense of humor.

Two seconds before the final buzzer, Tennessee's famous forward made a perfect nothing-but-net three-pointer and the fans went wild.

Jane ended up in his lap.

It was lunacy born of adrenaline. She wrapped her arms around his neck and kissed him enthusiastically. "They did it."

She wasn't sure Ethan shared her excitement. He'd been oddly silent for the last hour. And now that she had more or less attacked him, he seemed stunned.

But before she could draw back in embarrassment, he came out of whatever funk he'd been in. He dragged her the rest of the way into his embrace, leaned back into the sofa, and arranged her legs on either side of his hips. "They sure as hell did," he muttered. And then he kissed her back.

If she ever had the opportunity to observe a nuclear detonation from a safe distance, Jane was pretty sure it would feel like this: a brilliant flash of light, a blow of energy to the chest, and then a mushrooming cloud of intense heat. Ethan might have been shocked by her kiss, but he wasted no time catching up.

His tongue slid into her mouth. He tasted like pizza and passion. There was nothing tentative about his embrace or his kiss. He took her mouth as if it was his to claim, his to plunder.

She smoothed her hands over his chest again and again, just because she could. Even clothed, he was hard, with warm skin over sleek muscles. She trembled violently, her heart racing. Ethan was kissing her. She was kissing Ethan. Was this why he had invited her here tonight? Was this why she had accepted?

She whimpered and tried to get closer. In some corner of her brain, she knew she might regret what was happening. They had barely even come to terms with the rebirth of their friendship, and now they were playing tonsil hockey.

And she had no idea at all if he felt even a fraction of the emotions that were singing through her veins. She loved him. She had loved him forever, it seemed.

But Ethan was a man, and men enjoyed having sex.

He nipped her throat with his teeth, and she groaned. It didn't matter what his reasons were. She was tired of waiting and wanting and wishing. It was time to live in the here and now.

He took her breasts in his hands, and her brain shut down. Period. Gut instinct took over. The need to mate was as violent and urgent as her need to survive a fire the week before. She honestly thought she might die if he didn't make love to her tonight.

He was hot to the touch, his broad shoulders clad in a thick sweatshirt. She grasped the hem and pulled it up his chest, watching impatiently as he leaned forward and helped her take it off.

Oh, God, he was beautiful. She had forgotten how much. His skin was naturally bronze due to a Cherokee ancestor back in the family tree. A light dusting of dark hair arrowed down his sternum to the belt that cinched his jeans.

She studied his flat, copper-colored nipples, dazed by their beauty. When she lowered her head and tasted each one, he bit out a curse and buried his hands in her hair so hard that she winced.

Since he showed no signs of stopping her, she took her time feasting on his gorgeous body. She licked her way across his collarbone, sucked at his neck hard enough to leave a mark, nibbled the sensitive spot beneath his ear.

His chest heaved with ragged breaths. It stunned her to realize that she was having such an effect on him. She pulled back a fraction and met his gaze. He looked like a warrior, like the man he might have been two centuries earlier. His cheekbones were sharp slashes of color, and the thrust of his clenched jaw gave testament to the immense restraint he was exercising.

Heat flooded the secret places between her thighs as she realized that when the dam broke, the resultant flood would devour everything in its path.

She kissed him softly, learning the flavor and contour of his lips, his mouth. His hands went back to her breasts, and he kneaded them slowly, pausing now and again to tug at the nipples. When he did that, fire shot like a hot wire directly to her womb, making her squirm restlessly.

The ache in her sex urged her to press closer to the thick ridge of male flesh beneath the zipper of his jeans. He had to be hurting, but he let her set the pace, despite his flagrant arousal.

They kissed for hours it seemed. She was drunk with pleasure, hovering on the knife-edge of an unrealized orgasm. All it would take was one touch on her sensitive flesh, but Ethan had allowed her to remain mostly clothed.

He rested his forehead against hers, his hands on her back, his thumbs tracing the edges of her tank top. "Were you really kidding the other night when you suggested I make love to you?"

She played with his ears, making him move restlessly. "No. That was for real. But you were so shocked, I backed off."

He chuckled roughly. "I *was* shocked. But I was also damn interested."

His irises were so dark they appeared black. She ruffled his shiny, straight hair. "I'm glad." There was more she wanted to say, but she still felt a need to protect herself. Loving Ethan had been a painful experience in the past. And like a child who has been burned on the stove, she was wary and fully cognizant of the danger to her heart.

He slid his hands beneath the back of her tank top and toyed with the clasp of her bra. His face was buried in the curve of her neck. "Will I seem unmanly if I tell you I'm a bit scared?"

The self-deprecating humor in his voice touched something deep inside her. Tenderness replaced lust for a moment, or at least cohabited with it. "Why?"

She felt him sigh, his big, solid frame vibrating with the depth of it. "After four long years, we've finally reconnected. I like having you back in my life. Tonight seemed familiar—good, really good."

"But?"

"But I'm afraid that if we do this, things will change. And I don't want to lose you again."

Her heart sank. He wanted to have sex, but he wanted to maintain the status quo. Not quite what she was hoping for. "Change can be good," she whispered, resting her cheek on his shoulder.

She understood his reservations. Heck, she could write a book on the subject. But unlike Ethan, she was no longer satisfied with the comfortable and familiar. She was willing to take the risk, willing to gamble a pleasant present for a fairy-tale future.

He took her face in his hands, his gaze sober. "You've always been special to me, Jane."

She ignored the dart of pain. Sometimes it took men longer to say the words. "Don't be afraid of me, Ethan. Of this. I promise you won't be sorry."

And then her hands went to his belt.

Ethan felt ice-cold and burning hot at the same time. His hands were clumsy, his throat tight. At no other time in his life had he felt such a violent need to get this right. Jane deserved to be cherished. He wanted to convince her in deeds, if not in words, that she meant the world to him. If he tried to wrap it up in pretty sentences, he'd come off looking like an idiot. But he could show her.

Carefully, monitoring every nuance of expression on her face, he flipped open the fastener on her bra and lifted the lacy fabric and her top over her head. The resulting view of Jane's breasts hit him square in the chest with a jolt of lust that left him breathless.

She was a woman at the peak of her beauty, smooth, soft, ripe. Her nipples were a pretty pinkish brown, tightly furled at the moment, begging to be nibbled.

He did just that, his hands splayed on her back as he bent his head and sucked gently. Jane squirmed and groaned, increasing his discomfort. His jeans felt two sizes too small, his dick crammed painfully against his boxers and an unforgiving metal zipper.

But he shoved his own physical aches away and concentrating on giving pleasure to Jane. It was no hardship. She responded to his touches and caresses with natural sensuality. He paused again to return to her lips. And every time he did, she kissed him eagerly, sending his arousal one notch higher.

Finally, he pulled her tight to his chest, feeling her breasts crush against his torso. It was almost enough to soothe the beast within him. But when she wriggled her crotch against his aching cock, he was a goner.

Next he attacked her belt. He had it unfastened and out of the belt loops in seconds. When he moved to the button on her jeans, she tried to help him.

But in their current position, he couldn't undress her the way he'd like to. He kissed her nose, her chin, her lush, sweet mouth. "I want you in my bed, sweetheart. Any objections?"

She smiled at him, her eyes cloudy with arousal, the color of a stormy lake. "I thought you'd never ask."

He stood up, with her still in his embrace, his hands slipping under her butt to steady her.

"Ethan. Your back."

He panted, urging her legs to tighten around his waist. "Screw my back."

He carried her down the hall as fast as he could. The grip he'd kept on his control was fraying at the seams. He wanted her naked and beneath him.

He lowered them both to the bed, not bothering to toss back the covers. The light from the hallway was illumination enough. He fumbled at the opening to her jeans, while she did the same to his.

Their hands stilled at once, and he heard her giggle. She shoved his hands away. "Time management, Ethan." Then before he could protest, she rolled away, got on her knees, and ripped her pants down her hips. Her socks and shoes were next.

He dragged his own jeans off, taking a few seconds longer than Jane had, simply because he was struck dumb by the sight of her wearing nothing but tiny lavender panties. His throat dried even more, and he knew he was a goner.

He took his boxers off, as well, in the interest of efficiency. When Jane's big blue eyes widened as she surveyed his dick, he decided the decision was the correct one. He was painfully hard. The last time he'd had sex was several months ago. It might as well have been years. That was how eager he felt, how desperate.

He took her hand and tumbled her off balance onto her back. Then he straddled her hips on his knees and looked down at her. Her skin was soft and pink and warm, her waist narrow, her legs the stuff of fantasy.

At the moment, her thighs were demurely pressed together, but he'd caught a glimpse of her lovely rosy sex in the transition.

She bit her lips, still eyeing his bobbing erection. "Do you have a license to carry that thing?" she asked wryly.

He barked out a laugh. No other woman he'd ever known could make him feel sexually ravenous and amused at the same time.

He stroked the head of his erection, spreading the drop of fluid over his taut, supersensitive skin. Her gaze locked on every motion of his hand. And the more she watched, the more his penis swelled. He got off on seeing that wide-eyed fascination. Some weird rush of caveman-inspired testosterone made him want to impress her. Jane. The woman who'd always been in his court. Except for that one time he made a fool of himself.

He shoved the unwelcome memories away. The past was past. Tonight was all they had, all he wanted. He scooted off her and moved toward her feet. He leaned back on his heels and ran his hands from her knees down to her ankles. Gently, ever so slowly, he tugged her legs apart.

Her thigh muscles tightened instinctively, but she relaxed after a split second. Hot color rushed from her throat and flooded her face. Her long-lashed eyes were glazed with hunger, but he also saw uncertainty in the way her teeth mutilated her bottom lip.

When he eased her ankles even farther apart, her chest rose

and fell in a choked exhalation of breath. She was exquisite. His hands trembled as he ran them upward along the sleek curves of her inner thighs.

When he touched her clitoris with a teasing fingertip, she groaned and twisted restlessly on the sheets, her hands clenched in fists at her sides. He ran his finger down the moist cleft at her core, not easing inside, though he wanted to . . . badly.

Keeping the pace leisurely was a mammoth challenge. But he didn't want to rush. Not with this. Not with Jane. She was too precious to him.

He moved to his belly, sprawling full length and kissing his way from one of her narrow, classy ankles up to her glistening sex. The scent of her made him dizzy. He was torn in a million different directions, wanting it all. It was a gluttonous feast for a starving man.

He tasted her with a light flick of his tongue, and she went wild. His hands clamped down on her upper thighs, holding her immobile so he could pleasure her.

The intimate flesh was hot, slick with her arousal. He licked her slowly, keeping her poised on the brink, deliberately not allowing her to come. He was determined to give her as much as she could handle. Maybe more.

Her voice was shaky, weak. "Please. God, Ethan, I can't take any more."

"Oh, I think you can," he muttered. He bit down gently on her clitoris and then suckled her as her climax roared through her to the accompaniment of her keening moan. He thrust his tongue in her vagina, feeling her release, sweet as honey, on his lips.

She had barely come down to earth when he rolled on a condom, positioned himself between her thighs, and centered the head of his aching cock at the entrance to bliss. "Look at me, Jane." He growled the words.

She focused on his face, licking her lips. The sight of her pink tongue made him shiver. When she remained mute, he nudged her intimately with his prick. "Tell me you want this."

Her hands came up to stroke his flanks. "I want *you*," she said, her voice surprisingly strong. In his muddled head, he realized there might be a distinction between his words and hers, but it was enough that she was in agreement.

"Thank God." He entered her slowly, though it practically killed him not to shove deep and hard. Her passage was snug around his cock, almost virginal. But he knew she had been with other men.

The knowledge barely registered. He didn't care. She was his now. He drove deeper, feeling her muscles squeeze him. The sensation was indescribable. He was fucking Jane. His Jane. For a moment, a blinding wave of tenderness threatened to derail his lust. The poignant moment struck at his heart. He wanted to make love to her so thoroughly and so often that she would understand how special she was, how utterly unique.

She wrapped her legs around his back and tilted her hips. He gained another inch. Now he was buried to the hilt, his lungs screaming for air. Until that moment he hadn't realized he was holding his breath. Looking at her beneath him was like looking straight into the sun. He couldn't speak, couldn't move. He'd never seen anything so lovely.

She put her hands on his shoulders, her fingernails biting into the flesh of his forearms. "Ethan." The single word was barely audible, but he heard her plea.

He eased out of her and then thrust like he wanted to, a mighty flex of his hips that joined them irrevocably. Her strangled cry urged him on. He repeated the motion . . . once . . . twice. Each time he slid deep, her inner muscles grasped him and dragged him toward ecstasy.

He tried to keep up a rhythm, but Jane was having none of it. She played dirty, teasing his nipples, scoring his ass with her fingernails, dragging his head down to hers for a carnal kiss that zapped his strength.

And then he broke, lost to reason, lost to reality, his only focus the woman beneath him and the challenge in her sky blue eyes. He slammed into her again and again, his chest heaving, sweat dampening his forehead.

"God, Jane," he cried out, and every bone and muscle in his body went rigid as he emptied himself over and over, caught up in a spasm of pleasure that bordered on pain.

In the final seconds, as he ground the base of his cock against her clit, he sensed that she came again. But he was almost insensate with the force of his climax.

In the aftermath, he slumped on top of her, weak as a baby. He felt her hands in his hair, her gentle fingers combing through the damp strands, massaging his scalp, easing the tension that had bound him from the first moment he saw her the night of the break-in.

Every day since then she had been in the back of his mind, smiling a challenge at him, waiting for him to process the weird mélange of feelings.

As he drifted into exhausted sleep, he rolled to his side, taking Jane with him. He knew things had changed. But it would take time to sift through it all.

In the meantime, Jane was in his bed. That was all that mattered.

# *Ten*

*J*ane waited until Ethan's steady snores signaled his uncon-
scious state. She extracted herself from his embrace and,
on shaky legs, made her way to the bathroom.

If she had known what sex with Ethan would be like, she
might have quit being a coward a lot sooner.

Sweet, holy hell. The man was a freaking sex machine. Her
thighs were sore, and her womanly parts felt as if they had been
pummeled relentlessly. Which, if you looked at it literally, they
had been.

She turned on the shower and stepped under the warm spray.
As she ran the soapy rag over her body and between her legs,
tingles of latent arousal reminded her that she was nowhere near
being sated by Ethan's lovemaking. Perhaps after a little rest she
could coax him into a second round.

She was giddy with the knowledge that she was able to touch
him at will, no longer hiding her fascination with his fit, hard

body. The first moment his cock had entered her was emblazoned in her memory. The incredible feel of his thick, hot flesh penetrating her had been so universe altering, it was as if she were a virgin again.

Only this time there was wonder and joy instead of pain and lingering disenchantment. Ethan's lovemaking was all that she had expected and more.

And the thing that struck her the most—the truth that she had suspected but not completely been sure of until tonight—was that Ethan was her one and only. He was her true love. The man she was meant to share her life with.

It was sentimental and schmaltzy and maybe even a tad overdramatic. But there was no escaping destiny.

She stepped out of the shower and dried off with one of Ethan's oversize towels, then decided to chance a look in the steamy mirror. It took only one swipe of her hand on the wet glass to reveal the sappy smile on her face. Dear God, she was actually glowing. How embarrassing was that? But she couldn't seem to erase the grin.

When she tiptoed back into the bedroom, Ethan was still dead to the world. Poor man had been working fourteen-hour days all week. It would be cruel to wake him.

She slipped between the covers, careful not to dislodge the blanket and comforter from his shoulders. Her skin was covered in gooseflesh, and entering the snug cocoon created by his big body was like being wrapped in radiant heat.

She scooted close and spooned his back, but was shy about the last few inches. With her eyes closed, she tried to absorb the barrage of feelings—contentment topped the list. She didn't know what would come of this. And she wasn't naive enough to imagine that one night of sex led to happily ever after.

But she was determined to enjoy the moment. Being here, with

Ethan, was more than she had hoped for. Maybe she would aban-
don the valentine plan . . . and maybe she wouldn't confess. After
all, fate had brought him back into her life without any help from
her. So maybe she should simply go with the flow and be happy.

He muttered in his sleep. She took a breath and shifted across
the small bit of space separating them. Now her breasts cuddled
against his back, and her hips cradled his ass. Her heart made a
funny little jerk, and her pulse skittered. Too much stimulation.
How would she ever fall asleep? It seemed criminal to waste time
when all she wanted to do was hold on tight to this incredible
moment.

But she'd been working like a madwoman as well, and as
hard as she tried, she couldn't keep her eyelids open.

The next morning, Ethan kept perfectly still, giving himself time
to process alien sensations. His head was groggy, his mental pro-
cesses slow. The sluggish feeling reminded him of the aftermath
of one too many drinks.

But he was fairly certain he was stone-cold sober.

And then it hit him. Jane. In his bed. All night.

The memories came back in a trickle and then in a rush,
bombarding him with images that made his cock leap to attention. He and Jane had made love four different times, every one
an off-the-charts, world-altering, explosive encounter.

He rolled carefully to his back, and breathed a sigh of relief.
She was still there. Sometime in the night she had migrated to
one side of his big mattress. That was a mistake on his part. He
should never have let her get more than three inches away.

He glanced at the clock. It was still early. His internal body
clock usually woke him before the alarm went off. And despite
last night's sexual excess, it still had. Carefully, he reached out
and turned off the knob above the digital readout.

As much as he might want to, there was no time for another round of sex with Jane. He had to get to work. But he'd let her sleep while he got ready. No point in both of them cranking out early.

He did his best to ignore the flutter of panic ricocheting in his chest. If he could go face-to-face with armed criminals and come out unscathed, surely he could survive the "morning after" with Jane. But to be on the safe side, he'd give himself a little time to come up with a plan before he woke her up to say goodbye.

He needed a script for this most treacherous of conversations— call it backup, if you will. Maybe he'd find inspiration in the shower.

Jane waited until she heard the bathroom door close before she started to breathe normally. She'd awakened minutes before Ethan and was aware of his every move. Moments ago he had slipped from the bed, retrieved clothes from the bureau and closet, and left the bedroom.

The still-aroused, sexual Jane was deeply disappointed that her newfound lover had made no move to drag her to his side of the bed and have his wicked way with her.

But the practical Jane squashed all feelings of letdown. Ethan had a job to do, and besides, a man and woman couldn't spend a full twenty-four hours in bed. Not that she wouldn't mind testing that hypothesis.

When the bathroom door opened, letting out a waft of man-scented steam, Jane froze again. Ethan's shower had been quick. Really quick. He tiptoed silently through the bedroom and out into the hall, presumably on his way to the kitchen for breakfast.

When the coast was clear, she rolled out of bed with a wince. Odd muscle aches in strange places made her smile. She didn't rehash any memories at the present. That could wait for later

when she had time to savor, time to enjoy and absorb the flash-
backs of incredible pleasure.

Her shower was shorter than Ethan's. She didn't want him
to come into the bathroom to say goodbye. She wanted to be
dressed and prepared for what was bound to be an awkward
encounter.

She had her clothes on, her hair in a ponytail, and her minimal
makeup applied in less than five minutes. When she heard the
front door open and then shut, she frowned. Surely he wouldn't
have left without speaking to her.

Cautiously, she peeked into the living room just as Ethan
came back into the house. He didn't have his coat on. Apparently,
he'd been out to the mailbox.

She froze, her heart in her throat. He was flipping through
a rather large stack of catalogs and envelopes. The moment he
came to her missive, she saw him visibly react. He frowned
slightly, looked at his watch, and tucked it unopened in the large
pocket of his winter coat.

Jane forced her feet to move. She entered the room where he
stood and folded her arms across her chest as she leaned a hip
against the sofa. "Good morning."

He looked up, and the flash of hot male appreciation in his
eyes soothed her nerves a tiny fraction. His grin made the hair
on the back of her neck stand up. "Hey, there, gorgeous. I was
trying to let you sleep."

She clenched her hands, fingernails biting into her skin.
"Anything exciting in the mail?"

He evaded her gaze as he slipped his arms into his coat. "The
usual." His voice was gruff.

Wow. The jolt of pain left her breathless. He wasn't going to
tell her about the erotic valentine. Clearly he planned to read it
in private. Which meant what?

In the past, her good friend Ethan would probably have opened it, read it aloud, and handed it to her to see if she could help him locate the sender. They would have laughed about it together, studied the syntax and the handwriting to solve the puzzle of the mystery woman.

But Ethan had tucked her naughty card into his pocket as if it was a note from his lover.

Which it was. But he didn't know that. So why was he hiding it? Did he not want her to be jealous? Or was he so intrigued by his mystery admirer that he longed to track her down and sleep with her, too?

Jane's stomach tightened with disappointment and the knowledge that her little plot had backfired. How could she give her heart to a man who was keeping secrets from her? A man who was interested in another woman . . .

Even though she knew his naughty pen pal was not a threat in the truest sense of the word, the fact that Ethan was being clandestine about the note was damning. Good Lord, what a tangle.

He ran his hands through his hair, smoothing it down where the wind outside had tumbled it. "What do you have planned for the day?" His voice was stilted, awkward.

She forced herself to relax. "I promised Mr. Benson that I'd cook lunch for him. It's his birthday. And I'll bake him a cake while I'm there."

Ethan cocked his head, his smile more genuine. "You're a nice woman, Jane Norman."

*Nice.* Yeah, bloody hoorah. She managed to shrug instead of grimace. "He's been really good to me. And besides, with all my grandparents gone, I enjoy having him in my life. He's a sweetheart."

Finally, Ethan moved. He crossed the room and took her face

in his hands. "So are you, Jane. So are you." He kissed her softly, letting his lips linger long enough to rekindle a visceral memory of the night before.

It was a brief kiss, but it left her breathless.

He rested his forehead against hers. "We'll talk about last night. But I can't right now."

She pulled away, feeling the need to protect herself. "We don't have to. I know men hate stuff like that."

He frowned. "I *want* to. We need to."

She shrugged. "If you insist. Would you like me to make dinner for us tonight?"

"What if I take you out instead? Somewhere nice."

"I'd rather stay here." *And have gobs of passionate messy sex.* Yikes. Had she said that last part out loud?

Perhaps not, but Ethan's amused smile seemed to say he could read her mind. "Well, if you insist. I'd like that a lot."

Ethan functioned at work with only half his brain. The other side of his gray matter was engrossed in reliving a night of incredible passion with Jane. The memories were so intense, it was all he could do to keep his boner under control.

Thank God, it was a quiet Saturday.

Midmorning he snatched a cup of the sludgelike coffee most of the guys enjoyed, and then he closeted himself in his office with the third mysterious valentine.

He'd been afraid to open it at home, worried that it might hurt Jane's feelings. And there was no way under the sun he was going to do that. Their relationship was new and fragile. He couldn't take the chance that she might misunderstand the provocative mail. If it weren't for the slim possibility that the sender was someone dangerous, he would have merely tossed the notes as they arrived. But the cop in him had caution ingrained in his DNA.

He slid his finger beneath the flap and opened the envelope. This particular note wasn't decorated. But the same beautiful calligraphy flowed across the paper.

*Ethan, my love,*

*Last night as I slept*
*My heart and soul leapt.*
*You were there in my bed,*
*Toe-to-toe, head-to-head.*

*I felt you so real.*
*Your fate is now sealed.*
*I'll not find my rest*
*Till our union is blessed.*

*My need is intense*
*I can't bear the suspense.*
*Will you make me you lover*
*And play under the covers?*

*I swear you'll find pleasure*
*In a cup without measure.*
*Your hard flesh will swell*
*As I've stories to tell.*

*My thighs will spread wide*
*You'll thrust deep inside.*
*A gasp and a moan*
*Is it yours or my own?*

*By the light of the moon*
*Please marry me, soon.*
*I promise you bliss*
*And a wedding night's kiss.*

Damn, damn, and double damn. He was in deep shit. Some psycho chick wanted to marry him, and he'd already been down that road once.

He slid the incriminating note beneath the desk calendar in front of him. But the words on the paper danced in his head. Though he was loath to admit it, the woman, whoever she was, had an appealing way with words. That part about thighs and thrusting made him squirm in his chair. Despite the origin of the note, the naughty words made him think of Jane and last night.

God, he wanted her as much as he had before they ever touched each other.

He shoved the heels of his hands in his eyes and rubbed. His sleepless night was beginning to catch up with him. When he finally emerged from his office and strode back into the fray, Randy Temple was the first person he saw, and the man looked like shit. Oh, hell, that might mean the date with Sherry hadn't gone well.

Ethan nodded tersely to the other man. "Mornin', Randy. Thanks for coming in today. I know it's not your regular shift."

A bleak flash of something in the man's eyes flickered and disappeared, leaving his expression impassive. "No problem, sir."

Ethan realized with a shot of shame that he hadn't checked on Sherry all week. He'd seen her three times when she catered lunches, but they hadn't been able to talk about anything personal. And considering the stuff she was dealing with right now—namely Deb's move to Florida—it might behoove her brother to be a little more intentional about making sure she was okay.

After lunch and in between crises, he managed to squeeze in a phone call. Sherry didn't pick up. That was odd. He tried her cell. Still no answer.

Wondering if he was doing the right thing, he buzzed the receptionist and asked her to track down Temple.

The younger man was in his office immediately. "Sir?" His face was shadowed, his eyes dull.

Ethan was standing, and he leaned forward to sign something on his desk, breaking eye contact. "My sister is not answering her phone. Would you mind dropping by and making sure she's okay?"

When Ethan finally looked up, Randy was staring at him, his mouth slightly open. And then he frowned. "Not sure that's a good idea, sir. She doesn't want to see me."

Ethan would have given a thousand dollars not to have this conversation, but his sister's happiness was very important to him. And he had a hunch that Randy Temple might be just the medicine she needed. Ethan had watched Sherry react to the man, and her body language was a dead giveaway. She was fascinated . . . wary but fascinated.

Ethan sighed. "If you're really interested, give her time. She's been way too hard on herself over the years. I'm not sure that she believes she deserves to be happy."

"That's a load of horseshit, sir, if you'll pardon my French."

Ethan managed a grin. "Well, we're on the same page there." He took a key off his ring and handed it to Randy. "Don't barge in. Be discreet. But my gut tells me something is wrong, and I've learned to trust it."

"Understood, sir. I'll let you know what I find out." He was gone before Ethan could say thank you.

*    *    *

Jane was glad she had Mr. Benson as a distraction. The cleanup at her shop and the possible fallout from her night with Ethan were too much to think about without her head exploding.

So she practiced the time-honored art of avoidance.

Mr. Benson shouted for her to come in when she rang the bell this time. She found him ensconced in his favorite recliner in front of the fireplace, a small wool coverlet over his legs.

She pulled up the footstool and took his hands. "A bad day?"

He managed to look chipper, despite his apparent discomfort. "They've got rain in the forecast. Does it to me every time. But don't you fret. I'm fine. Been looking forward to this all week."

He had a photograph album in his lap, so she leaned forward curiously. "What are you looking at?"

He turned the pages so she could see them, his smile wry. "Just some family photos."

He didn't have to explain. She knew that his three children and his assorted relatives were a disappointment to him. But she could also see the love in his eyes as he pointed them out to her and named them one by one. Despite their shortcomings and the lack of love and attention they had given the old man, he clearly still cared for them.

She thought she recognized one of the boys. "Isn't this the young man I saw painting your house?"

He nodded. "That's my great-nephew, Dougie. I'm happy to say the lad has an entrepreneurial spirit. I suppose he might actually make something of himself."

After flipping through the final few pages, Jane closed the album and put it aside. She stood and kissed his forehead. "Why don't you close your eyes for a bit? And I'll get busy with our lunch."

She threw the cake together and put it in the oven. Then she started on the meal. It was never easy to work in someone else's kitchen, but Mr. Benson's wife, long dead, must have been an awesome cook. Her shelves and cupboards were fully stocked with all the right pans and gadgets.

Mr. Benson had gleefully chosen the menu for today's birthday feast. At his request, Jane was preparing chipped beef on toast, fried green tomatoes, and candied apples. It might not be the most healthful or aesthetic menu, but for the dear old man, she would fix fried bologna if it would make him happy.

They ate in the kitchen nook. Mr. Benson liked to watch his bird feeders, particularly in winter. Jane was heartened to see him take small second helpings of everything. Sometimes his appetite was nonexistent, and she worried about his health. There was really no one who checked on him regularly except Jane.

While the cake cooled, they played a few hands of gin rummy. Then Jane iced the applesauce cake and cleaned up the kitchen while Mr. Benson watched his soap. At three she popped a couple of candles in the caramel icing and carried it into the living room.

Although she was no singer, she made it through "Happy Birthday" without incident. Mr. Benson blew out the candles and beamed like a kid as she sliced each of them a piece of cake and served it on delicate china dessert plates.

By three thirty, she began winding things down. She knew if she left, her elderly host would probably take a nap, and besides, she had promised to cook for Ethan as well, so she had to get cracking.

Mr. Benson reached for her hand and urged her into an armchair when she returned from putting the cake away and washing the last few dishes. She was pleased that there were plenty of leftovers. He'd be eating well for at least another meal or two.

At his urging, she subsided into a comfy seat, pleasantly tired. "You don't look a day over sixty," she teased, expecting him to respond to her humor.

His face was serious. "I want to talk to you, my dear."

She leaned forward. "Of course."

His hands trembled as he grasped the arms of his recliner. "This business with your building has worried me. I'd be devastated if anything happened to you."

She smiled reassuringly. "The police are working on the case. I'm fine, I promise. It appears to be nothing more than malicious mischief."

He wasn't placated. "I'm not sure it's a good idea for you to be living there alone."

Her heart sank. Surely he wasn't planning to evict her. "I love my apartment," she said slowly, not sure what he was after.

"I'm getting old," he said baldly.

She didn't want to say it, but he'd passed "old" about a decade ago, and gone straight on to ancient.

He ignored her silence. "I'm afraid I'll be at the point soon where I won't be able to handle all my business interests. Tell me, Jane, have you thought about your future?"

Sheesh. She wasn't ready for this. She gnawed her lower lip. "Well, I do wonder from time to time if Paper Pleasures is a longtime venture. I enjoy it. But occasionally I think about going back to school . . . maybe finishing up a four-year degree. Why do you ask?"

He frowned. "If I sell the building, I worry about what will happen to you."

She swallowed her instinctive protest. "Of course you need to do what is right for you. I'll be fine. I have lots of options."

He leaned his head against the back of his chair and looked exhausted suddenly. "You need to have a husband and babies," he mumbled, his expression morose. "Don't know what the men in this town are thinking."

She managed a smile. "Twenty-first-century women can take care of themselves, Mr. Benson. We're tough."

He snorted. "You can do or be whatever the devil you want to. I'm not disputing that. But it's hard to curl up at night with a ledger book. I may have one foot in the grave, but I know what it's like to love someone, and I know what life is like alone."

For a brief moment, their eyes met, and she saw in his faded gaze every bit of the grief he had carried around for twenty years since his beloved wife had died.

Her throat tightened and she blinked back tears. "I do love someone," she said impulsively. "But I don't know if he loves me."

Mr. Benson's eyes narrowed. "Have you told him? I thought you modern gals didn't sit back and wait on men to do the whole romance thing."

She laughed unsteadily. "Let's just say I've put out some feelers. Things are progressing, but nothing is certain yet."

Last night was too new to discuss even in cloaked terms. So she changed the subject. "If you make the decision to liquidate your real estate assets, don't you dare worry about me. You have to do what is best for you. Life is full of changes, and sometimes it does all of us good to face a bit of a shake-up."

He played with the fringe on his blanket, his gnarled arthritic fingers restless on the soft plaid. "Well, then, I'll tell you this. My plan is to make a decision by the first of the summer. That will give you plenty of time to see if you want to keep the shop open, or if you want to take a new direction."

She nodded. "That seems fair. But in the meantime, you have to promise me not to worry. I'm a big girl. I have plenty of opportunities. And no matter what happens, we'll still be friends."

*    *    *

As she drove back to the supermarket to buy a second round of groceries—this time to prepare a meal for Ethan—her mind spun in circles. If this thing with Ethan didn't work out, she'd probably move away from Statlerville long before the summer. So whatever Mr. Benton did or didn't do with his property would be irrelevant.

Her heart quivered as she tried to imagine saying goodbye to the man and the home she loved.

But no one ever died from a broken heart. And maybe she was wrong. Maybe there *was* another man out there for her. Someone who would take one look at her and fall madly, deeply in love. It was a nice fantasy.

But no matter how hard she tried, she couldn't picture a life somewhere else. She was the kind of person who put down roots, deep roots. This town was full of childhood memories, rife with the rhythms of her life. She felt a connection to the place, the people.

And at the center of it all was Ethan. Always Ethan. As she pushed her buggy down one aisle and up the next, tossing food items into the basket, all of the emotional memories she had ignored during the day came flooding back.

Ethan hovering over her, his rigid, hot sex ready to enter her. Ethan muttering words of praise and passion. Ethan slumped exhausted in her arms, his heart beating in sync with hers.

She dropped a jar of tomato sauce from nerveless fingers. Thankfully, it was plastic and not glass. It bounced once and rolled underneath the nearby shelf.

As she bent to retrieve it, she glanced at her watch. Ethan would be home in an hour and a half.

And then, God only knew what would happen. . . .

## Eleven

Randy stood on Sherry's doorstep and bolstered his courage. As he jingled his keys in his hands, he glanced around him. Last Monday night he had been too preoccupied with the evening ahead to notice the yard.

Now he saw that it was immaculate. The grass in the lawn was pale and brittle, but the winter foliage at the base of the porch and the low evergreen shrubbery along the driveway looked healthy and recently trimmed. Like everything else about Sherry, her plant life was neat and under control. Did the woman ever rest?

When he rang the bell, no one answered. Sherry's car was in the driveway, but her brother said she hadn't answered either of her phones. Randy wouldn't assume the worst, but he was definitely concerned. After a loud knock still produced no results, he used the key.

Inside, he hovered in the foyer. "Sherry?"

The house was quiet as a tomb. Slowly, feeling like an intruder, he moved forward. "Sherry?"

This time he was almost certain he heard a noise. He followed the hallway, pausing to check at each open door. The left-hand side of the house was clearly the living area: kitchen, den, etc. The small bedrooms were opposite. The first one was a guest room. And the second one, judging from the artwork on the walls, belonged to Sherry's daughter. He had to grin when he saw the heavy-metal posters. Sherry must love that.

He found his quarry at the back of the house. If Sherry at one time shared a large bed with her husband, it had long since been replaced by a small double mattress and frame. And lying in the middle of a tempest of tumbled covers was the woman he was falling for, hard and fast. She barely made a discernable mound under the bedding.

"My God." Even at his shocked exclamation, she never stirred. For a split second he thought she might be dead, but then he saw her chest rise and fall, and his heart started beating again.

He went down on his knees beside the bed. She was wearing a sleeveless cotton gown, and her exposed arms and legs were burning hot to the touch. Her face held not a drop of color, and her breathing was ragged and harsh.

It didn't take a genius to deduce that she had the flu. He found a thermometer on the nightstand and eased it under her tongue. She stirred restlessly, but didn't try to spit it out. When he pulled it from her mouth and read the number, he scowled. 105.4. Jesus.

He considered bundling her up right then and there to take her to the emergency room, but he knew how long that could take, and he was worried about any delay in getting her temp down. Instead, he dialed his doctor's weekend answering service and waited impatiently for the minute and a half it took for someone to call him back.

The instructions were simple and familiar. Grim-faced, Randy hung up the phone and contemplated calling Sherry's brother. But Ethan had sent him here, and he knew the boss wouldn't have done that if he didn't trust him.

Hell, Sherry might be furious with him, but she could bloody well live with it. He was trained to deal with emergencies, and this sure as heck qualified. And in the end, even if she was royally pissed, he'd be no worse off than when she begged him to take her home last Monday night. That had come close to crippling him.

He wasted no more time brooding over his failed date. Instead, he scooped Sherry up in his arms and carried her into the bathroom. He sat down on the closed lid of the commode and reached to turn on the bathwater, all the while keeping a tight hold on his precious cargo. She seemed as light as a child.

It scared him spitless that she was dead to the world in his arms. Her hair was a tangled mess, and he brushed it from her face with an unsteady hand as he waited for the tub to fill up. At the doctor's orders, the water was deliberately chilly.

Randy took off his shirt, first one arm, then the other. After a moment's consideration, he removed his watch as well. Eventually, Sherry's gown would have to come off, but in the meantime, he would preserve her modesty.

As he lowered her into the uncomfortably cool water, he expected her to fight him. She opened her eyes and tried to flail in his grasp, but she was too weak. Her lack of protest left a sick feeling in the pit of his stomach.

People died from the flu.

Carefully, he wet her hair and sponged her face. Every time she tried to lift herself away from the deliberate torture of the water, he gently pressed her down. After fifteen minutes, her lips were blue.

He couldn't bear it anymore. He lifted her from the tub and tried to stand her on her feet, but her legs collapsed like soft rubber.

Cursing and struggling, he stripped her wet nightclothes off her chilled body and wrapped her in a towel. Later he would pause to appreciate her beauty. Not now.

In the bedroom, he tucked her beneath the covers. She curled instantly into a fetal position, and he smoothed the blankets around her. When he checked her temp again, it had come down to 103.8. It was a start, but it wasn't enough to suit him.

He left her only long enough to retrieve a glass of orange juice from the kitchen. He'd already spotted the bottle of ibuprofen on the nightstand. When he got back to the bedroom, Sherry was deeply asleep. It seemed cruel to wake her, but he had no choice. He pulled her into a seated position, supported her back, and shook her gently.

Her head lolled like a broken flower. "Sherry, wake up, baby. You have to take some medicine."

She made a tiny noise and tried to bury her face in his shoulder. He held her chin in one hand. "Sherry, open your mouth." He made his voice harsh and authoritative. Somewhere beneath the layers of fevered sleep, her subconscious responded to his demands.

He forced three tablets between her lips and put the glass to her mouth. At first nothing happened, and he damn near spilled the juice down her chest. But finally she got the message and drank slowly, swallowing the pills and moaning as the cool, wet liquid slid down her throat. He made her finish all eight ounces, and then lowered her once again beneath the covers.

When he was convinced she was sleeping normally, he went into the other room to call Ethan and report in. Randy managed to convince a worried brother that he had things under control and, at the same time, ask for two vacation days.

After that, he collapsed into a chair and sighed. He was pretty sure he wasn't going to win any brownie points for his Clara Barton routine. At least not from Sherry. Ethan might approve, but that was irrelevant. Randy didn't need to kiss up to his superior officer.

Ethan had mentioned coming by, but Randy persuaded him not to. It wouldn't help matters if the boss came down with the flu as well.

Randy turned on the TV and lowered the sound. He wouldn't be sleeping much tonight. His plan was to alternate acetaminophen every two hours with the ibuprofen. If it became necessary, he'd repeat the cold bath. But he hoped it wouldn't come to that.

It actually hurt him to cause Sherry distress, a giant ache in his chest that still sat like a stone. God knew if she would allow him to help her when she woke up. But he'd be damned if he was going to leave her to fend for herself. As far as he could tell, Sherry had devoted her life to being a perfect mom.

It was high time someone took care of her.

Ethan made it home by six thirty, which was something of a miracle. He'd pulled a killer ten-hour shift, not even stopping for lunch. The candy bar he'd crammed into his mouth midafternoon had long since vanished in a poof of empty calories.

So when he opened his front door and smelled the aroma of home-cooked food, he was ready to drop to his knees and whimper in gratitude. But even his ravenous stomach couldn't quite edge out his hungry cock.

All day he'd kept an image of Jane in the back of his head. Jane smiling at him. Jane laughing. Jane sighing and stretching in the aftermath of orgasm. Jane, bare-assed naked, ready to make love to him. He couldn't erase the vivid memories of last night. Nor did he want to.

He took a deep breath. "Lucy, I'm home." His Cuban accent was atrocious, but when he entered the kitchen, Jane was smiling. A pot of spaghetti sauce bubbled on the stove, the source of the fabulous smells, and a pan of rolls sat on the counter, ready to be warmed.

She wiped her hands on a dish towel. "Don't get used to it, *mi amigo*. My culinary repertoire is narrow at best. I need to learn some stuff from Sherry." He'd told Jane about the catered lunches and invited her to drop by the station one day and eat with them.

Ethan's gut urge was to grab her and bend her over the kitchen table. He resisted. Barely. Clamping down on his jittery lust, he waved a hand at the stove. "Will this keep if I take a quick shower?"

Jane was hovering in front of the oven door, barricading herself behind the kitchen table. She nodded. "We can put the noodles in whenever we want."

He escaped, feeling dangerously on edge. He wanted her again. To hell with supper. To hell with etiquette. He had a boner the size of the Empire State Building, and he realized with dumfounded amazement that he'd completely lost his appetite for dinner.

How could he sit down and eat, pretending that everything was the same?

When he stepped out of the shower, dried off, and went into his bedroom to get clean clothes, he stopped dead in his tracks. Jane was in his bed . . . nude. Smiling bravely with a seductive gleam in her eyes. She was on her back, resting on her elbows, one leg out in front of her, the other bent at the knee. She licked her lips, nerves visible despite her provocative pose. "I thought we might wait on the spaghetti. If you don't mind." She held a condom packet in her hand.

His throat—hell, his whole entire body—felt like he'd been given one of those drugs that paralyze the muscular system. Shouldn't they talk about last night before they dove into round two? Wasn't it important to clarify exactly what they were doing?

Jane's smile faltered. "Have I goofed?"

Trust dear Jane to be direct and to the point. He glanced down at his cock. Couldn't she tell? He inhaled roughly. "God, no. You're right on the money."

He stumbled to the bed and came down on top of her, burying his face in her hair and shivering from the feel of her bare skin touching his. His hips molded to hers. His painfully erect dick pushed into her soft belly. He kissed the side of her neck, smelling the light, sweet scent of her perfume. "I've thought about this all day long."

He felt her chuckle. "Me, too."

He'd told himself he would be the best lover she had ever known. Lots of slow, practiced, erotic foreplay. Plenty of soft words and romance.

He took her like an animal, shoving roughly between her legs and mounting her as if he hadn't been with a woman in a lifetime. Over and over he plunged into her tight, wet passage.

Jane didn't seem to mind. Her fingernails scored his back, and she wrapped her legs around his waist. She nipped his lips with her teeth, kissing him over and over, practically smothering him with her enthusiasm.

Halfway through, he rolled their bodies and put her on top. Now he could play with her breasts and see her face go all soft and rosy with embarrassment when he found her clit and teased it. He grasped her curvy, firm ass. "Ride me, honey."

She was eager. She was good. And those fabulous long legs enabled her to rise above him and then sink down for a million agonizing seconds until their bodies were fully joined.

She learned a wicked rhythm. Ethan panted, trying to stay with her. God, he wanted to come. The stab of fire in his gut ripped at him, offering sweet release. Ethan beat it back, his body damp with sweat, his fingers locking in a bruising grasp on her hips.

He concentrated on her face, watched every flutter of pleasure that painted her feminine features with a glow of eroticism. She was an earth goddess, natural and stunningly lovely.

She squeezed him with her inner muscles, caressing his cock so that he bit back a curse. He smiled tightly. "You don't play fair."

She leaned forward and lowered her mouth to his. "Fair is for sissies." Then she reached behind her, caressed his balls, and ground her hips down on his as he shouted and climaxed with enough force to rattle his eyeballs. The wave of searing pleasure seemed endless.

He was embarrassingly weak in the aftermath. His breath still came in great, shaky gasps, and his heart rate might never be the same.

Jane was slumped on his chest, her lips dangerously near his nipple. If she touched him again on anything remotely approaching an erogenous zone, he might have a heart attack. He brushed her soft, silky hair from his chin and put a hand on the back of her head.

She didn't move, so he ran his fingers gently from the top of her spine to the base of her skull, caressing the baby soft skin at her nape. She murmured and shifted her legs against his. He figured this was as good a time as any to discuss their new situation.

He whispered her name. "Jane?"

She still didn't open her eyes, but she yawned delicately, her soft puff of breath tickling his chest. He liked the feel of her slender, relaxed body on top of him. A lot.

When she didn't answer, he tried again. "Jane . . . honey. Are you awake behind those pretty eyelids?"

She sighed and pushed up, supporting herself with a hand on his chest. "You ready for some spaghetti?"

Ethan chewed and swallowed in a state of shock. He and Jane had just had incredible, hotter-than-hell sex, and she was acting like nothing out of the ordinary had happened. It made no sense.

In his experience, women loved postmortems. They wanted to talk about relationships and the future and whether or not their partner had achieved nirvana.

Jane, being Jane, did none of that. Instead, she served up a steaming plate of spaghetti with meat sauce, offered him a garlic roll, and proceeded to eat her own dinner with enthusiasm.

He was mildly insulted. And strongly indignant. And seriously confused.

She quizzed him as they ate about his day at work. He suddenly realized he hadn't told her the latest about her two break-ins.

He wiped his mouth on his napkin and took a swig of sweet tea. "One of the men first on the scene the night of the fire recovered the imprint of a shoe in the soft dirt beneath the window. He's processed it, and the good news is, it matches a high-end athletic shoe popular with adolescents."

"And the bad news?"

"That brand is sold in at least three locations here in town, not to mention in Knoxville and on the Internet. But the fact that the shoe is expensive may mean we're dealing with drug money. Or perhaps even a gang initiation." Statlerville had managed to stay exempt from a lot of organized activity, but Ethan wasn't naive enough to believe the status quo would last forever.

Jane frowned as she studied his face. "But it still seems odd that nothing was stolen either time. And what motive could there possibly be for setting off the smoke bombs?"

"We're still looking at possible scenarios." It pissed him off that they had so few leads. He wanted to prove to Jane that the Statlerville Police Department was hard at work keeping her safe at night.

But so far, they were coming up empty-handed.

He decided to test the waters in light of the recent carnal activity. "It occurred to me that you would be a lot safer staying with me for a while."

She didn't blink an eye, but her body language grew still. "Surely that's a bit extreme."

He'd never asked another woman to move in with him, not even his ex-fiancée. So Jane's reluctance hit a nerve. "What if whoever is doing this decides to up the ante? A real fire, maybe. Or even an explosive device."

She cocked her head, a faint smile crossing her lips. "Somebody has been watching too many episodes of *Law and Order*."

His temper flared. "This is nothing to joke about. You don't know who this jerk is. Be sensible, Jane."

Her eyes narrowed. " 'Sensible' is my middle name. But I'm also smart enough to know that both attacks happened on a weekend. Obviously, the cleaning crew is working around the clock this weekend, so I'd say if anything is going to happen at all, it will be next Friday or Saturday night. So in the meantime, I'm relatively safe."

"You assume too much," he said, his words stiff with frustration.

She took a bite of spaghetti, chewed it, and swallowed, as if she hadn't a care in the world. "I appreciate your concern, Ethan. Really I do. But I have a cell phone, and I keep it right beside my bed."

"Cell phones only give the illusion of safety."

She put down her fork and leaned her elbows on the table, her hands clasped below her chin. "Let's assume for a moment that I might take you up on your offer. Are there any women in your life who might be unhappy with that arrangement? Anyone at all?"

It was the perfect opening. Jane offered it to him deliberately, praying he would take the bait. But Ethan said nothing. Not one damn thing. He merely shook his head and muttered a negative.

She decided then and there that this new physical awareness between them would not be allowed to make her stupid. She was not going to permit herself to be blinded by sex, no matter how incredible.

She stood and gathered the dishes, suddenly realizing what she had to do. Spending another night under Ethan's roof would be foolhardy in the extreme. Until she could believe in his sincerity . . . until she could know beyond the shadow of a doubt that he wasn't interested in the woman sending him mysterious valentines . . . then and only then would she trust him.

Was it entrapment to continue the string of erotic notes? No. Not really. All he had to do was show them to her. And ask her opinion about the identity of the sender. It was that simple.

She wanted to stay so badly, it was tearing her apart. She wanted another night in his bed, in his arms. But this was too important. She had to be strong.

When Ethan finished loading the dishwasher and turned it on, she faced him with a smile that was hopefully natural. "I appreciate you letting me stay here last night. But I think I'm going to drive to Knoxville now and be with my parents until tomorrow. They've really been worried about me with the break-ins and all. I'm sure they would feel much better if they can see me in the flesh . . . be positive that I really am okay."

Ethan's expression went from shock to disappointment to stoic calm, with maybe a fillip of anger thrown in along the way for good measure. He shrugged. "If that's what you need to do. I have a pile of paperwork to go over before Monday anyway."

His easy acceptance nicked her pride. Her bags were ready. All she had to do was retrieve them from the bedroom. She swallowed her own disappointment. "Would you mind running me back to my apartment? I won't go in, but I need my car."

The brief trip was silent and strained. Ethan was brooding, all dark-eyed displeasure. She did her best to ignore him.

Standing in front of Paper Pleasures, she bade him goodbye. She even managed to press a quick kiss to his firm lips. "Thanks for everything, Ethan. You're a good friend. I'll talk to you later in the week."

And then she walked around to the rear parking lot with his gaze boring a hole in her back.

Sherry wrinkled her brow and wondered what sadistic person was responsible for the ice pick that had been jabbed into her skull. Little snatches of memory teased her consciousness . . . nothing concrete . . . just bits and pieces of tantalizing images.

She tried to move and groaned. Her body was one big mass of pain. Holy cow. She'd recognized the unmistakable signs of the flu coming on, but after that, she had a giant hole in her memory.

She turned her head slowly and gazed at the clock on the bedside table. It was eight a.m., but what day? She remembered feeling wretched on Friday night . . . so maybe this was Saturday.

Several items near the clock caught her eye and made her frown. The thermometer and medicine made sense. But the other thing did not. It was one of her great-grandmother's crystal goblets. Sherry used them only on special occasions. No way would she have filled the glass with water to take a pill.

Maybe Ethan had stopped by. But that didn't make sense either. Ethan knew she cherished that glass. He would have been more likely to give her a paper cup from the cabinet. Oh, heck, too much thinking was making her poor head ache even worse.

She closed her eyes again and floated in and out. The sunshine streaming through the open drapes was cheerful, but not enough to ease her misery. And why were the drapes open, anyway? It was her habit to close them at night. Maybe she had been too sick to do even that.

She needed to go to the bathroom, but the thought of trying to get upright was daunting. Perhaps she would sleep a little more.

The next time she looked at the clock, thirty minutes had passed. She could barely focus long enough to make out the numbers on the clock.

Suddenly, tears of self-pity filled her eyes and squeezed out beneath her closed eyelids. She hurt all over, and there was no one to care. Ethan was horribly busy. Debra was hundreds of miles away in Florida, and the only other person who might be concerned was . . .

Randy.

She tried to ignore her poor, restless body by remembering the beautiful date last Monday night. Everything about it had been perfect. Right up until the moment she freaked out.

But, God help her, the blinding river of joy that had crashed through her long-held defenses had scared her to death. She was just as likely to drown in it as she was to swim. And the temptation . . . Dear Lord. She had been inches away from ripping Randy's clothes from his body.

If she had ever felt such sharp, shining sexual desire, she couldn't remember it. And the tenderness in the way he had held her had made her want to weep.

But she had ruined it all. She must have seemed like an immature lunatic to him. Not only was it utterly embarrassing to know she had overreacted—it was not fair to Randy. He had done everything right.

She, as usual, had not.

She tried to swallow and winced when her dry throat protested. Was there any liquid left in that glass?

She opened her eyes, even though the light seemed unforgiving and harsh. She put out her arm and braced herself in an effort to sit up.

But her hand didn't land on the mattress. Her fingers ran into smooth, warm male flesh.

# Twelve

It was a miracle she didn't scream. But honestly . . . it would have taken more energy than she could muster. And besides, some innate sense of self-preservation warned her that screaming would likely make her head explode.

She took a deep breath and brought her hand back to her side. It was Randy. He was lying facedown on his stomach, his head turned toward the wall. The pillow was half under him, clenched in one arm. The only thing he was wearing as far as she could tell was his uniform pants.

Which left huge expanses of his smooth, golden-skinned, muscular back completely bare. Her fingers itched to explore all that gorgeous masculine real estate.

She couldn't resist the impulse to touch the arm closest to her. It looked very uncomfortable, bent as it was at his side. She skated her palm over his lightly hair-dusted forearm.

He jerked upright so suddenly, she squeaked in surprise. As

he twisted his body into a seated position, she studied him. Dark smudges under his bloodshot eyes did nothing to detract from his appeal. He scrubbed his hands over his face. "What time is it?"

She tried to clear her throat. "A little after eight." She paused. "Is it Saturday?"

He shook his head, his brown eyes solemn. "It's Sunday morning, Sherry. You've been out of it for quite a while. I've been here since Saturday afternoon."

She lay still and quiet as she tried to process the bizarre information. How did a woman lose track of an entire day?

He took pity on her confusion. "Ethan sent me to check on you. He was worried when you didn't answer either of your phones. When I got here your temperature was over a hundred and five. I called the doctor. He said to get your fever down with a cold bath. That and alternating ibuprofen and acetaminophen every two hours finally did the trick. You've been sleeping naturally for the last little bit."

He rattled off the information with a cop's impassivity. Just the facts, ma'am. Just the facts.

But his no-frills recitation left a heck of a lot to the imagination . . . such as how the aforementioned bath took place, and why she was not wearing her usual nightgown. In fact, she wasn't wearing anything at all.

Holy crap. One of her arms was still under the covers. She scooted her hand over her chest. Yep. Buck naked. If she hadn't felt so lousy, she was pretty sure she would have been blushing from her toes all the way up to her forehead. Sherry McCamish did not sleep in the nude, not even when she had been a newly married teenager.

She managed to look at Randy without moving her head. The drums beating inside her skull were starting to make her nauseated. "I'm sorry," she said dully. "Ethan shouldn't have called you."

He shrugged. "I'm glad he did. You needed help."

Her chin trembled as her stomach rolled, and her head throbbed. "I was so mean to you," she muttered. And then she burst into tears.

Randy sighed and pulled her into his arms, settling his back against the headboard. "Don't be silly, Sherry. One rejection wasn't going to get rid of me." He reached for the medicine and the half-full glass of water. "Here . . . take this and try to relax."

She lifted her head long enough to swallow the tablets. Then she slumped back onto his chest.

He stroked her silky hair, enjoying the feel of her in his arms. The sheet was protecting her modesty, but now that her fever was down near one hundred, she might be getting cold. He brushed her cheek with his thumb. "Would you like me to get some pajamas out of your drawer . . . to keep you warm?"

She burrowed deeper. "I'm warm," she said, her voice slurred. "This is nice." Seconds later, he realized she was asleep again.

It touched him that she had accepted his presence so easily. And she hadn't turned him out on his ass. Of course, that was probably because she was too weak and sick to do anything else.

Nevertheless, he would enjoy this time while it lasted. He loved taking care of her . . . would be honored and pleased to do it more. But her compliance no doubt had an end. About the time her body shook off the flu and her stubborn spirit was once again in charge.

He was pretty sure that Sherry was the one for him. The feeling had struck hard and fast. They'd barely known each other two weeks. But he was old enough to recognize that she appealed to him in ways no other woman ever had. He felt a connection that couldn't be denied.

The knowledge was scary. Although he didn't see the difference in their ages as any big deal, Sherry would. He already knew her that well. She was a woman who lived by rigid rules, perhaps because she had broken a big one at an early age. Or so it seemed to her. It was a good bet that if he tried to take things in a more serious direction, she might bolt.

Her reaction when he kissed her Monday night had hurt, but he wasn't really surprised. Sherry was an extremely private person, her emotions held in check at all times. So the passion that had blown up out of nowhere had shocked her. Hell, it had shocked him.

But now that he knew how it could be between them, he was damned if he'd let her walk away.

When he was sure she was sound asleep, he eased her out of his arms and laid her down. The sheet fell away as he got her settled. The sight of her soft, round breasts struck hard at his heart and his self-control. With shaking hands, he pulled the covers to her chin.

He wanted her. He needed her. He had no more than seventy-two hours to insert himself into her life and her heart. He prayed it would be enough time.

Ethan was pissed. It was Wednesday, and Jane had been avoiding him ever since her abrupt departure from his house on Saturday. After sharing a night and an evening of wild, deeply satisfying sex, she was suddenly too busy to see him. Hell, she wouldn't even answer his phone calls.

And he was pretty sure she was trying to drive him out of his mind. She'd deliberately returned one or two of his messages by calling at times when she knew good and well that he was tied up and unavailable.

His personal life was the pits, but thankfully, the police department was beginning to return to normal. Sherry had still been too weak to bring lunch on Monday, but she swore she was feeling well enough to fix today's meal. And judging by the fact that Temple was hovering by the door to the parking lot, she must be on her way.

Ethan would check up on his sister in a bit, but for the moment, he escaped to his office and shut the door. He reached in his desk drawer and extracted the three valentines. One by one he spread them out and examined the verses. Try as he might, he couldn't see any evil intent behind the unusual mail he'd received. The words were loving—highly sexual, yes, but almost tender in places.

As much as it galled him to admit it, he was intrigued by the handwriting, the erotic wordplay, and the ultrafeminine paper. Because he was a man, the bold effort to seduce him was flattering and even amusing.

More than once, he had debated showing the notes to Jane to get a woman's point of view. But two things stopped him. First was the slim possibility that the mystery poet was some kind of psychopath. If the woman behind these notes knew he was in a relationship with someone else, Jane's life might be in danger. So it was better to keep the two females separate. And the second thing that had kept him from asking Jane's opinion was the possibility that she would be hurt. She might even think the sender was someone with whom Ethan had been involved in the past and who now wanted him back.

He had already been careless with Jane's feelings once in the past by getting engaged without telling her. She might interpret his interest in the erotic valentines the wrong way. Jane was the only woman he wanted, the only woman on his radar. So until he nailed down the identity of the mysterious admirer, he'd keep his own counsel.

But tomorrow, come hell or high water, Ethan was going to stake out the post office to learn once and for all who was behind the string of anonymous mail. And when he knew the woman's identity, he'd clean up the situation with Jane none the wiser.

Jane stood with her hands on her hips and surveyed her progress. Returning home Monday morning had been a pleasant surprise. The cleaning crew hired by Mr. Benson had done an amazing job. The hardwood floors shone, her display cases were spotless, and unless she tried really, really hard, she couldn't smell a whiff of smoke.

Her apartment upstairs was even better. So she was a happy camper.

On Tuesday, the first of the replacement stock she'd ordered had begun arriving. It was almost as exciting as when she had first opened her shop. With the sales floor literally wiped clean, it was a good chance to rearrange her displays and reroute the traffic flow in the shop.

It was hard work, but at the end of the day, the results were rewarding. She was actually starting to believe that things would get back to normal. The deductible on her insurance was a hefty chunk, but with spring and summer ahead, her business would pick up.

She decided to take a chance and beef up her bridal supplies in hopes that extra revenue in that sector would help her recoup some of her losses. And not for the first time, she debated adding a small case of baked goods. Mrs. Fitzhugh had a friend who used to own a catering business, and the other woman had indicated an interest in supplying Jane with homemade cakes, tarts, and cookies if Jane decided the time was right.

Mrs. Fitzhugh was itching to get back to work, and even though Jane continued paying her, she hadn't wanted the elderly woman to be exposed to the smoke smell because of her asthma. Even now that the air was clean again, the physical nature of the restocking job was not suitable for her older employee. But Jane called her each afternoon to report on the shop's progress.

Ethan was not so easily appeased. He'd bombarded her cell phone and home phone with messages, all of which she had ignored for the most part. Tomorrow, she was going to send one more valentine, the fourth one, and then evaluate Ethan's response. She would give him every opportunity to talk to her about it. And if he didn't . . . well . . . she'd confront him if she had the guts, and they would have a serious heart-to-heart.

Wednesday evening she took a bath right after dinner and put on her comfiest pair of soft knit pajamas. They were covered with little pink and yellow and green hearts that said things like *Kiss Me, I'm Yours, Will U Be Mine?*

She'd bought them for half price last year after Valentine's Day on a whim. They weren't the sexiest pajamas in the world, but they were bright and cheerful, and right now Jane needed some serious perking up.

Outside, tiny, icy snowflakes swirled in the wind. They weren't the big, fat, wet flakes that promised to pile up in a picturesque blanket of white. These were the painful, needlelike, wind-driven shards that made a person want to hunker down and never go back outside.

She adjusted the thermostat up a notch and pulled a pair of fuzzy white socks on her feet. Then she curled up in her big armchair and began composing the most important note yet.

*Ethan, My Love,*

Ha. That was even better than the *Dearest Ethan* she had used before. She was pulling out all the stops.

*Ethan, My Love,*

*I've waited in vain,*
*My heart full of pain.*
*I thought that by now*
*You'd have figured out how*
*To find my true name*
*And to finish my game.*

*A girl shouldn't be,*
*As you might foresee,*
*A sly, lustful tease.*
*But you won't believe*
*What's right under your nose*
*And my frustration grows.*

*Just give me a chance*
*In passion's sweet dance.*
*I'll be all you desire.*
*Our passion a fire*
*That blazes so bright*
*We'll cling to the night.*

*I won't wait endless days.*
*There's a price you must pay.*
*Once the treasure is lost*
*My heart turns to frost.*

Jane nibbled the end of her pencil. Was that last stanza too forbidding? She didn't want him to think she was a stalker.

She sat through two *Friends* episodes on TBS and brooded about her latest verse. The poetess was beginning to sound desperate, about like Jane herself. How and when was she supposed to reveal her identity? And if Ethan didn't share this wicked valentine with her, what then?

Would she send the last two? Would she tell him she was jealous of the mystery lady sending him mail? Would she snoop through his drawers and confront him with the evidence of his infidelity?

She pulled her pajama top up over her head and groaned. Things were completely out of control, and she wasn't sure if she had any hope of getting them back on track.

When her cell phone rang shrilly, she jumped two feet in the air. She snatched it up and stared at the caller ID. Oh, glory, it was Ethan. And even the man's ring tone sounded irritated. She flipped open the phone with shaky hands and pressed a button.

Ethan's voice was definitely on the frustrated side. "I've called you a dozen times. What's with the silent treatment?"

Trust Ethan to put her on the defensive. "I've been really busy."

He made a rude noise. "Come down and open the front door." And then he hung up on her.

Her heart started racing. She jumped to her feet, tucked the valentine out of sight, and looked for her robe. Then she remembered. She'd had to throw her old one away. And she hadn't had time to shop for a new one yet. Blast.

As she hurried down the stairs and crossed the shop floor, she gave herself a pep talk. She wouldn't have sex with Ethan. She wouldn't have sex with Ethan. She was a woman with self-control and strong moral fiber and a keen sense of danger.

Through the opaque glass of the entrance, she could see his large silhouette. Even his outline looked cranky. She unlocked the large wooden door with the ornate pane and pulled it back.

Immediately, bitterly cold air and a flurry of snowflakes swirled into the shop, propelled, it seemed, by the big, menacing figure of the man she loved. Ethan entered like the abominable snowman, his uncovered head and shoulders already dusted with white. He didn't look like a happy camper, his scowl dark, his expression implacable.

She stepped back, shivering violently.

Ethan shut the door without her assistance. The muted *thunk* of the dead bolt chased a chill down her spine. And when he turned to face her, every bit of snow in the room melted in simultaneous wisps of steam.

If she'd been a Victorian maiden, she might have swooned. Ethan radiated heat, determination, and aggressive sexual hunger that even a blind nun couldn't miss.

She licked her dry lips. "Why are you here?" The question was brave, even if her voice did crack a bit on the last word.

He stripped off his heavy coat and tossed it on the floor. Then he folded his arms across his broad chest and let his gaze make a lazy journey from her flushed cheeks, to her whimsical pjs, to her sock-clad feet. She was dressed for a quiet evening at home . . . alone. Nothing about her attire suggested sex.

But apparently Ethan was not put off by the fact that she was wearing fuzzy cotton instead of smooth silk. He lifted one eyebrow. "You've been avoiding my phone calls." His jaw was granite hard, and she was pretty sure he was spoiling for a fight.

Seeing the normally placid Ethan so riled made her want to laugh, but the nervous sexual tension in her stomach overrode any humor in the situation. She straightened her spine and wiped damp palms on her hips. "I am a business woman with many demands on my time."

He took two steps closer. "Bullshit."

Her eyes flared wide in shock and then narrowed. "Are you calling me a liar?"

Two more steps.

She held her ground. She was pretty sure she saw his lips twitch.

He reached out and fingered the lapel of her pajama top. "I think you're scared of what happened between us. You don't know where it fits in your tidy little life, so you're pushing me away."

The "tidy little life" comment stung. Her arms were by her sides, and she resisted the impulse to wrap them around her waist. Calling on all her latent acting ability, she shrugged nonchalantly. "I don't know what you mean."

He traced the V where the bare skin of her throat met the neckline of her top. Despite the fact that he had just come in from the cold, his hand was warm. Holy Hannah, the man was only using one damn fingertip, and already Jane was close to stripping off her skimpy layer of armor and saying, *Take me, you fool.*

His breath was warm on her cheek, their faces almost touching. He unbuttoned one of her buttons . . . just one. "I felt used," he deadpanned. "Surely you want me for more than sex . . . right?"

She cocked her head. "Well, there *is* the matter of my unresolved break-ins. I could definitely use some assistance there."

He licked the shell of her ear. "And if I promise you an arrest by the end of the week?"

She shuddered, her knees threatening to buckle. He was barely touching her. But her breath was coming in short jerky pants, and she was trembling like a maple leaf in autumn. "Then I would be suitably grateful," she whispered, the prim words a croak.

A second button popped open, aided and abetted by her big, handsome policeman boyfriend. Could she call him that? Even if they had never actually been on a date?

He put one hand on her shoulder, one on her hip, and pushed her neck to the side with his mouth so he could bite her neck. He mumbled something against her throat. His hair smelled of winter and wood smoke.

It was hell not to touch him. Now she did tighten her arms around her waist, holding on to her sense of preservation. "What did you say?"

He lifted his head for a split second, his eyes hot and glazed. "In about five seconds I'm going to fuck you up against a wall. So you'd better stop me now if you have any objections."

Her knees gave out, and as her limbs melted, he scooped her into his embrace. His mouth came down hard on hers, moving over and between her lips with determination. His tongue stroked her teeth, even as a growl of masculine satisfaction rumbled through his chest.

It was everything she had wanted and everything she was afraid of. Nothing was resolved. The notes. His secrecy. Her confession.

But when his thumb brushed over her nipple with reverence, and his lips stroked hers with cajoling passion, she was lost. Her whispered affirmative was almost swallowed up in his groan of relief.

Had he really thought she would refuse?

He walked her backward, true to his promise, toward the nearest wall. And all the while, he kissed her, fondled her breasts, nudged her hips with his powerful thighs.

Somehow, her arms finally let go of their death grip on her waist and linked around his neck. The remaining buttons on her top magically fled their constrictive holes, and now the pajama shirt fluttered open, leaving her aching breasts free.

In Ethan, she sensed something snap. It was the unmistakable shattering of his control, the helpless surrender to a hunger that gave no quarter. Jane knew, because she felt it as well.

He unfastened his belt and pants with one hand. "Help me," he muttered, his plea hoarse and urgent.

She wrestled with his zipper and freed his cock. It was thick and hot and pulsing with eagerness.

His hands pushed at the sides of her pajama bottoms, shoving them to her knees and off her feet. He lifted her with muscles straining in his arms. And then he joined their bodies with a mighty thrust.

Jane cried out, feeling stretched beyond belief from this angle. She sobbed and buried her hot face in his neck. "Ethan."

He went dead still. "Did I hurt you?"

The shocked anguish in his voice combined with dazed remorse for her pain.

She rested her cheek against his, feeling his life force deep within her, relishing the amazing sensation of being joined with him. "Don't stop. I'm fine. I'm better than fine."

He whooshed out a breath, chuckling hoarsely. "Thank God."

And then he moved again.

Jane locked her ankles behind his back and held on. He took her slow. He took her fast. He took her with shallow, teasing probes and firm, steady thrusts. And the wilder he got, the more she liked it.

The wall bruised her shoulder blades. She never noticed. How could she, when it took all her concentration just to breathe?

He changed his rhythm suddenly, his entire body rigid with the effort it took to maintain the new, lazy, almost tender moves. He rested his forehead against hers. "Have I told you you're amazing?" The words came out in quick, short pants.

She played with the soft hair at his nape. It was silky and smooth beneath her fingers. "No," she said softly. "Nice, yes . . . amazing, no."

He found her mouth and kissed her roughly. "Not nice," he muttered. "Spectacular. Sexy. Hot as hell."

Her heart turned over in her chest. That sounded more promising than "good old buddy Jane." She squeezed her inner muscles and grinned when he shuddered and cursed. Then she nipped his ear with her teeth. "I believe you've already breached the castle, so I'm pretty sure flattery is superfluous at the moment." She was barely able to string words together. The feel of him inside her was a huge distraction. Really huge.

He moaned and moved in and out slowly, making them both crazy. "Sweet Jane." He murmured the words so softly she was barely able to hear.

Maybe later she would analyze the word "sweet" . . . might wonder why a man in the midst of a really powerful fuck wanted to describe his lover by such a syrupy endearment. But for now, all she really, really wanted was an orgasm.

She rubbed her breasts against his chest, feeling the light tickle of his chest hair. "Ethan?"

"Hmmm?" His hands beneath her ass tightened.

"Don't make me wait. . . ."

He straightened suddenly, startling her into an undignified squeak. "Change of venue," he ground out between clenched teeth.

He strode toward the back of the shop, closed the distance to the staircase in record time, and sat down on the third step with her astride his lap. When he dragged her hard against his chest, the base of his cock ground against her clit. That was all it took. She trembled and cried out as fire shot through her body, stole her breath, and left her limp and gasping in his embrace.

His smile was feral. "Hang on, baby. There's more where that came from."

## Thirteen

eons later, or maybe just an hour, Ethan tugged Jane against his chest and spooned her with a sigh of contentment. He had no desire to dress and go back out into the frigid night, so he was banking on Jane's willingness to let him spend the night.

But she hadn't offered that as an option . . . yet. They had just completed a second round of rock-his-world-to-hell-and-back sex, and he was trying to regain his equilibrium before he broached the subject of sleeping over.

He liked it here. Jane's place was homey and warm. On the table beside her bed lay the mystery she was reading. A single stuffed animal sat in an old-fashioned rocking chair. Her closet door was ajar, and the top of her dresser was covered with a variety of female stuff.

Jane wasn't a neat freak. But she wasn't a slob. She was just . . . Jane.

He played lazily with her breasts, stroking the incredibly soft skin and teasing the nipples in turn. Jane stirred restlessly, her long legs tangling with his. Their bodies fit together perfectly. He couldn't imagine a woman more physically suited to be his lover. Even though they were unaccustomed to physical intimacy, there had been virtually no awkwardness in their coming together, perhaps because they knew each other very well.

The sex was explosive, but at the same time perfectly comfortable, powerfully satisfying.

He liked this newly resurrected relationship, this fresh incarnation of what they once enjoyed. But he was baffled by Jane's behavior.

Every day since last weekend, and even now, he'd expected her to demand some sort of explanation . . . to talk about the future. But she had been almost cavalier about the whole thing. And though he refused to admit that it piqued his pride, on some level, her refusal to do so was insulting and disturbing.

Was Jane merely indulging in fun and games? Did she see him as temporary entertainment? His stomach churned with acid, and he stirred restlessly.

Before he could stop her, she slid out of bed and went to the bathroom. He heard water running, listened for the soft pad of footsteps, and finally noticed her return. But she was dressed in her pajamas, and he sensed that her emotional armor was firmly back in place. She paused in the doorway, her slender figure a shadow against the harsh light from the hallway.

She hovered there. "Would you like something to eat? I have part of Mr. Benson's cake left over from Saturday." Her voice was tentative, and the hint of vulnerability he heard made his heart turn over in his chest.

"Come here," he said gruffly. Maybe she wasn't as nonchalant as she seemed. Maybe she was protecting herself from him. It was a sobering thought.

She climbed into bed, and he cursed with a laugh when her icy feet touched his legs. "Damn, woman, where are those cute fluffy socks?"

She burrowed against him with a flurry of feminine wiggles, making his dick snap to attention. Her words were muffled. "Socks aren't sexy."

He kissed the top of her head, carefully keeping his hands in noninflammatory positions. For now. "Trust me, Jane, if you're wearing them, they're sexy."

For several long minutes, they snuggled in silence, a warm, cozy, new-but-not-weird tangle of limbs and breath. He felt his chest tighten with all sorts of impulsive, heartfelt words. But he choked them back. It was no time to be rash. He couldn't risk doing or saying something stupid. Not when he was finally back in her life, close to her in every way that counted.

So he did what any smart man would do. He played to his strengths.

She had to have noticed his boner. It throbbed between them like an overeager adolescent. But he ignored it. He stroked her back, tracing her spine. "We think your intruder may try something again this Friday or Saturday."

She stiffened in his arms. "Why?"

"I had a couple of men swing by on patrol this past weekend when the cleaners were at your place. It's possible your fire bug showed up again, because Sunday morning one of the officers found a cigarette butt beneath that same alley window."

She moved restlessly. "You think he was planning to break in a third time?"

He shrugged. "Maybe. If we're right and the perp is a teenager, it would make sense that he has more freedom on the weekends.

He would have assumed the downstairs was empty as usual at night. Then he shows up and realizes the shop is crawling with people. He got spooked and took off."

She rolled to her back and ran a hand through her hair. "I just don't get it. What could he possibly want?" It tickled Ethan that she sounded pissed, not scared. Jane was no pushover.

He rolled up on an elbow and toyed with her buttons, wishing she hadn't been so quick to cover up all that luscious, warm flesh. "I don't give a damn what he wants. All I care about is busting his criminal ass so I know you're safe again."

She lifted a hand to his cheek. "My hero."

He chose to ignore the saccharine sarcasm. "I don't think you're taking this threat seriously."

When she linked her hands above her head, he caught a glimpse of pale skin at her waist. Even in the dim light, he could tell she was rolling her eyes. "Be honest, Ethan. He broke a window and set off a few smoke bombs. I don't think this is going to turn into the script for a Hollywood slasher movie."

His temper flared. The fact that Jane was the one person who could provoke him so easily was not something he wished to dwell on at the moment. He wanted to shake her. "Bad things happen to nice people, Jane." He saw it all the time. The innocent caught in unspeakable situations because they didn't take precautions or because they had no one to stand up for them, to protect them. He wouldn't allow it to happen to Jane.

His fingers clenched in a fist on her belly. "I'm staying here this weekend."

Her eyes narrowed. "Have I invited you?"

He heard the irritation and the female pique, but he didn't give a rat's ass. Jane's safety was his responsibility, both professionally and personally. And if that offended her, tough shit.

He battened down the urge to play bad cop. Sometimes coaxing was better than coercion. Deliberately, he relaxed his fingers and splayed his hand on her abdomen. He could feel her quick intake of breath and the faint shiver that rippled from her breasts to her thighs.

His head bent. His lips nuzzled that tiny strip of naked skin above the elastic waist of her pants. "I don't snore. You should know that by now." Alluding to their first night together, at his house, was a calculated risk. He wanted her to remember the heat, the raw passion, the aching hunger. But he risked scaring her away, because since that night she had definitely kept her distance.

Slowly, he lowered her pants an inch and probed his tongue in her navel.

Her narrow hips came off the bed. "Ohmigod, Ethan." Both of her hands clenched in his hair, threatening to yank him bald.

He slid his hands under the elastic and pushed at the fabric until it crumpled at her knees. Her pale, lush thighs nearly derailed his plan. He wanted to shove between them and take her again.

*Patience, man, patience.* He licked a lazy line from her navel to the top of her mound. It tickled him that Jane shaved there. It seemed a very un-Jane thing to do. All that was left for him to tease with his tongue was a tiny, almost heart-shaped puff of pale gold hair.

He shifted positions and moved on top, his hips resting on hers, pinning her to the bed. Because he hadn't completely removed her pajama pants, she couldn't spread her legs. She was his prisoner. Deliberately, he rubbed his erection over that silly heart. On the down stroke he brushed her clitoris with his shaft.

Jane mumbled something under her breath and closed her eyes. Her hands gripped the bedsheet, threatening to rip the soft, brushed flannel.

He smiled—even though she couldn't see him—and shoved her shirt to her armpits, not bothering with the buttons this time. When his mouth closed over her breast, she pulled his head closer, whimpering his name. As he tugged at her nipple with his teeth and tongue, Jane went wild.

She bucked and twisted, threatening imminent harm to his boys.

He choked back a laugh that was three parts frustrated lust and yanked the two sides of her top apart, flinging buttons across the room.

When Jane's eyes flew open in shock, he grinned through clenched teeth. "Always wanted to do that," he panted.

He was playing with fire, and he knew it. His hips ground restlessly on hers, and he savored the feel of skin to skin. But it wasn't enough, not even close.

Jane's skin was damp, her breath a harsh rasp. He rolled off her and pushed her feet toward her butt. Now her knees spread wide, but her ankles were still trapped.

He knelt before her and brushed a finger through the lush, wet folds of her sex. When he lightly rubbed her clitoris, Jane came with a raw groan. He slid two fingers inside her as she climaxed, feeling her muscles clamp down and grip him.

Finally, he ripped off her pants and moved his body into position, bumping the head of his cock at the entrance to her still quivering channel. "Invite me to stay this weekend." As he bit out the words, he entered her a fraction and then withdrew.

Jane licked her lips. Her eyelids rose slowly. "What?" The word was slow, slurred.

He teased again, in and back out. "Tell me you want me to sleep here . . . in your bed."

He could see on her face the moment she understood the sexual blackmail. Her mouth opened and closed and her chest rose and fell. To her credit, she tried. "I'm used to sleeping alone. It's more comfortable that way." Her stubborn words might have been more convincing if her old-fashioned brass bed wasn't in disarray with rumpled sheets and the scent of sex.

He kept his expression austere. "I want an invitation, sweetheart. And I want you to mean it. 'Please, Ethan,' " he mimicked. " 'Please sleep with me and keep me safe.' "

She managed to laugh. "I might take my chances with the punk."

Now she was just being mean. He pulled all the way out and got to his knees. "Okay," he said calmly. "If that's the way you want it."

He slid off the bed and stood up. "Make sure and keep that cell phone charged," he mocked.

Jane practically vibrated with outrage. "You're leaving?" She pulled up her pj pants and straightened her gaping top. "That's police brutality or entrapment or something."

He leaned against the wall. "Try making *that* stick. You're the one turning down a genuine offer of police protection."

She sat cross-legged on the bed, glaring at him. "Nice. Real nice. The assistant chief of police has to use blackmail to get sex from a woman."

He leaned against the wall, still nude. Jane's hair was tousled, and her breasts were only partly covered. His dick was so hard, he ached. He managed a grin, hoping he looked more nonchalant than he felt. "I believe we've established that the sex was freely offered. I'm trying to finagle an invitation to sleep in your bed this weekend. But, hey, if that doesn't work for you, I'm fine sleeping on the couch, sweet thing. Your call. Either way, I'm staying."

Despite his deliberate provocation, her face softened. "I can't let you sleep on the couch," she said, her smile wry. "You might hurt your back."

He shrugged. "A chance I'll have to take."

She scooted off the bed and stood before him, her gaze locked on his bobbing erection. "Do you really think our mystery intruder might try something again?"

When Jane took Ethan's rigid flesh in her fingers, a sharp, startled breath hissed through his teeth. "It's a distinct possibility."

She stroked him slowly, cupping his balls with her free hand. His knees locked, and sweat broke out on his forehead. Her gentle but firm touch was torture and pleasure in a potent cocktail.

She dropped to her knees without warning and guided his cock to her lips. "Okay, then. Consider this your official invitation to have a sleepover. In my bed." And then his world shifted to black as she took him into her mouth and began to lick and suck and destroy him, inch by inch.

Jane was little better than a novice when it came to oral sex. But having the freedom to tease and arouse Ethan was exhilarating. She didn't waste time wondering if she was doing this right. Ethan was hard and male and so wonderfully responsive to her touch. His penis reared proudly against his belly, the skin velvety soft over hard, ready flesh. The broad purplish head of his cock leaked fluid that was salty on her tongue.

The taste of him . . . his scent . . . the way his big hands tangled in her hair and massaged her scalp—all of it seemed surreal. But God, how amazing. He was strong and tough and a man of honor. In centuries past he might have been a knight in chain mail ready to defend his lady's virtue. It touched her that he cared so much.

The fact that she was well able to take care of herself didn't negate his call to arms.

She sensed when he neared the breaking point. For a moment she considered taking him over the edge. Wondered how it would feel to have that much power over a man. Craved the experience of having him come in her mouth.

But she wanted him too badly to wait.

She stood up and leaned into him, shocked to feel the tremor in his strong arms when they encircled her. His breathing was harsh, his chest rising and falling with each gasp of air. She shimmied out of her top and slid her arms around his waist so she could feel her naked breasts against his hair-roughened chest.

His hands clamped onto her hips. "Jane." He groaned her name, his face buried in her hair.

She felt the press of his erection at her stomach. For one brief moment of fluttery feminine anxiety, she wondered how something so large could fit inside her. He seemed impossibly large, overwhelmingly aroused.

Bravely, she released him, turned around, and bent at the waist. With slow, teasing movements, she tugged her pajama bottoms an inch at a time off her butt, over her hips and down her legs. Behind her, she heard Ethan curse.

She kicked the unwanted clothing aside and stood there, waiting.

Without warning, Ethan tackled her onto the bed. If she knew more about football, she probably could have called the play. But in an instant, he was on top of her, surrounding her, locking her on hands and knees into a submissive carnal embrace.

His hand parted her legs. The head of his cock nudged at her opening, seeking entrance, demanding she let him in. As he moved inside her, she groaned. Her body stretched to accommodate him, and nerve endings she wasn't aware of sang with pleasure.

Colors swirled behind her closed eyelids. Every cell in her body seemed to coalesce into a sharp dagger of need deep in her belly. She shifted to accommodate him. He thrust deeper. Hot tears stung her eyes, but she didn't let them fall. For years she had dreamed of this, wanted this. Had she known the truth of it, she might have run. If he couldn't love her, this might destroy her.

To have so much and not all. How could she bear it when he moved on?

He had stilled inside her momentarily, giving her the chance to adjust to his forceful penetration. Now he whispered silly words in her ear, syllables of praise, lust, cajoling, grunts of pleasure.

Her hair fell over her hot face. She felt his sharp teeth at her nape, biting her, marking her. Where their bodies were joined, a tidal wave drew back and waited, poised. Ready to destroy everything in its path.

Ethan's hips pistoned now, the swollen head of his erection battering her womb. Her arms trembled. Her mouth dried as she gasped for air. Instinctively, she clamped down on his cock and squeezed with all her might.

Ethan gave a roar, thrust wildly, and reached his peak, just as her world shattered in scalding pleasure that went on and on and on.

Ethan knew he needed to say something, but his mind was blank. All his data wiped clean. He blinked his eyes in the darkness, stunned by the magnitude of the quake that had shaken him to his core. Nothing in his life had prepared him for this.

Sex with Jane.

It didn't compute. Sweet, quiet, amiable Jane. The girl who baked a mean chocolate-chip cookie. The woman who had just jerked him to the top of Mount Everest and flung him headfirst, deprived of precious oxygen, from the high peak and left him to find his way back home.

What did it mean?

She was quiet, too quiet, sprawled flat on her stomach now. He was still inside her, his quiescent flesh drained, but still partially erect. He was loath to break the connection, and even though he was on his elbows sparing her the full force of his weight, perhaps she might appreciate it if he moved off of her and gave her some space.

It was the polite thing to do, but he couldn't quite follow through.

He stroked her forearm, squeezing her narrow wrist in his big hand, feeling the delicate bones. Inside the warm cocoon of Jane's pussy, his dick came to life. He should withdraw, get a fresh condom. But he couldn't bear to sever the cord of intimacy that bound them there in this safe, dark sanctuary. He never wanted to leave her.

Snatches of memories flitted across his mind's eye like an old silent movie. He saw Jane laughing, Jane talking, Jane teasing him and challenging him and urging him on—all with animated joy and refreshing candor.

Though it took an effort, he managed to shut down his brain and concentrate on the physical. Stroking, pushing, rotating his hips to make Jane gasp. She was soft everywhere he was hard, mysterious and familiar all in the same breath. He was drunk with the sheer physical pleasure that funneled through his veins like licks of fire from head to toe. He felt invincible, godlike, as if he could fuck for hours far into the night.

Finally, so close to the edge he could taste the promise of sweet release, he paused and rolled them carefully, putting Jane on top. The five seconds he wasn't inside her stretched like hours.

Jane's hands went to his chest for support. Her eyelids were at half mast, her slender frame drooping in exhaustion. He used his thumb to tease her clit. Her whole body trembled. "God, Ethan . . ." Her voice trailed off, as she tried to sit upright.

He bent his knees, feet flat on the bed as he gave her something to lean against. Deliberately he probed where their bodies were joined and found the tiny nub of sensitive nerves. He toyed with it. "Look at me, Jane."

He could barely get the words past a tight throat, but she obeyed. With her eyes locked on his, he rubbed harder. She gasped. Her back arched. He shoved his dick upward, and Jane cried out, her inner muscles milking him violently as he exploded with a curse and a hard, wild stroke.

It seemed to last forever. Her eyes were closed, her body limp as he supported her waist.

Carefully, he lifted her to one side and laid her down gently. She didn't stir when he left long enough to dispose of the condom and wash up.

When he returned to the bedroom, he scooted under the covers and pulled her close. She went to him as naturally as if they had been lovers for years.

He felt something tight in his chest. If you'd asked him a few weeks ago, he'd have said he was a pretty happy guy. But this gut-deep contentment was something new. A feeling he couldn't have imagined, because he had never experienced anything close.

Jane stirred, her hair tickling his chin. He felt and heard her sigh. She tested the stubble on his chin with her fingers. "Ethan, can I ask you something?"

His stomach lurched, and he frowned inwardly. What was he afraid of? He swallowed. "Of course."

"Why did you never ask me out on a date?"

He opened his mouth to speak, and she held up a hand before he could get a word out, clearly anticipating his answer.

"I was under no illusions," she said flatly. "Those things we did together, places we went, were buddy outings. I was your pal. But I want to know why. Surely you knew I had a huge crush on you back then, and you dated just about every single woman in town but me. Why, Ethan. Please tell me why."

He felt like a little boy being scolding for swiping the last of the chocolate cake. Her question was valid. He'd asked himself the same thing on a number of occasions. "Lots of reasons, I guess." He needed space for this conversation, but he didn't want to let her go.

"I'll settle for a couple," she said wryly.

He exhaled, his heart beating loudly in his ears. No doubt about it. This was a minefield. "Well, in the first place, you were special to me. You were my best friend. I didn't want to mess that up. If you'll recall, I never dated any of those women more than a couple of months. I didn't want that for us."

Jane sighed inwardly. It had taken more courage than she knew she possessed to ask the question. And even more to hear the answer. She paused to regroup. It made sense in a weird, guy-code sort of way. "And the other reason?" Her hand was on his thigh, so she felt him tense up.

Silence ticked on for several seconds before he spoke. "I think I knew instinctively that you were the kind of woman a man settles down with. And I sure as hell wasn't ready for that. I may have been serious about my career, but that was about it. The thought of home and hearth gave me hives. I was selfish and immature, but I never meant to hurt you, Jane. That was the last thing I wanted to do."

"And now?"

It was a valid question. And it deserved an answer. But until he cleared up the mess about the valentines and the stalker, he didn't want to muddy the waters.

He had some thinking to do. About Jane. About the future. No need to rush.

So, to his shame, he didn't give her what she asked for. He prevaricated. "I'm here, aren't I? With you."

Jane absorbed the disappointment, felt its bitter taste, and then locked it away. She would not let anything sour this moment. She sighed, suddenly sleepy. "So you are, Ethan. So you are."

As they both drifted off to sleep, she remembered the valentine hiding in the other room. She would send it. And she would pray he decided to share it with her.

If he didn't, she wasn't sure what she could do. What she *would* do. To carry on an affair with Ethan and not have even a smidgen of hope for the future was suicidal. She was smarter than that, wasn't she?

And was the promise of great sex enough to mask the disappointment of knowing Ethan was keeping things from her? She closed her eyes. She wished she could go back in time and unsend those damn valentines.

But it was too late. Way too late.

She pulled the covers to her chin and snuggled into Ethan's arms.

She might not have the future, but she had tonight.

# Fourteen

Thursday morning Sherry stood in the rear of the Victoria's Secret store at the mall in Knoxville and flipped through a rack of merry widows. She couldn't believe she was shopping for such intentionally provocative underwear—skimpy items that she planned to wear while having intimate relations with Randy Temple.

She was a grown woman. She was horny. And she was planning to have sex just for the hell of it. It was no one's business but hers: not Debra's, not Ethan's, not anyone's. For once, she was putting herself first. And it felt darn good and hugely liberating.

She took an armful of the risqué garments back to the dressing room and started trying them on. The lime green made her look like a little girl playing dress up. The violent candy pink satin turned her into a hooker.

But the soft ivory trimmed in delicate black lace was perfect. Her small breasts plumped up nicely over the top of the corset, and her legs looked longer than they were. The hourglass shape emphasized her slender waist. When she added the thigh-high stockings, it was perfect.

She looked in the mirror and brushed the swells of her cleavage with shaking fingers. The dampness between her legs and the jittery sensation in her belly were alarming. She'd deliberately made herself into an asexual being for years. Getting pregnant out of wedlock, and the accompanying guilt, had screwed up her attitudes about sexual intimacy. After her divorce, it had been a relief to be single and celibate. Now her libido was roaring to life, and she didn't know how to handle it.

But with Randy, she was willing to try. It wouldn't last. She was certain of that. But unlike days of old, she was ready to live for the moment and enjoy the relationship for as long as it played out.

She wouldn't marry again. She knew the truth. One day she would watch her daughter fall in love. Hopefully Debra would give her mother grandchildren to love. It would be a good life . . . a full life.

But for the moment Sherry had a fleeting opportunity. A chance to resurrect the sexually deprived woman buried deep inside her.

Randy Temple wanted her, and she wanted him back. If she didn't die of a heart attack in the meantime, she was going to seduce him tonight.

As she drove back to Statlerville, the innocent pink bag resting beside her on the other seat, she remembered the tender way he had cared for her when she was so sick. If she hadn't already been halfway in love with him, those hours would have done the trick.

Lots of men wanted an easy lay. It took someone special to give unselfishly, expecting nothing in return. In her misery and suffering, she had let him stay the remainder of Sunday. But come Monday morning, her head slightly clearer and her temperature mostly gone, she had forced herself to be strong. With gratitude and faint embarrassment for the things he had done and seen, she booted him, ever so gently, out the front door.

Yesterday, when she took food to the police station at lunchtime, she and Randy had chatted. But it was a brief conversation and ultimately unfulfilling. So last night she had screwed up her courage and called to invite him for dinner. This evening.

His voice had sounded taken aback, but he accepted immediately. Now all she had to do was remember how to act like a woman—a sexual woman, not a mom.

Hopefully it was like riding a bicycle. But then again, she'd never had much luck with that either.

Ethan clamped down on his guilt over using his badge for a personal agenda, and proceeded doggedly ahead with Operation Valentine. It was the only time he could ever remember deliberately crossing the line between professional business and selfish priorities.

He soothed his conscience by reminding himself that his mystery admirer might prove a threat to the public. It was a stretch, but it was all he had.

After 9/11 and the anthrax scare, the postmaster in Statlerville had applied for and received a grant to install security cameras in the main downtown branch. The tapes were logged and filed away on a regular basis, but to Ethan's knowledge, no one had ever had any reason to study them. After twelve months, the old tapes were wiped clean and the process started over.

When he called the Statlerville postmaster and swore him to secrecy, Ethan alluded to the possibility of mail fraud. The middle-aged man was beside himself with excitement. It was all Ethan could do to impress upon him the need for discretion.

The idea was simple. Ethan, to keep things on the up and up, took a personal day. He entered the post office by a back door thirty minutes before opening. The postmaster told his staff of three that Chief Oldham was investigating a private matter and was not to be disturbed. Ethan was then ensconced at a small table near the monitor that played the feed from the live cameras.

It was deadly dull work. By ten a.m. he already had a headache. He took bathroom breaks only when absolutely necessary, and each time afterward he rewound the tape to make sure he hadn't missed anything.

He ate a pack of peanut-butter crackers from the vending machine for lunch and washed them down with a Coke.

The day dragged on. Though many people used the Statlerville "local" slot to post items, none of the envelopes being dropped in resembled Ethan's valentines. And in truth, there were only a few females who were conceivably the right age to be the woman he was looking for.

And then at one thirty, things got interesting. Jane entered the lobby of the post office. He waited for her to walk up to the counter and buy stamps. But she didn't approach the postal employees at all.

Instead, she loitered in the outer lobby. Ethan hunched over the screen with the grainy gray image and studied the woman who was acting so strangely. It was Jane all right. No mistaking her tall, graceful posture.

Finally, she approached the "local" slot and took an envelope from her purse. She looked surreptitiously to the left and right, ascertained that no one was watching her, and dropped her mail into the Statlerville chute.

Ethan's jaw dropped. It couldn't be . . . could it? As he watched, stunned, Jane hurried to the front door, opened it, and disappeared outside.

He ran his hands through his hair and stood up, his heart pounding. On the inside, where employees held court, the slot opened into a narrow metal bin. Jane's letter, or whatever it was, lay on top of a day's worth of mail. The envelope was baby blue. Sadly for him, the piece of mail had landed upside down. There was no way to read the address without picking it up.

And since Ethan was not an authorized postal employee, if he were to bend over and touch Jane's envelope, he would be committing a felony.

If national security was at risk, Ethan could make a judgment call. Under the circumstances, he was shit out of luck. It was one thing to bend the rules for a personal matter. But tampering with the U.S. mail was a bridge too far.

He always had the option of asking the postmaster to pick up the piece of mail and show Ethan the address. But that would require more explanation than Ethan was willing to give. And if the envelope did have his own name and address on it, what would he do then?

His only real option was to go home and wait for tomorrow's mail delivery. Which sucked, because he was fresh out of patience.

He closed up shop and gave the postmaster a garbled explanation about what he had or had not discovered. Ethan felt his neck getting red as he stumbled through the awkward conversation. As soon as he decently could without being rude, he exited the building with relief. Since he had the day off, he dropped by Sherry's house, but her car wasn't in the driveway.

Frustrated and hyped up on adrenaline, he went home and paced the floors. The possibility that Jane might be sending him erotic valentines shook him to the core. He was partly excited, partly confused, and completely stymied. If it was her, why resort to cryptic notes? Why not just tell him how she felt?

On a whim, he picked up the phone and dialed her number. Wanting to hear her voice was uncomfortably needy. But it wasn't out of line to call the woman with whom you just shared a night of smokin'-hot sex . . . right?

After all, they'd been so exhausted, they barely heard the alarm go off this morning, and they had both jumped out of bed and scrambled to get ready for work.

It was only later that he remembered he was taking the day off, and then it was too late to go back to Jane's and coax her into bed again.

She answered on the second ring, her voice slightly breathless. "Paper Pleasures. May I help you?"

He grinned, holding the phone to his ear and opening the fridge to reach for a beer. "It's me," he said simply. "Thought I'd see how you were doing."

A long silence on the other end. And then the sound of Jane clearing her throat. "Ethan . . . hello. I'm fine. How about you?"

He popped the top on his beer and took a swig. The subtext beneath the platitudes was making him hot. He adjusted his crotch. All he could think about was getting Jane naked again.

He set down the can and walked into the living room. As he sprawled on the sofa, he decided to play dirty. "What have you been up to this afternoon? Running errands, I guess, while Mrs. Fitzhugh was there."

If he hadn't been listening so intently, he might not have noticed the flustered note in Jane's voice. "No," she said, her voice painfully breezy. "I've been working all afternoon on bills and orders and such. I might head out for a pizza after we close."

Ethan blinked, not believing what had just happened. Jane lied to him. But why? Unless she didn't want him to know she'd been anywhere near the post office. He thought about asking if he could tag along for the pizza outing, but there was no way he'd be able to look her in the eye without demanding an explanation.

And there was still a possibility that he was wrong. Maybe Jane really had been working hard all afternoon, and had forgotten one quick trip to the post office . . . or didn't consider it worth mentioning.

He gripped the receiver. "I missed you today." The words came out of nowhere, startling even him.

Jane voice was softer now, and he could swear he heard her smile. "Me, too."

It was his turn to speak, but his throat closed up, and he didn't know what it was he wanted to tell her. Everything in his head was all jumbled. Last night had been the most incredible night of his life. It was that simple and that complex.

Something had changed or was changing. He and Jane had things to work out. But not over the phone.

He thought longingly of Jane and pizza and sex. But he shored up his resolve. "I'll see you tomorrow night then. And dinner's on me. Goodbye, Jane."

Her response was barely a whisper. "Bye, Ethan."

Sherry took a sip from her glass of iced tea and realized that her hand was shaking. After finishing a leisurely dinner, she and Randy had moved into the living room and were now sitting on the sofa together, a safe distance apart. Something was wrong. Ever since she had opened her front door and invited him into the house, things had been awkward. They had talked about the weather and politics and even the flu epidemic, for heaven's sake. It was more boring than listening to C-SPAN.

This wasn't how she had anticipated the evening unwinding at all. She thought they would flirt and laugh and get to know each other better. And later . . .

Randy glanced at his watch. "Dinner was great, Sherry. But I'd better be heading home."

Shock punched her stomach. He couldn't leave. Not yet. Not when she had bathed and perfumed and primped just for him. She was wearing a pretty faux-cashmere dress in deep burgundy. It was a grown-up dress, not at all suitable for PTA meetings or church or even a business affair. It was a "date" dress, and beneath it, she wore her brand-new underwear.

But Randy had barely noticed, damn it. For the last two hours he had been as jumpy as a cat in a room full of rocking chairs.

She frowned. "So soon?" She thought about leaning over to show off her cleavage, but couldn't quite bring herself to do something so silly. She wet her lips. "We could watch a movie." She was laying her pride on the line, but she didn't want him to leave.

He wasn't even looking her in the eyes, and she suddenly realized that he had crossed his legs and was sitting oddly upright, his face a mask of discomfort.

Holy cow. Did he have an erection? The possibility made hot color bloom at her throat and flash to her hairline. How was a woman supposed to know if a man wanted her? She hadn't dated in two decades, and back then all it took was a backseat and an overload of hormones.

She scooted a foot closer. "I never thanked you properly for being so sweet to me when I was sick. I don't know what I would have done without you." She kept her voice soft and low.

Now it was Randy's turn to flush. He shot her a glance and swallowed so hard she saw his Adam's apple bob nervously. "Ethan would have showed up eventually. But I'm glad you're feeling better." Any more stiff, and the words would have shattered on the floor.

It was do-or-die time. Sherry placed a hand on his thigh. The muscles jumped beneath her fingers. She leaned in to him. "I was kind of hoping you would spend the night, Randy."

As soon as the last word left her mouth she felt like fainting. Her eyes squeezed shut, and she prayed for a puff of smoke to swallow her up. She had never in her life done something so bold. Not in any context. Unless you counted the day she had stood up to her parents and told them unequivocally that she would not give her baby up for adoption.

Randy hadn't made a single sound. She opened one eyelid and chanced a peek at his face. He looked like a fellow police officer had used a stun gun on him, his eyes blank and glassy.

"Randy?" Now she stroked his thigh, marveling at the firm muscle beneath the fabric of his casual slacks. The boner was no longer a what-if. His pants were tented at the front, his excitement plain to see.

It gave her a weird feeling. Thankfulness mixed with happiness and soft awe. To know that this man wanted her melted her heart.

Encouraged by the fact that he had made no move to leave, she scooted closer until they were shoulder to shoulder. He might have been carved out of stone. Maybe he thought she was a tease and would freak out at the last minute the way she had on the riverboat.

She reached up and kissed his cheek. "It would be nice if you helped me out here. I'm not in the habit of throwing myself at men." Despite her bravery, her voice wobbled. Maybe she had misread the situation entirely. Her stomach flipped and settled in a tight knot.

He sighed, a huge rattling gust of breath that seemed to come from his gut. Finally he looked at her, really looked at her. His gaze was unguarded, allowing her to see his hunger, his shock, his pleasure. He took her hands in his, and even though she saw excitement in his expression, it was banked, overlaid with a look of concern. "Are you sure about this? You seemed pretty adamant that night on the boat. I don't want to take advantage of you."

She squeezed his fingers. "Feel free," she said, her voice husky. "And yes . . . I'm sure. I like you Randy, a lot. You're sweet and gentle and sexy, and God knows how, but you've made me feel like a woman for the first time in forever."

The moment hung, poignant and pregnant, between them. And then he kissed her. Like on their first date, the kiss was neither tentative nor awkward. Their lips met in easy harmony, seeking and taking, exploring and giving. She wanted to cry and laugh, because it was so perfect.

He cupped her breasts through the soft fabric of her dress. She moaned, feeling her nipples harden and strain toward his touch. "Randy . . ." She didn't know what she was saying. Or asking.

But thankfully, he took control, lifting her in his arms and carrying her to her bedroom. All the way down the hall, he never took his eyes off her face. His intense scrutiny made her blush, but not nearly as much as when he set her on her feet at the foot of her bed and started undoing the buttons on her dress with restrained eagerness.

When he slid the whisper-soft garment from her shoulders and down her body so she could step out of it, he got his first glimpse of the new lingerie. He cursed beneath his breath, and his hands clenched in fists at his sides. Slowly, his hot gaze roamed from her toes up her silk-clad thighs to her waist and then to her breasts.

She stood frozen, feeling both terribly vulnerable and feverishly excited. He traced a finger along the lacy edge at the top of her merry widow. She had gooseflesh there, even though the room was reasonably warm.

The expression on his face was dazed, longing. His eyes met hers. "You're beautiful, Sherry. Exquisite." The raw sincerity in his voice brought tears to her eyes, but she blinked them away.

No more thinking about the arid past. Here, with Randy, she felt sexual, ripe, ready for anything.

He led her to the bed, not bothering with the lamp. The light from the hallway spilled into the room. Together they lay down on the soft comforter, hands touching, exploring, caressing.

She felt the need to warn him, perhaps in a remnant of feminine anxiety. "I haven't been with anyone but my husband. I don't want you to be disappointed."

He heard her plea for gentleness, for reassurance, and he smiled down at her, his gaze filled with tender amusement. "Not gonna happen," he muttered, bending his head and nuzzling her cleavage. "I'm already so primed, I'm in danger of disappointing *you.*"

She giggled finally, releasing the tight hold she had on herself. It was okay. This was Randy. There were no expectations, no hoops to jump through, nothing to prove. He wanted to make love to her. She wanted him, too. And she needed to show him how wonderful he was and how much he made her yearn.

It was easier after that . . . and infinitely more intense. Every spot he touched on her body brought a million little nerve endings to life. Skin and bone and muscle she'd thought nothing more than ordinary sang with sensuality. It was like waking from a long, troubling dream and feeling sizzlingly alive.

Randy was still clothed, and she decided that was a shame. She worked at the buttons on his shirt, his belt, his zipper. His chest heaved through it all, his hands clenched in fists at his sides as she knelt over him, intent on her mission.

Finally, he rolled off the bed and finished the job, shedding socks, shoes, and clothing with clumsy haste. His body was pleasing to the eye, sturdy and strong. And between his legs, that part of him she had fantasized about rose stiff and eager.

When he rolled on a condom, she didn't stop him. She trusted him, no matter if he had been with other women. Randy would have a clean bill of health. She knew it. But this was not the right time to tell him that pregnancy was not an issue.

She swallowed a gulp of trepidation and held out her hand. He joined her, resting on his side still on top of the covers, and ran his hand down the silky fabric that covered her ribcage. "Do you want to keep this on?"

She wasn't sure of the correct answer. "Do you want me to?"

His quick smile was rueful. "Yeah. You look damn hot."

The answer was what she needed to hear. She wiggled out of her panties and tossed them aside. Now, clad in nothing but the merry widow and the thigh-high stockings, she felt like a seductress. It was heady stuff.

He moved over her, not giving her all his weight, but covering her body with his. The heat pouring off of him warmed and soothed the last of her nerves. Even the stiff erection probing her hip was more exciting than alarming. His lips touched hers.

Oh, glory. She wrapped her arms around his neck and kissed him back. She loved the way his hands tangled in her hair, the slight catch in his breathing when she daringly nipped his tongue with her teeth.

He buried his face in her neck, and a hard shudder racked his frame. "God, Sherry, I want to make this special for you, but I don't think I can hold off. I swear the next time will be better."

She bumped her pelvis against his. "Wow. Already talking about the next time. We must be doing something right."

Her teasing broke the tension momentarily, and he reared up to look at her face. The slam of emotion that took her breath away was frightening. She couldn't feel this much this fast. She wouldn't allow it.

He locked his gaze with hers as he shifted his hips and lodged his firm, hard flesh at the aching spot between her legs. She was plenty wet, but the first steady push made her wince.

He stilled, his breathing ragged. "Stop me if you need to." The look on his face said it might kill him, but she had no intention of stopping him. Not now.

He moved deeper, his watchful eyes gauging her discomfort. She managed not to wince, but it was an effort.

Damn. Maybe if she had indulged in the use of some adult toys in the last decade she wouldn't be so damn out of shape, so to speak.

She wiggled her hips. "More," she stuttered, trying to breathe. It felt like he was never going to fit, his eager rock-hard flesh parting her tight passage steadily, making her ache in the best possible way.

Finally, he was all the way in. They both breathed sighs of relief. His complete and total possession left her floundering in a sea of confusion. She had asked for this, wanted it beyond reason. And now that it was here, there was fear mixed in with the passion.

How could she give him up? How could she let him walk away and think to herself that this was nothing more than scratching a sexual itch?

He started to move, and she forgot to worry, forgot to breathe. The sensations were incredible. Everywhere her body stretched to accommodate him, her sensitive flesh gripped his shaft eagerly, squeezing, stroking, trying to keep him inside her.

Again, she heard him curse. He thrust more quickly now, shaking the bed, shaking her soul.

The power in their joining stunned her. The beauty in their instinctive rhythm captivated her.

A hot stream of raw physical pleasure trembled in her belly, spread upward and outward, and connected with a pop and a sizzle to the spot where their bodies met.

She gasped as she felt the orgasm build and swell. It hovered just offstage, taunting her with the empty years, her young body barren, bereft both of fertility and of release. Badly, so badly, she wanted it. Wanted the sheer physical oblivion promised by his bold strokes.

He slid a hand between them and found her clitoris. Her body jerked and arched from the electric shock, and with a strangled cry, she exploded, dimly aware that his shout followed on the coattails of hers.

The sweat had not dried on their bodies when he said the cruelest thing of all. "Marry me, Sherry."

Without processing her panicked response, with no filter at all, she let fear take hold, her voice far sharper than she intended. "You've got to be kidding."

# Fifteen

Randy might have been wallowing in the glow of male postcoital smugness, but he wasn't stupid. The physical connection between them remained intact, his flesh still inside her. But his two quiet words had snapped the emotional bond like a matchstick.

Sick at heart, he rolled off her. Deep hurt made him want to lash out, but he tempered his bitter response. "I'm guessing that's a no." The sarcasm was something he couldn't or wouldn't disguise.

She shot off the bed like he'd attacked her, escaping into the bathroom and shutting the door with a quiet motion that might as well have been a mighty slam. While she was gone, he turned on the light, found his shoes, socks, and clothes, and got dressed. He felt nauseated, angry, and scared shitless. Sherry McCamish had the power to destroy him. He'd fallen hard the first time he saw her. And every day since, she had wormed her way into his heart and made him dream about a future that clearly didn't exist.

He contemplated walking out, but he couldn't do it. So he sat motionless on the side of the bed and waited. When she returned, she was covered from head to toe in a thick black terry bathrobe. The color seemed symbolic—a death knell for their budding relationship. Her knuckles were white where she clutched the lapels.

He shrugged. "Any explanation you'd care to give me?" He said it with insolence, barely able to look at her. He felt like a fool.

Sherry hovered in the doorway to the bathroom, her lips pale, her skin even more so. "You said something impulsive, and it shocked me."

He shook his head slowly. "Not impulsive." He made sure his voice was flat, impassive. If he let go of the anger, it might spew out and make things worse. "I've thought about marrying you ever since the day we first met."

She frowned. "That's ridiculous."

He thought he was numb, but the dart found its way to his heart. "Again, thanks."

She twisted the ends of her belt. "Randy, you can't possibly be serious. I'm nine years older than you. You want a family and I had to have a hysterectomy after Debra was born. We might be attracted to each other, but that's all."

"I'm not attracted to you," he said slowly. "I'm in love with you."

If possible, she went even whiter. "You're not."

His control wasn't as complete as he would have liked. "Don't fuckin' tell me what I feel."

She looked like the wall behind her was the only thing holding her up. Her throat moved as she swallowed. "I'm sorry."

He bowed his head, feeling sick. "Do you care for me at all, Sherry?"

Her silence was deafening.

He got to his feet, the pain so deep and black in his gut he could barely breathe. "Next time you decide you want to break a decade of celibacy, do me a favor and call someone else."

She went to pieces when he left, sobbing and screaming and wetting the mattress with her wild, panicked tears. Twenty years of penance, and with one false step, she had screwed up again. Only this time, the sin was far worse. She couldn't claim getting caught up in the moment as she had at seventeen.

This time she was a grown woman with years of life experience and plenty of perspective. She had deliberately made the choice to use sex as recreation . . . to prove something to herself. And her selfish lack of consideration for Randy's feelings was unforgivable.

She debated calling him back, making him listen as she explained the right he had to marry a young woman who could bear him children.

But she knew he would argue and try to wear her down. And since the bright, shining future he was offering was what she wanted more than life, she might in the end grow weak and accept.

But it would be wrong. And one day when he realized his mistake, she would have to suffer through another divorce, another failure.

The only saving grace was that she had managed to choke back her genuine response. Did she love him? Of course, she did. How could she not? He was everything a woman could want in a man. The real deal, through and through. But if she had admitted that, had told him how she really felt, he would have used it against her. And she wasn't sure she was strong enough to resist him if he had begged.

Though it was barely nine o'clock, she stumbled through the house, turning out all the lights and finding her way back to the bedroom in the dark. Feeling old and broken and dead inside, she climbed under the covers, closed her eyes, and prayed for the oblivion of sleep.

Ethan made it through Friday on autopilot. And he couldn't wait until the end of the day. He raced home at lunchtime to check the mailbox. Thank God, the carrier had already delivered.

He reached in and pulled out a stack of mail. With jerky hands, he riffled through it. There in the middle, as pretty as you please, was a baby blue envelope.

Sweet Jesus . . .

He glanced at his watch. He had a few minutes. With his heart bouncing around in his chest, he unlocked the door and went inside. Deliberately taking his time, he dropped the mail on the coffee table, took off his coat, and sat down hard on the couch.

He slid the blue envelope free and placed it on top of the pile. Then he stared at it, willing it to reveal all its secrets.

Finally, he picked it up and opened it. The sender was upping the ante. She meant business.

*Ethan, My Love,*

*I've waited in vain,*
*My heart full of pain.*
*I thought that by now*
*You'd have figured out how*
*To find my true name*
*And to finish my game.*

*A girl shouldn't be,*
*As you might foresee,*
*A sly, lustful tease.*
*But you won't believe*
*What's right under your nose*
*And my frustration grows.*

*Just give me a chance*
*In passion's sweet dance.*
*I'll be all you desire.*
*Our passion a fire*
*That blazes so bright*
*We'll cling to the night.*

*I won't wait endless days.*
*There's a price you must pay.*
*Once the treasure is lost*
*My heart turns to frost.*

He read it three times. The fact that his hands were slick with perspiration didn't occur to him. But he was shaken. He tucked the card back in the envelope and slid it with the other three into his inside jacket pocket. The earlier notes were definitely dog-eared, a sign of how much time he'd spent studying them.

For the rest of the afternoon, he worked in a fog. The truth was staring him in the face, and he couldn't quite wrap his head around it. Jane had been sending him naughty, seductive valentines. And the first one had been mailed a day before the night of the initial break-in. Which meant if Jane had indeed been the sender, she had mailed a valentine to a man she had barely spoken to in four years. It didn't make sense.

*Never make assumptions. Let the evidence speak for itself.* He tried to step back and assess the situation objectively. But it was damn hard. Now, each time he reread one of the notes, he digested the words in the context of a mental picture of Jane naked in his arms, which tended to shoot his objectivity to hell and back.

By the time he went off duty, he still hadn't come to any conclusions. The only thing he knew for sure was that he had seen Jane mail a blue envelope—one that showed up in his mailbox a day later.

He ran home, showered, and shaved, all the while struggling with indecision. Should he go to Jane's and act as if nothing had happened, wait for her to confess? On the other hand, wouldn't she have already said something if she was the sender? After all, he and Jane had been sexually intimate for a week now, plenty of time for whispered confessions of true love.

It stood to reason that if she was sending him explicit valentines, the time was right for her to come clean. And based on her admission that she'd had a crush on him four years ago, surely it wasn't that much of a stretch to think she might be in love with him now.

Or was that his ego talking?

And then a nasty thought occurred to him. The whole thing might be a coincidence. He had seen Jane mail a blue envelope. But after it passed through the Statlerville slot, the envelope had flipped upside down. Ethan hadn't seen the address. The fact that a blue envelope showed up in his mailbox today could conceivably be nothing more than a damn coincidence.

He didn't want to believe it. His brain rejected the idea. He wanted the hot, suggestive notes to be from Jane, not from some weirdo stranger. But wanting it didn't make it so.

When he was clean and had stuffed a few personal items in a duffel bag, he picked up his cell phone and tossed it from

hand to hand a few times. If he wasn't feeling so damn awkward, he would call and offer to pick up dinner. But now he
didn't know what the hell to do. He didn't know if he was coming or going.

As he held it, the phone vibrated sharply, startling him so
much that he dropped it on the carpet. Feeling foolish, he bent
and grabbed for it before whoever it was hung up. The caller ID
made him smile.

He flipped open the phone. "Hey, Jane."

She sounded cheerful, open, not at all like a woman who was
trying to seduce him with erotic valentines. "Ethan, we never
talked about dinner, so I wanted to let you know I put a roast
and veggies in the oven this morning. If you don't mind, bring
something for dessert, and we'll be all set."

He gripped the phone. "Sure. No problem. I'll see you about
six thirty?"

"Perfect." And then she hung up.

He cursed under his breath. How in the hell was he going to
go over there and pretend he hadn't seen her at the post office?
And how would she react if he admitted to spying on her? Not
that his covert activities had been directed at her in particular,
but still . . .

He shut down that line of thought as best he could and concentrated on the task at hand. Jane was cooking for him . . . again.
The least he could do was bring a dessert that would show her he
remembered the past, that he knew her likes and dislikes.

As he slid into the car and headed for the grocery store, his
mind was a blank. And then it hit him. It was almost February.
And he knew just what to get.

Jane was having some serious second thoughts. Why had she
allowed Ethan to talk his way into staying at her apartment to-

night? Despite what he said, she really doubted there was much chance that her vandal would return to the scene of the crime.

The way she saw it, she was in far more danger from Ethan. Every moment she allowed him into her life was just going to make it that much harder to see him go.

She was already nuts about the man, and now that she had been in his bed and he in hers . . . now that she knew what it was like to be the focus of all that steely-eyed determination . . . well, she was in big trouble. She was in love with Ethan. And she was terribly afraid that all he felt for her was sexual attraction laced with a strong dose of nostalgia.

She didn't want him to make love to her for old times' sake. She didn't want him to make love with her because he was fond of her and they were both healthy, young adults in their prime. She wanted to be his one and only, the love of his life. She wanted to be his Valentine. For keeps.

She was still in the shop when Ethan arrived. It was a deliberate move on her part. With the front door still unlocked, and away from the intimacy of her upstairs apartment, she was able to greet him casually.

It was a balmy early evening, and he came in wearing jeans and a gray cotton sweater that matched his eyes. His black hair was still damp from the shower he had obviously taken before coming over. Her stomach curled in anticipation as she imagined his hard chest covered with soap, his big hands stroking over his torso, cleaning up just for her. Imagining their bodies twined together in her bed made her breathless, so instead of greeting him with a breezy kiss, she stayed behind the counter, where she was straightening some gift bags.

She smiled brightly. "Guess what. Cupid's been at work already."

Ethan stilled midstep. He carried what looked like a cardboard cake box in one hand and a small bag from a local discount store in the other. "Cupid?" He had an odd look on his face. Almost as if he was expecting her to say something in particular.

She frowned inwardly, but kept her expression friendly instead of lustful, as she was feeling. It was a terrible cliché, but he looked good enough to eat. And she was a hungry female.

He was waiting for her to continue. She tucked a strand of hair behind her ear and grinned. "Do you remember the window guy you sent over to replace the glass—Tony somebody? Well, apparently he and Mrs. Fitzhugh hit it off, and now they're going out on a first date tonight. I think it's really sweet."

Ethan rolled his eyes. "What is it about women and the need to play matchmaker?"

She held up her hands. "Don't look at me. You're the one responsible for this. I'm an innocent bystander. But I do feel happy for her. She deserves a little romance in her life."

He set the cake box on the counter and waved a hand. "Turn around. I have a surprise for you."

She hesitated. Surprises weren't always good. But Ethan looked so eager, she obeyed. She heard the rattle of the plastic bag, and then he spoke again. "Okay, you can peek now."

When she faced him, he was smiling at her with that look she remembered from years past—the sexy, teasing, happy expression that made her go all soft and yearning inside. She licked her lips. "What is it?"

He tapped the box. "This is German chocolate cake . . . for later. But the real dessert is this."

He handed her a folded piece of thick white paper. She opened it slowly, and hot moisture filled her eyes. He remembered. Glued to the paper was a series of candy conversation hearts. They spelled out a sentence. *Hey, Hot Stuff. Will You Be Mine? Kiss Me. I'm Yours.*

She swallowed the lump in her throat. Every year for the

longest time Ethan had bought her multiple boxes of the colored candies. She'd loved eating them, and she and Ethan had laughed together over the silly phrases.

She looked at him, her eyes still misty. "Thank you. This is sweet." She wouldn't torment herself by wondering if there was any deeper significance to the carefully crafted message. It was enough that he had taken the time to try to please her with a fond memory.

He handed her the bag with an abashed grin. "I got you a six-pack of boxes. That ought to last you until Valentine's Day."

She couldn't help herself. She abandoned the relative safety of her position behind the counter and hugged him tightly, feeling his strong arms come around her and lock her to his chest. It touched her deeply that he recalled her simple enjoyment of the childish treat.

Beneath her cheek she could feel the steady beat of his heart. Strong. Dependable. That was Ethan.

The kiss happened slowly. A lazy, gentle mating of lips and tongues and whispered breaths. He feasted on her mouth, his hunger banked, giving her romance in keeping with a string of colored candies.

She wanted to believe he was wooing her. And for the moment, she allowed herself to be courted, cherished. There was a certain sense of wistful regret in the kiss, at least for her. Even if Ethan could never love her as much as she did him, it was clear that she meant *something* to him. They had been friends before. They were friends again—this time friends who had gone one step farther to intimacy.

But ultimately, it would not be enough. Unless he could give her his heart.

He shifted his feet, pulling her tighter into the embrace. His erection pressed between them, eager, hard, ready to get started.

Ethan's hands were tangled in her hair, his fingers pressing into her scalp, angling her head so he could take the kiss even deeper. The scent of his soap and the warmth of his body made her dizzy.

The yearning that flooded her chest actually hurt. She came very close to blurting out her love, but something held her back. Some small part of her brain that remembered what it was like to be hurt.

The sudden tinkle of the bell over the front door, followed by a gusty breeze and feminine laughter, broke them apart.

Jane turned, automatically glancing at her watch. "Sorry. We're closed."

But the visitor was not so easily dissuaded. Ethan's sister, Sherry, was unapologetic. "I saw Ethan's car outside. But I didn't expect to find my brother lip-locked with you, Jane."

Jane managed not to blush. At one time she and Sherry had been close, but after the rift with Ethan, the two women had drifted apart. She smiled at the older woman. "Lock the door behind you, and come on in. Are you shopping or visiting?"

"Both, if you'll let me. And I'm sure my baby brother will tell me to mind my own business, right?"

Ethan kissed his sister's cheek. "You're a smart woman, Ms. McCamish."

Jane smoothed her hair where Ethan had disheveled it, and tried not to rush their visitor along. "Anything in particular I can help you with?"

Sherry was already perusing the displays on the first aisle. She glanced over her shoulder. "Debra's twenty-first birthday is in a few months, and I'm hoping to throw a big coming-of-age party for her. So I'm thinking invitations, decorations, guest favors—the works."

Jane nodded, the businesswoman in her momentarily taking charge. "I can fix you up with all of that."

Ethan watched the two important women in his life chatter away, and realized that they clearly had forgotten his presence. He didn't mind. It was a good opportunity to study Jane. She was wearing a pair of black knit pants that hugged her fabulous long legs, along with a cream cowl-neck sweater striped in red and pink.

She looked like a valentine herself. Her cheeks were flushed, her face animated. And just like that, the penny dropped. He was head over heels in love with her.

The knowledge smacked him in the face like a two-by-four, and his stomach did a weird flip and jolt. Of course he was. Why else had he invented a not so subtle reason to spend the weekend with her? It was hardly police procedure to seduce potential crime victims in order to be on the scene.

Idiot that he was, he'd probably been halfway in love with her five years ago. But for whatever reasons, including the ones he'd given Jane, he'd been content to preserve the status quo. But no more.

He was damn lucky no other man had scooped her up in the meantime.

He stared at her, knowing she was too busy with Sherry to see his shock and bafflement. Everything about her was perfect. Her sweet, sometimes naughty smile. The elegant way she carried herself—all long legs and ripe breasts and narrow waist. And that soft, mixed-breed hair, a dozen shades of gold and yellow and bronze . . .

He swallowed hard, his hands trembling. What in the hell was he going to do about this? Should he come right out and ask about the notes? Tell her he was madly passionately in love with her? Woo her with hot sex and plenty of begging? He owed her something for being a blind fool.

But if Jane hadn't sent the notes . . . shit. He'd be hung out to dry.

He strolled to where the two women stood discussing the merits of various shades of crepe paper. Ethan hugged his sister and grinned at Jane. "What you don't know, Jane, is that my sister is dating one of Statlerville's finest."

Jane bounced. "Who? Tell me, who?"

In an instant, Ethan realized his mistake. Sherry's face had gone gray, and she looked even more miserable than when her daughter moved away.

He and Jane sobered simultaneously. Jane patted her arm. "Don't let your brother bully you. Some things are private. Let's finish up your shopping list."

But Sherry shrugged and sighed. "It's no big secret. Randy Temple and I have been out a couple of times. But I'm too old for him. So it's kind of pointless to continue. He needs a young woman his own age who can give him a houseful of children."

At Jane's distressed look, Ethan explained in a low voice, "Sherry had some complications after Deb was born. She had to have a hysterectomy."

Jane hugged the petite woman. "I'm sorry that happened to you, but honestly, Sherry, some men wouldn't care. You're a beautiful woman, with or without any potential babies. I don't think you should write him off just yet. I've met Randy, and he's a hottie."

"Hey!" Ethan protested. He recognized the shot of jealousy, marveled at it, rolled it around in his head. "I'm standing right here."

Jane put her arm around his waist and laid her head on his

shoulder. "Don't be such a baby. Women are allowed to look these days."

He realized he didn't like that thought. Not one bit. "And that goes for me as well?"

She gazed at him, for the moment seeming to forget that his sister was watching them. The gleam in her eye made his spine, and other parts, stiffen. "Don't worry, big guy. I'll keep you too busy to be distracted by lesser women."

He barked out a laugh, and even Sherry joined in the chuckle. His sister glanced at her watch. "Oh, heck, I've gotta run. Jane, if you'll ring this stuff up for me, I'll get out of your hair."

While Jane did her thing at the cash register and bagged Sherry's purchases, Ethan studied his sister with troubled eyes. Temple was a good guy, solid in every way. But Sherry was stubborn as a mule. It would take a miracle to change her mind.

When the two women said their goodbyes, Ethan helped carry the packages out to Sherry's car. When he came back in, he locked the door, turned the sign to CLOSED, and pulled down the shades. Then he turned and faced Jane.

She was watching him, her eyes narrowed. In a split second, the mood in the room had changed. He crossed to where she stood. "I know it's probably a social faux pas, but would you be terribly offended if we postponed dinner for a half hour?"

The corners of her mouth kicked up in a smile. "You got something in mind, Chief? Police business you need to take care of?"

He reached into his back pocket and pulled out a pair of regulation handcuffs. "I have a vulnerable woman I need to take into police custody. For her own protection . . . of course."

## Sixteen

Jane managed not to choke on her tongue. Holy cow. She might have had a few law enforcement fantasies about Ethan over the years, but that was the result of an overactive imagination in a dark, private room.

Heat flooded her belly and she felt her nipples tighten. She crossed her arms over her chest, in case her sweater was too thin to disguise her current state of mind . . . and body. She bit down on her bottom lip. "Um, well . . . I'll just keep the roast warm until you come back."

His quick grin was all male. He headed her way with determination written on his face, following her step by step as she backed up instinctively. "Oh, don't worry, my delectable Jane. I'm not going anywhere . . . except upstairs . . . to your bed."

Even with the evidence in clear sight, she was still sputtering in intrigued outrage when he pulled her sweater over her head, dispensed with her bra, and dragged her arms behind her back.

By the time she thought to struggle, it was too late. Her wrists were tightly secured with cold metal handcuffs.

Fortunately, she and Ethan were near the rear of the shop and not in danger of being seen from the street. Thank God. She could see the headlines now: *Assistant police chief apprehends partially nude shop owner.* Of course, it might be good for business.

He swung her around to face him, his narrow, laser gaze taking in every detail of bare skin from her waist to the top of her head. She was red-faced and aroused. He was dark-eyed and inscrutable.

Deliberately, he flicked first one nipple, then the other with his fingernail. Her thighs clenched instinctively as moisture bloomed in the secret places between her legs. Her breathing was all over the map.

Ethan dropped to his knees and dragged her pants and panties with him. Her cotton slacks had a bit of Lycra in them, and they cooperated easily. For long, tense seconds, he looked. That was all. Just looked, making her even hotter, if that was possible. And then he blew warm air over her mound, murmuring something she couldn't quite catch. The tickle of his breath on her damp flesh was subtle torture.

When he probed her aching sex with his tongue, she struggled wildly, feeling the metal of the handcuffs bruise her wrists. "Ethan, oh, God. Please." She had never been aroused so quickly . . . had never known she could be.

The first orgasm hit fast and hard, bowing her body and leaving her breathless. The second one was hotter still, a bright starburst of pleasure that radiated from her clitoris in a million tiny waves. She barely even noticed when he stripped her rapidly of her pants, panties, shoes, and socks. But the bite of the cold floor on the bottoms of her feet made her flinch.

She begged then, not sure she could stand any longer. "I

can't," she panted breathlessly, her face red, her eyes dazed. "No more."

He stood slowly and faced her, his eyes hooded. "Oh, there's more," he promised. "There's always more. Let's hope you can hold out."

Without warning, he ground his mouth down on hers. In his wild kiss she felt the same desperation that made her shake. He might be calling the shots, but he was no less crazed than she was.

He steered her by the arm. "Up the stairs. And no funny stuff."

She stumbled ahead of him, painfully aware that her ass was on eye level with his face. Halfway up he stopped her, gripped her butt in two hands, and nibbled on her chilled cheeks. Her fingers twisted restlessly as she fought to keep her balance with knees the consistency of cooked spaghetti noodles.

He licked the base of her spine, his tongue rough on her hot skin. "Spread your legs. I need to see if you have any concealed weapons."

He didn't wait for her cooperation, but merely knocked her ankles apart and stroked up her inner thighs with his palms.

In another situation, she might have giggled, but she was so hot, so needy, so ready for him to screw her, she could only whimper and obey.

He reached around her with his left arm and put one big hand on her belly. Then she felt something probe between her ass cheeks. She tensed in alarm, but he bypassed that area, and in an instant, she felt the fingers of his right hand invade her swollen vagina. She came instantly, crying out and almost losing her balance.

But he controlled her every move. He moved up onto the step behind her, pressing his body against hers. His breath was hot on her nape. "Have you hidden anything from me, Jane?"

She blinked her eyes, trying to get them to focus. She felt dizzy and weak, and she wanted him inside her. "No," she croaked, "I haven't done anything wrong."

He played with her breasts until she thought she might scream in frustration. "I hope you're telling the truth, little lady."

When he tugged hard at her sensitive nipples, she moaned. His touch was too much and not enough. The sound seemed to galvanize him, because he pushed her forward again. "Climb. All the way to the top. Hurry."

On the landing of her small apartment, he left her standing alone as he went through the place, turning on lights. Bound as she was, she would have preferred the cover of darkness, but apparently the chief had other ideas. When he came back to her, she saw streaks of color staining his cheekbones, the sharp angle of his jaw, the gleam of pure sexual hunger in his eyes.

He stood before her, hands on his hips. "I'll ask you one more time," he said gruffly. "Are you hiding anything from me, Jane?"

She blinked in confusion. Was this a game, or did his pointed question mean something else? Her throat dried and nerves skittered. Surely he hadn't found out about the valentines, had he?

Oh, Lord, what should she say? She slid her gaze past his, wondering absently if her nice dinner was ruined. She felt suspended in time, hanging in limbo, sensing a crossroads ahead. It was difficult to have a serious conversation with a man when one of the parties was buck naked.

Surprisingly, Ethan wasn't looking at her nude body at the moment. His eyes were locked on her face, his expression sober. Was this how he looked in an interrogation room? All grim and serious?

She could do it. Spit it out right now. *Ethan, I'm the woman who has been sending erotic valentines. I'm in love with you, and I got tired of waiting to see if another guy was going to come along.*

*But turns out, no one measures up to you in my book. So tell it to me straight. Are we merely fooling around for the hell of it, or do you love me at all? I'm a big girl. I can handle it.*

It seemed like hours dragged by as she debated her options. But when she glanced at the clock, she knew differently.

Ethan was still waiting.

But she chickened out. "No, Officer, I'm not hiding anything."

Something flashed across his face—a look she could swear was disappointment. Had he expected her to make up a confession? For the game? Or did he really know she was sending the notes and wanted her to admit it?

She told herself there was no way he could be sure it was her. Which still ate away at her confidence. Why not ask Jane's advice? Why not share the contents of the valentines with her? She couldn't think of a single reason, except for the fact that he might, even now, be planning to seek out his mystery admirer and see what developed.

And if he did know it was Jane, the only reason that she could imagine for him not to acknowledge it was because he didn't feel the same and didn't want to embarrass her. That possibility was one she didn't want to dwell on, not even briefly.

She realized she was shivering. "Officer," she said softly, her eyes pleading with him to understand, "don't you think I've done my time?"

His face cleared, making her wonder if she had imagined his troubled reaction. He slid his hands into her hair and pulled her toward him. "I'm open to bribes and sexual favors," he muttered.

His sweater tickled her breasts. His belt buckle pressed into her belly. She arched closer, wanting him so badly, loving him beyond reason. He'd called her a vulnerable woman. And she was, but not in the way he meant, not because of some teenage troublemaker.

She was vulnerable to Ethan. He had the power to make her dreams come true, or to hurt her deeply.

Soon, she would push for an answer. Soon she would know the truth. But not yet. Not while they were in the midst of this delicious "getting to know you" phase.

Ethan was a generous lover—fun, playful, single-minded in his devotion to making her body sing with pleasure. If this was all he had to give her, she would not end it too soon. Because she might have to live on these memories for a long, long time.

Her decision made, she nipped his chin with her teeth. "You could give me time off for good behavior."

He lifted his head, his hair rumpled. "But that's just it, my lovely Jane. I want you to be bad."

Ethan choked back his disappointment at Jane's reticence, and concentrated on the exquisite woman in his arms. The handcuffs might not have been such a good idea. He was ready to devour her, and his lust was dark enough, greedy enough to give him pause. Perhaps all men, beneath the skin, were animals. He'd made Jane helpless, had taunted her, teased her. And every second she was under his control, he wanted her more.

But he grew impatient to have her hands on him. So he spun her abruptly and used his key to open the cuffs. When she held her arms in front of her, he massaged her wrists, feeling guilty that he had marked her flesh. He lifted her hands one at a time and kissed her palms. "You're the sexiest captive I've ever had in my cuffs."

She leaned into him, stroking his chest. "Come to bed with me, Ethan."

He liked the way she said it. Direct. No games. A woman's eternal invitation to a man.

He tugged his sweater over his head and tossed it aside. "Lead the way, honey."

As he followed her, enjoying the view from behind, he shed the rest of his clothes, dropping them where they fell. By the time Jane scooted onto her bed, he was right behind her. The raw urgency that had been momentarily tamped down flared up in a supernova of need.

They tumbled together, limbs entangled, hands seeking, lips clinging. She took his cock in her hands, and he groaned, falling back on the bed, panting, striving not to come like a green boy.

Already she had learned what he liked. Her gentle fingers hit magical spots, coaxed gasps and curses from his gritted teeth.

He wanted to let her have her way with him, but the naughty foreplay had brought him to flash point with no chance of banking the flames.

He lifted her astride him with trembling arms, waiting with fevered impatience for her to slide down onto his rigid dick.

The docking maneuver threatened to blow the top of his head to the moon.

He was shaking like a malaria patient, his hips thrusting upward, even as Jane bore down, her hands at his shoulders, her eyes closed as she rode him slowly.

He held her waist, marveling at the delicacy of her bones. She was so strong, so determined, and so very dear. They came within seconds of each other, bound by a thread of heat that raked up his spine and flashed in his skull. She literally took his breath away.

In the aftermath, he knew he had to tell her the truth. He loved her. If God was smiling down on Ethan Oldham, Jane might love him back.

He floated, sated and wonderfully content. Jane lay on his chest, her body lax, her hair tickling his chin. He never wanted to move.

In that quiet moment, he had an epiphany. Valentine's Day was coming up very soon. He would shop for a ring, plan an unforgettable night, and propose to the woman he loved. It was an awesome idea. And on that encouraging thought, he closed his eyes and dozed off to sleep.

Hunger woke Jane up. She rolled to one side and gazed at the clock. No wonder she was starving. It was eight o'clock. She saw Ethan's watch and the handcuffs on the bedside table, and she couldn't squelch a grin.

Sex that good had to include love . . . right? The connection between them had transcended the physical. She felt it, knew it in her bones.

She slipped out of bed, pressing one last, soft kiss on Ethan's shoulder along the way. It took her barely fifteen minutes to get dressed and bring the waiting dinner up to par. By then Ethan had surfaced, made himself respectable, and was now sprawled in a chair at the table.

He raked his hands though his hair, his eyelids drooping. "What can I do?"

She kissed the top of his head. "I'll handle it. But don't get too used to this treatment. Next time it's your turn to feed me."

He yawned. "Duly noted."

For Jane, it was a magical evening, one she would always remember. It felt right having Ethan in her home, at her table, in her bed. And as odd as it sounded, they were comfortable, easy with each other.

With a single look, they could generate heat in remembering, anticipating. But the hunger was banked for the moment, allowing a dangerously addictive tenderness to take its place.

After the meal, they cleaned up the mess, watched a movie, flirted lazily.

At midnight, she daringly stroked his hard thigh. "Ready for bed?"

His eyes gleamed in a now familiar expression of intent. "I could be persuaded."

They took turns showering, Ethan grumbling all the while about the lack of room in her antiquated bathroom. She laughed at him. "Yours isn't any bigger. And besides, I think the shared-shower thing is more romantic fiction than practical."

He snorted. "Where's your sense of adventure, Jane? Who gives a damn about practical? I have dreams about screwing you with your hair all wet and your tits—" He broke off suddenly, his face turning bright red.

His obvious mortification was too funny. She laughed out loud. "Don't stop on my account. It was just getting interesting." She handed him a towel, enjoying the view of his muscular body all squeaky clean and sporting an impressive erection. When she brushed him casually, acknowledging his readiness, he groaned and trapped her hands, urging her fingers to cup his balls. They stood in her tiny bathroom, locked in a quivering moment of anticipation. The air was charged with electricity.

He found her mouth, brushed his lips over hers, covered her eyelids with a kiss, her nose, the side of her cheek. "I want you," he said softly, his eyes unguarded, his sincerity unquestioned.

She took his face in her hands and kissed him back. "Then take me, Ethan. I'm yours."

The noise woke her somewhere around three a.m. The muffled tinkle of glass, the muted thump of a heavy foot in the inky darkness.

Her heart beating like she had run a marathon, she shook her lover urgently. Damn, she hated it when he was right. "Ethan, wake up. We have company downstairs."

He awoke instantly. It amazed her that he could go from a dead sleep to robo-cop in less than thirty seconds. He was already in his pants and shoes, reaching for his gun, before she could blink.

He kissed her hard. "Call nine-one-one. Tell them I need backup. No sirens. I think Temple is on duty." And then he was gone.

She did as he commanded, then hung up the phone and dressed with shaking hands, suddenly terrified that Ethan was going alone to face the intruder. Her heart in her throat, she tiptoed soundlessly down the stairs.

She could see the dim outline of Ethan's body crouched near the base of the stairs. He was perfectly still, listening, locating his target. Without looking in her direction, he waved her back.

She froze, huddling on a stair midway up, praying with all her might. She'd never actually seen Ethan in the midst of a dangerous situation, and she realized in sudden alarm that he must put his life on the line far more often than she realized.

A strange sound toward the front of the shop caught her attention. It was a hissing noise, muted but familiar . . . like hairspray. Oh, hell. It was paint. The vandal was destroying her newly stocked merchandise with spray paint.

She wanted to get up and yell at him and demand an explanation. But she bit down on her bottom lip and stayed where she was. Any stupid move on her part might put Ethan in danger.

The seconds ticked by, each one longer than the last. Ethan appeared to be tracking the suspect's movements. It was clear that the kid, if indeed he was a juvenile, had no idea they were on to him.

Now that her eyes had adjusted to the dark, Jane caught a

glimpse of their intruder as he rounded a corner. Still the quiet hiss of the spray can. To their right, visible only to Ethan and Jane, a man appeared in the broken window. Temple was being hoisted, with his partner's help, high enough to slip over the ledge.

He and Ethan made silent hand gestures. The kid moved closer, intent on his graffiti.

Suddenly Ethan lunged to his feet. "Freeze. Police. Hands in the air."

The young man cursed violently and hurled the can of paint in Ethan's direction. It didn't hit its mark, but the boy had already darted around the end of an aisle and was heading in a panic for the broken window.

Randy Temple pulled his weapon, ready to fire, but the boy jumped sideways and shoved a display case with all his might. Temple never had a chance. The heavy piece of furniture smashed down on top of him, glass breaking and shattering in a sickening cacophony.

Jane heard Ethan curse, and she jumped to her feet. Ethan tackled the kid in a flying leap, rolling around on the floor with him, using his strength to subdue the wildly flailing adolescent. Jane hit the light switch, flooding the room with harsh illumination.

The place looked like a war zone, but she didn't stop to mourn the third destructive visit. Ethan shot her a stone-faced glance over his shoulder. "Open the front door. And help me with that damn case."

She flew to do his bidding, her stomach in knots, her hands shaky with adrenaline. In mere seconds Ethan had the boy handcuffed and facedown on the floor. As soon as the kid was no longer a threat, Ethan was across the room. The other officer had climbed through the window already, and now the three of them surrounded the bulky piece of furniture and lifted with all their might.

Jane felt pitifully useless. Without the two men, she couldn't have moved it an inch. Carefully, with painfully slow movements, they raised it off the floor. They dared not risk losing their grip and dropping it on top of the injured officer.

A split second after the cabinet was upright and secure, Ethan and his fellow officer were kneeling by Randy Temple's side. The man was still as death, a nasty purplish gash near his temple already swelling into a knot.

But that wasn't the worst of it. When the glass had shattered, it had embedded itself in Temple's flesh. His uniform had protected him in part. And he had clearly thrown up his arms to cover some of his face. But protruding from the side of his neck was a four-inch shard of glass. Blood oozed around the edges.

Jane's vision grayed and nausea billowed in her stomach. Taking several shallow breaths, she knelt beside the three men. "What can I do?"

Ethan's face was shadowed with fear. And that scared her more than anything that had happened so far. "We can't remove the piece in his neck. He might bleed out. The EMT's will be here any moment." Already in the distance, the scream of sirens drifted on the night air.

Jane hadn't even realized she was shivering until the other officer handed her his jacket. She accepted it with murmured thanks, her eyes never leaving Randy's still white face. They were six feet from the broken window, and cold air funneled in. Not as cold as the first night this had happened, but still . . .

Without thinking about it, she draped the jacket over Randy's chest. And then she ran upstairs for blankets. She had to step past the cursing, screaming male on the floor. He hurled epithets at her feet. She never paused.

In less than two minutes, she was back. Ethan and his officer were working on their comrade, checking his vitals, making sure he was breathing. As she watched, they gently removed the smaller pieces of glass.

To see two such big, powerful alpha men touching their fallen brother so tenderly brought tears to her eyes. She blinked them away and offered the blankets. Ethan accepted them with murmured gratitude and tucked them around Randy's bleeding body.

Thankfully, the paramedics burst through the front door at that moment. Things moved quickly after that—a methodical, restrained chaos ending with Randy's body being lifted onto a narrow gurney and carried to a waiting ambulance.

Jane glanced around the shop, dazed, weary, and jumpy with nerves and stress. Ethan had followed the medical personnel outside, but he returned now and hugged her tightly. "You okay?"

She nodded jerkily, biting down hard to keep her lips from trembling. "Will he be okay?" She was terrified, not only for Randy but for what might have happened to Ethan. Life was so terribly fragile and precious.

Ethan's face was grim and exhausted. There were tiny cuts on his big hands where he had been plucking glass fragments from Randy's body. "He's stable. Removing the glass from his neck will be tricky . . . and the head wound is serious. But I think he'll make it."

She wanted to burrow into the comfort of his embrace, have him take her back upstairs and comfort her, but she knew his job was not over. Now that Randy was in good hands, Ethan and the other officer approached their suspect.

Ethan rolled him to his back none too gently, his jaw rigid with disgust and restrained anger. "Playtime's over, punk. Let's head down to the station and get you booked. It's gonna be a long list."

Jane inched closer to the trio of men, intrigued and repulsed at the same time. Who was this destructive intruder who meant her harm?

Ethan's body was shielding the guy's face, but Jane could see skinny legs clad in ripped denims, and a paid of gangly, too-large-for-his-body feet wearing fancy athletic shoes. She stepped to the side and gasped in startled recognition. "Oh, my God." She had seen this teenager twice, once in a photograph and once when he was on a ladder painting.

Ethan's head shot around, incredulity carved on his face. "You know him?"

She nodded slowly. Sorrow filled her chest, and she felt a giant tug of sympathy for what this would do to her dear old friend. "I've seen him at Mr. Benson's house . . . doing odd jobs. I'm pretty sure that's his great-nephew Dougie."

# Seventeen

emple's partner took Dougie out to the waiting cruiser. Ethan lingered, wanting one last moment with the woman he loved before the rest of his night went to hell and back. It would be hours before he'd be done wrapping up this mess, not to mention keeping tabs on Temple.

He brushed the tumbled hair from Jane's face. She was pale, with dark smudges beneath her blue eyes. "You were a trooper," he said, feeling so very proud of her. Never once had she panicked or shown even a smidgen of hysteria. And she would have been justified.

For a civilian who was unaccustomed to any kind of real violence, tonight's dustup had been pretty damn traumatic. It had been no walk in the park for Ethan himself. He was more concerned than he cared to admit about Randy Temple's condition.

Her expression was troubled. "Mr. Benson will have to be told, but I don't want to wake him up in the middle of the night.

Tomorrow morning is soon enough, don't you think? It won't hurt Dougie to spend some time in a jail cell." She paused, and her eyes flashed. "I'm so angry with him. That sweet old man has gone out of his way to do nice things for Dougie, and now this."

Ethan rubbed his thumbs over her cheeks. "Can you think of any reason for the vandalism?"

She wrapped her arms around her waist. "That's just it. I can't. Dougie barely knows me. And if he wanted to get back at his uncle for some imagined offense, it seems like Mr. Benson's house would have been a more logical target. None of this makes sense."

Ethan glanced toward the front door and stifled a curse. He had to go. He hugged her close, feeling her warmth, her softness. His hands stroked her back. "Go back to bed, honey. I'll call you in the morning and let you know what's happening."

She leaned into him, her slim arms clinging to his neck as he kissed her gently. He wanted to give her beauty in the face of ugliness, but sadly, his job would always be filled with more darkness than light.

As her lips clung to his, he felt her shiver. Belatedly, he remembered the shattered window, and he scowled. How could he leave her like this?

She stepped back, her posture fatigued, but her gaze steady. "Go, Ethan. I'll be fine. I'll lock myself in upstairs. The window is not a problem. We'll talk tomorrow." Her smiled was crooked. "Don't worry about me. You have more important things on your plate."

He felt brutally torn in two directions. But Jane was right. She was a strong, confident, self-reliant woman. Though he might want to coddle her, she didn't *need* his protection.

With his jaw clenched, he turned his back on her and walked away. She followed him only long enough to lock the front door.

As he slid into the cruiser, he could see her silhouette against the opaque glass.

He spoke to his officer, pointedly ignoring Dougie cursing in the backseat. "Let's roll."

Jane wandered through her ruined shop, shaking her head at the mean, pointless, destruction. The new stock was worthless now, and she had serious doubts about whether or not insurance would pony up again to replace it.

She was exhausted, discouraged, and heartsick. So many people hurt by one spoiled, petulant teenager. Though Mr. Benton would be distraught, she was more worried about Randy Temple. His injuries were very serious, potentially fatal. And she prayed that he would be all right.

She flipped off the lights and climbed the stairs. It was fruitless to think about work right now. Time enough tomorrow to deal with such things.

But in view of what had happened tonight, she came to a decision. She opened her desk and stared at the two remaining pieces of note paper she had planned to use for Ethan's valentines: one a pale celery green; the other an elegant, stark white.

She had promised Ethan two more missives, but things had changed. No longer was she willing to muddy the waters with anonymous notes. From now on, she would deal directly with Ethan and his feelings for her. When things settled down after this latest incident, she would tell him she loved him. And his response would chart her path.

If his feelings weren't as involved as hers, she would gently extract herself from the relationship and move on. It would hurt. She wasn't kidding herself. Her heart might never be the same. But you couldn't make somebody love you. No matter how hard you tried.

Either Ethan wanted her or he didn't.

She took the sheet of green paper and sat down at the table with a pen. Stifling a yawn, she nibbled the inside of her cheek and tried to focus. It was almost five in the morning, and she wanted to get this over to Ethan's house while he was still occupied.

*Dear Ethan,*

*I think 'twas not wise*
*to deceive you with lies.*
*I'm done with this ruse,*
*and my bent to confuse.*

*I feel in my bones,*
*that your heart's not your own.*
*You're in love I believe,*
*with a girl who's not me.*

*I bid you adieu,*
*'cause there's naught else to do.*
*True love can't be forced.*
*It's a matter of course.*

*The heart casts its spell,*
*be it heaven or hell.*
*Be happy, my dear.*
*'tis the last you will hear . . .*

*From me,*
*Your devoted but secret admirer*

She studied the verse, the slightly shaky handwriting, the delicate paper. Her fingers were not quite steady as she folded the sheet and tucked it in the matching envelope. The game was over. All that lay ahead was plain speaking and either joy or despair.

Before she could change her mind, she dressed rapidly and bundled up in her warmest outerwear. She would not drive her car. She needed the brisk predawn air to clear her head and shore up her waning confidence.

It took her twenty-five minutes to walk to Ethan's house. His neighbors' windows were dark, the street deserted. She went straight up to his front door, not worried about anyone seeing her at this hour.

In keeping with the historic ambience of the town, Ethan had an old-fashioned mail slot. The postman used the official box out at the street, but for Jane's purposes, this more direct route was perfect.

She kissed the envelope and, with her fingers crossed, shoved it through the cold brass opening.

It was done.

Sherry hated middle-of-the-night phone calls. They were always bad news. Her heart pounding in her chest, she snatched up the receiver on the second ring. As she shoved her hair from her face and tried to focus on the voice at the other end, she saw by the clock that it was technically morning . . . six thirty to be exact.

She cleared her throat. "Hello."

Her brother answered, his voice strained. "I didn't know whether to call you or not, but it's Randy, sis. He was injured in an incident tonight. He's in pretty bad shape, and I thought you would want to know."

She held the phone, her fingers numb, as Ethan detailed what had happened and then described the surgical procedure now under way to remove a large piece of glass and repair a damaged artery.

Beneath her outward calm, her carefully constructed world was imploding. Dear God.

She bit down hard on her bottom lip, steadying her voice. "Thank you for telling me. I'll be at the hospital in half an hour."

Later, she would never remember how she dressed or even how she made it into the car and across town without running off the road. She'd shut out everything but the urge to see Randy, to reassure herself that he was okay.

When she stepped into his quiet private room, her heart stopped. Clearly, he had just come out of the recovery ward, and the nurses were getting him settled into bed.

No one was there to greet him. She remembered that his family was far away, and poor Ethan had his hands full down at the station.

Which left Sherry, the one person Randy would probably just as soon not see. But she couldn't leave, not with him hurting and alone.

After the trio of professionals exited the room, Sherry moved closer to the bed, her heart slugging away in her chest with nauseating thuds. In that split second, with the smell of antiseptic in the air and the muted beeping of monitors recording the life force of the man in the bed, she realized two things. She loved him. Love was all that mattered. Randy Temple. Dear, sexy, too-good-to-be-true, way-too-young-for-her Randy Temple. And she had been a fool.

No matter that it didn't make sense and would almost surely end in heartbreak, she loved him. And if he had died, her world would have fallen apart.

She had grieved Debra's absence in the way a mother loves a child. But if she lost Randy so soon after she had found him, it would cripple her. Life so seldom gave second chances, and

Sherry had come very close to squandering hers out of a mistaken sense of propriety or misplaced pride. She loved him.

She pulled a chair close to the bed and sat down. The knot at his hairline was alarming, but no more so than the bandage covering the side of his neck.

Even with his skin coloring, he was pale, his lips bloodless, their contours etched in pain.

She took his hand and whispered to him, silly, soft words of comfort, apology, heartfelt sorrow. He didn't respond, but she wasn't too alarmed. Postsurgery, he would still be floating in and out for a while.

Would he forgive her? Did he care if she had changed her mind? Could he give her an opportunity to make it up to him? She chided herself for her selfishness. None of that was important at this moment.

She would gladly give up any chance of a future just to know he was going to be okay.

He stirred restlessly, and his eyelids fluttered. The sheet was pulled up to his armpits, but his broad shoulders were bare. She reached for the small glass with the bent straw, touching it to his dry lips carefully. "Have a drink of water, Randy."

He cooperated slowly, his face taut with the strain, but then washed with relief. Three times he managed to swallow. Three times she blinked back tears at seeing him so weak and helpless.

His head moved restlessly on the pillow. He scrunched up his face and opened his eyes. "Sherry?"

She squeezed his hand and stroked his forehead, the side that was not injured. "I'm here, Randy," she whispered, her throat tight. "Go back to sleep."

*     *     *

Randy struggled through layers of drugged awareness, searching for something, needing to remember. He tried to open his eyes, but they were glued shut.

He concentrated on the bits of reality he could pin down. First and foremost was the pain. Like most men, he rarely complained, but oh, God. The slice of fire in his neck, the merciless throb in his head—the agony was barely muted. He tried to move and groaned when the suffering intensified. *Not a good idea, Temple.*

A chiding voice scolded him. Soft hands pressed him back against the pillows. He knew that voice, recognized it even in the midst of his discomfort. Sherry?

It was probably a dream. She wouldn't come within ten feet of him.

Now his heart ached in tandem with the rest of him.

The sudden familiar cadence of a nurse's voice broke the darkness . . . the words brisk, matter-of-fact. Seconds later, precious medicine flowed into his vein. He courted oblivion, in no hurry to face what was out there waiting to drag him down and defeat him.

It might have been hours or days later when he surfaced again. His pain hovered at a manageable level, the corners smoothed by drugs.

When he tried to swallow, unseen hands brought a straw to his lips, waited patiently for him to take a drink, touched his brow with a murmur of praise.

His eyelids felt like lead.

He drifted . . . content to do so as long as they would let him.

But soon a cuff tightened on his arm, a thermometer found

its way into his mouth, and his bedcovers were straightened, despite the fact that even his skin hurt.

*Leave me alone.* He tried to yell it, but the words wouldn't come.

The next time, he felt something new. Hunger.

He concentrated fiercely and opened his eyes. Or thought he did. His vision was blurry. Had they done something to him? Made him blind?

Panic clawed at his throat until he forced himself to breathe slowly. He tried to lift his eyelids a second time, and this go-round, he was more successful.

Without moving his head more than was absolutely necessary, he scanned the room. And his heart stopped. Sherry. Sherry. She was in a chair, tucked up beside him, with her arms folded on the bed and her head resting on them there at his hip.

He wanted to touch her hair, but he couldn't make his hand move. He tried to speak, but nothing came out. His throat was raw, dry as the desert.

"Sherry." This time his voice was an embarrassing rasp of nothingness, a mere hollow squeak.

But it was enough. Her head snapped up, her face painted with anxiety. "Randy, are you hurting?"

"No." A stud until the end. But he hadn't fooled her, particularly not when he groaned and cursed as he tried to sit up.

Firm, small hands on his chest pressed him back. "For God's sake," she muttered, her breasts near his face. She adjusted his pillows and stroked his hair. "Don't try to move. Not yet anyway. The doctor says they'll be bringing in dinner shortly. Time enough then to get vertical . . . if you think you can."

*Damn straight.* His stomach was demanding to be fed, and the woman he loved was here, in touching distance. He might be in a hell of a lot of pain, but he was highly motivated.

He went still, preserving his strength. Why was Sherry in this room with him? Pity? Guilt? Or simple compassion? None of those answers were acceptable.

She took his hand again, and he clenched his fingers around hers as tightly as he was able. Maybe if he held on to her and never let go, he could rewrite the ending of their relationship.

He'd tie her to him anyway he could, even if love wasn't the reason she had come. And perhaps in time she would find it in her heart to care for him. As deeply as he loved her, surely it would be enough.

He allowed himself to doze off again, dreaming of her, imagining them together as a couple. She was in his arms, her face alight with passion. Everywhere he touched her, she was soft, perfect.

He saw her pregnant with their child, and then in the dream, he frowned. No, that wasn't right. He winced in his sleep, feeling her sorrow. He wanted her to be happy. He'd make it so. No matter what.

Her gentle voice drew him back. "Wake up, Randy." She said it like a lover's caress, the depth of feeling in her words almost palpable. Or was he imagining things in a drug-blurred consciousness?

With dogged determination, he dragged himself out of the swamp, feeling the blessed relief of oblivion cling to him like twisted roots. Awakening was not pleasant. Now he had to deal with the pain.

But it was worth it to see Sherry's face.

The first thing he noticed beyond her pallor was the fact that her sweater was buttoned incorrectly. It was an incongruous detail, especially from a woman who kept her lawn manicured.

Had she been in that much of a hurry to get to him?

He turned his head to look at the clock on the far wall. Four o'clock. But what day?

Sherry took pity on him, her gaze kind. "It's still Saturday. You have a bad concussion, and you've had surgery to remove a piece of glass from your neck. The doctor says you'll recover fully. But you were in bad shape when they brought you in. . . ."

Her voice trailed off, and he saw her eyes fill with tears before she turned away and fussed with a pitcher on the table. Her shoulders shook, and he couldn't even hold her, damn it. He cleared his throat. "Come here, my love. I've got a hard head. Don't worry about me."

She turned, and her tears fell, tracing long, wet streaks down her face. She put a fist to her mouth, still three feet away from his bed. "I'm sorry." She sobbed softly. "Ethan called me. I was trying to be strong, but oh, Randy . . . I was so scared."

With a grimace, he held out his arms. "Come here, Sherry. Let me hold you."

He barely had four minutes with her before supper arrived. But God, having her in his arms was sweet. She nestled carefully against his unhurt side, not letting him take her weight. She smelled like a woman, his woman. He didn't want to let her go.

But when the young man with the perfunctory smile brought in a covered tray and plopped it on the table, Sherry jumped to her feet and began opening things, talking a mile a minute.

She tried to hand-feed him, and he bowed up. No man worth his salt would let his lover treat him like a helpless baby. When he said as much, she glared at him.

"Let me help you." She said it through clenched teeth. "You took care of me when I was sick. Why can't you let me return the favor?"

She had him there, damn it. So as much as it galled him, he

let her feed him broth and Jell-O and a stale roll. They were just finishing up the five-star cuisine when Ethan walked through the door.

His boss's face cleared when he saw him eating. "Good to see you on the mend, Temple. Everyone at the station sends their regards."

The words were prosaic, but in Ethan's eyes, Randy saw immense relief. The men and women on the police force were a close-knit team. And they looked out for their own.

Ethan kissed his sister on the cheek. "How about giving us a minute alone, Sherry."

She looked anxious, but she obeyed her brother's quiet request, stepping out into the hall and closing the door quietly.

Ethan's expression sobered. "How are you *really* doing, Temple?"

Randy grimaced. "I hurt like hell. But I've got my own personal Florence Nightingale, so I won't complain. But tell me what happened last night after I checked out. What went down with the kid?"

Ethan shook his head in disgust. "He's Mr. Benson's great-nephew. The stupid punk got the idea that if he made Jane miserable enough, she would move out and his uncle would rent or give the space to him. Dougie wanted to open up a comic-book store."

"Good Lord."

"My sentiments exactly. Not exactly the sharpest tool in the shed. Jane has been over at Mr. Benson's house all day, making sure the old fellow is okay. But he's a tough bird. And he knows it won't hurt Dougie to spend some time in juvie. Maybe it will knock some sense into him."

Randy shifted his hips and bit down on a helpless curse as raw pain streaked from his head to his feet, stealing his breath and making him nauseous. It was still thirty minutes until they would give him more pain meds. But the damn bed was starting to feel like a torture device.

Ethan helped him get settled more comfortably with a matter-of-fact manner that kept both men from feeling awkward or embarrassed. Then he stepped back, folded his arms across his chest, and smiled slyly.

Randy lifted a wry eyebrow. "What?"

Ethan's grin grew bigger. "They gave me your personal effects when they admitted you."

Randy frowned. "Okay . . . ," he said slowly, not sure of his boss's intent.

"So I though you might be needing this." Ethan pulled a small black item out of his pocket.

Randy felt his face heat. Shit. How could he have forgotten? He practically snatched the velvet-covered box from Ethan's hand. "Thank you, sir."

Ethan lifted an eyebrow. "I guess you'll have to drop the 'sir' crap when we're in private."

Randy frowned. "Excuse me?"

Ethan shrugged. "Looks like we might end up being family."

Randy's flush deepened. "No proof of that, sir. She's already turned me down once."

Ethan's gaze was kind. "She'll say yes, Randy. I saw how she looked at you when I walked in. I saw her face. She'll say yes."


Sherry returned when her brother departed. Randy was gray-faced with pain, and she pushed the call button for the nurse, even though the patient protested. The harried woman came moments later with an apology. "Sorry. We're understaffed at the moment." She inserted a syringe in the IV and injected the medicine.

In her wake, Randy fumed. "I could have waited," he grumbled, the narcotic already slurring his words.

Sherry sat down and held his hand. "You shouldn't have to suffer," she said. "I won't allow it."

The next time he surfaced, the room was filled with flowers. For a moment, he wondered if he had died and this was a funeral home. Then the fog lifted, and his eyes widened. Good grief. There were at least seven flower arrangements on the windowsills and counters.

And he'd thought of himself as a loner, an outsider. He felt a lick of shame as he realized that maybe he'd been the one to be standoffish. Maybe this small community had embraced him more than he realized.

Sherry was standing by the window, staring out into the dark. Night had fallen. She had to be exhausted. To his knowledge, she had never left his side.

His hand gripped the ring box beneath the sheet. He was petrified with fear. What if he asked a second time and she said no? There wasn't enough morphine in the world to dull that kind of pain.

He must have made a sound, because she spun around to face him. "You're awake. How do you feel?"

He frowned and did a quick mental evaluation. "Not as bad as I did twelve hours ago. But not quite well enough to go dancing."

Her smile warmed him. "That's good." But still she hovered by the window.

He decided he couldn't wait another minute. The suspense was almost as painful as the blow to his head. He lifted his hand. "Come sit by me."

She came instantly, her gaze never leaving his face. She

scanned every nuance of his expression as though checking to see if he was lying about his condition.

When she was seated, he took her hand. "I want you to promise me something, Sherry."

"Anything." The quick answer was solemn.

"I want you to promise me that you'll go home in a little while and not come back until morning. I'll take the damn medicine, so I'll sleep through the night, but I need to know that you're home in your bed getting some rest. You're exhausted."

She straightened her spine and her eyes narrowed. "No." She said the word simply, not dressing it up with explanations or equivocations.

His lips trembled in an effort not to smile. "But you just said *anything*."

She shrugged, her expression mulish. "Anything but that. I'm not leaving you. I heard the nurse. They're understaffed. So I'm going to take care of you. End of story."

"So if I ask something else, you'll say yes?"

She nodded slowly. "Within reason. I won't promise to bring you a cheeseburger, and I won't let you refuse your medicine."

He smiled, loving her so much his chest hurt with it. "Fair enough." He fumbled beneath the sheet, removed the modest diamond solitaire from the box, and held it out to her. "In that case, then . . . Sherry McCamish . . . will you please promise to marry me?"

Sherry was glad she was sitting down. Otherwise her knees would have buckled, and she would have keeled over. She shook her head, trying not to look at the beautiful ring he was holding.

How did a man with a concussion, a man who had recently come out of surgery, have the opportunity to procure an engagement ring? She cocked her head. Maybe she was dreaming.

She pinched her own arm. Then she pinched his.

"Hey!" His outraged protest echoed the pain she felt, as well. She must be awake.

She licked her lips, studying his face. Was it possible to know a man for such a short time and feel so desperately in need of him? "Where did that come from? They must have one hell of a hospital gift shop."

He waved the ring in front of her face. "Quit stalling. You promised me anything I want, within reason. I want you to be my bride."

An odd mix of relief and joy and stunned amazement began to swirl in her chest. He still loved her.

Desperate to hold on to a modicum of self-control, she ignored the ring. "Would it be?" she asked softly, her heart troubled, even now. "Within reason, I mean . . ."

He took her left hand and slid the small circle of gold onto the correct finger.

"No," he said softly. "It won't be reasonable at all. It will be passionate and crazy and messy and joyful and sheer, bloody wonderful."

Her chin wobbled. "And the babies?"

His smile was gentle as he rubbed the back of her hand. "We can adopt . . . if you want to. Either way, I'm okay. But I can't bear it if you walk out of my life, Sherry. I'm begging you. Say yes."

Fresh tears started, and this time she didn't try to hold them back. She stood, leaned over him, and found his mouth with hers. "Yes," she whispered. "Yes, yes, yes."

# Eighteen

Ethan unlocked his front door and practically landed on his ass when he stepped on a piece of paper and his right foot shot out from under him on the hardwood floor. He managed not to crash, but it was a close call. And he did bang his knee on the wall in the process.

Limping and cursing, he made it to the sofa and collapsed, facedown. God he was tired. He'd had a total of about two hours of sleep last night, and the entire day since had been grueling in the extreme.

Still, all the messy ends were finally tied up. Jane was safe. Dougie was in custody. Mr. Benson was disappointed and hurt, but in decent spirits, all things considered.

Ethan had spoken to Jane a couple of times on the phone. She wanted information about Randy. Ethan had asked about Mr. Benson.

Other than that, they hadn't been in contact.

And he missed her. Thinking about last night made him hard. And that made him frustrated and antsy, because he needed sleep, damn it.

He rolled to his side and sat up, staring balefully at the innocent envelope on the table. He knew without opening it what it would be.

But though he was right in theory, the contents surprised the hell out of him when he ripped into it and read the words.

*Dear Ethan,*

*I think 'twas not wise*
*to deceive you with lies.*
*I'm done with this ruse,*
*and my bent to confuse.*

*I feel in my bones,*
*that your heart's not your own.*
*You're in love I believe,*
*with a girl who's not me.*

*I bid you adieu,*
*'cause there's naught else to do.*
*True love can't be forced.*
*It's a matter of course.*

*The heart casts its spell,*
*be it heaven or hell.*
*Be happy my dear.*
*'Tis the last you will hear . . .*

*From me,*
*Your devoted but secret admirer*

His first reaction was disappointment. The naughty valentines weren't from Jane. After that registered, he realized he could forget about the notes. The sender had clearly moved on. A good thing all around.

He glanced at his watch. He'd sleep for an hour and then call Jane and see if she would let him come over.

Jane was trying not to be miffed. Ethan had a highly demanding job with far-reaching responsibilities. He didn't need a woman who got pissy because he didn't contact her when she expected him to.

She stayed up far too late, expecting him to call or drop by, but so far, neither had happened.

Her Saturday had been one crazy thing after another. Soothing Mr. Benson. Arranging for her smashed window to be fixed . . . again. Stopping by the hospital and dropping off flowers for Randy Temple. Trying to see if any of her new inventory was salvageable.

Through it all, she had bolstered herself with the knowledge that Ethan might share her bed again tonight. She was eager to know if he had seen her final note and how he had responded.

And she wanted a chance to decide if she had the guts to tell him she loved him. It was usually the man's prerogative and responsibility to do the deed. But in keeping with her New Year's resolution, she was going to be proactive.

Her plan was simple: wow him with amazing sex, and then when his defenses were down, tell him the truth. She was in love with him.

At one a.m., she gave up waiting. She turned off the light and fell asleep almost instantly.

In fact, she was still sleeping soundly when her phone rang some eight hours later.

She scowled at it, wanting to pull the covers over her head. But since the damn thing kept right on ringing, and because the caller ID was easily recognizable, she answered it with a snarl. "What?"

There was a split second of silence on the other end before someone responded. "Good morning, Jane." Ethan's voice, disgustingly fresh and cheerful, held amusement. "Have I called at a bad time?"

"About ten hours too late," she said sullenly. And then wanted to snatch the words back when he laughed.

His tone and his reply were apologetic. "I'm sorry about that. I was going to nap on the sofa for forty-five minutes when I got home last night, and the next thing I knew, it was morning. But I'll make it up to you. I'm fixing brunch. You'll recall that I owe you a meal."

Her stomach growled. "Waffles?"

"With real Vermont syrup and crisp bacon."

She moaned. "I'll be there in half an hour."

She had showered the night before, so she ran a brush through her hair and tore her closet apart, looking for something to wear. Just once, she'd like Ethan to see her in an outfit that was over-the-top sexy and sophisticated.

Sadly, not only was her wardrobe lacking in those qualities, but she and Ethan had yet to even go on a date, which pretty much negated the need for sexy and sophisticated.

She settled for a thin, long-sleeve silk tee in a deep violet shade topped with a lacy pullover. Both fabrics clung to her modest breasts and the two together were more trendy than her usual attire.

All that was left was to don her favorite pair of jeans and slip her feet into a pair of black ballerina flats. When she glanced in the mirror, she wasn't totally repulsed. She looked pretty damn good, if she did say so herself.

She pulled into his driveway three minutes shy of her promised thirty minutes. Her palms were damp. This was more than breakfast or lunch or even brunch. This was the beginning of what might be the end.

When she got out and walked to the door, Ethan opened it wide and scooped her into a bear hug. "God, I've missed you." He kissed her ravenously, in full sight of anyone passing by on the street.

She struggled halfheartedly, aware at some level that the assistant police chief probably shouldn't be caught necking outdoors. He smelled delicious, all woodsy pine and fresh bacon. It was a winning combination. She played with his hair and his ears, stroking and touching and toying until he dropped her to her feet with a muttered protest.

He put his hands on his hips. "I promised myself I would feed you before I fucked you."

She blinked. Twice. That was plain speaking for sure.

He drew her inside by the simple expedient of clamping her wrist in one of his big hands and pulling. Not that she was in any mind to resist arrest.

Once in the house, she concentrated on her host. He looked a damn sight better than when she had left him yesterday. His eyes were clear, his face was clean-shaven, and he had an air of purpose about him.

Her stomach wasn't filled with butterflies, but a whole colony of Mexican jumping beans had taken residence.

Over brunch, she managed to keep up her end of the conversation, all the while trying to plan out what she would say. *Ethan, I'm sorry, but I have to tell you that I love you. Do you want to get married or not?*

It didn't help that Ethan kept touching her with light casual caresses that bespoke a casual intimacy between lovers. But she didn't feel casual at all . . . not today. His kitchen table was tiny, and the two of them were very close. She could smell his soap and shampoo, and his body heat radiated, keeping her agitated and hungry.

In addition to the stupid valentines and the fact that Ethan had kept them under wraps, there was one other unresolved issue. It bothered Jane a lot that she had been the one to resurrect their friendship.

Without the break-in at her apartment, Ethan would have let things remain the same, their estrangement intact. Which seemed to point once again to the fact that her feelings were probably more involved than his.

She sighed and drew patterns in the syrup on her plate with the tines of her fork.

Ethan poured them each another cup of coffee. "What's wrong?"

Geez. She hated it that he could read her so well. "Nothing," she mumbled.

He sat down across from her and smiled—a simple, direct, uncomplicated flash of white teeth that made her dizzy. He was so damn handsome.

He took a sip of his drink and set it down. "I've been meaning to tell you something, Jane."

She leaned back in her chair. "Go for it," she said, her voice light. Better him than her . . . since she hadn't quite figured out what she was going to say.

He stretched his arms over his head, and she saw muscles flex beneath his Statlerville Police Department T-shirt. His chest was hard as a rock. He yawned and tipped his chair back on two legs, his hands clasped on his flat belly. "Sherry and I had a heart-to-heart on New Year's Eve."

Her ears perked up. "Oh, really?"

"Yep. We were chiding each other on our lackluster love lives, and Sherry asked me why I had never dated you seriously, or words to that effect."

"And what did you tell her?" Here it was . . . perhaps a moment of truth.

"I said that back then I thought of you as my sister."

*Ouch.* Her stomach tumbled to her knees. "I see." She didn't know what else to say. It sure as hell wasn't what she wanted to hear.

He was staring at her intently, and she had to fight the urge to squirm in her chair. She felt off balance, unsure of where this was leading.

He sighed. "She more or less called me a liar."

Jane leaned forward, propping her elbows on the table, her chin in her hands. "That's not very nice."

"Turns out it was true."

Her jaw dropped, and she closed her mouth rapidly, trying to look mildly curious instead of rabidly interested. "I don't understand."

He dropped the chair on all four legs and leaned toward her, tugging her hands into his and holding them tightly. His were strong and warm. Hers were icy and trembling.

He stroked the back of her hands with his thumb. "A while back I told you a couple of reasons why I didn't ask you out . . . but the truth is, Jane . . ."

She saw his throat flex as he swallowed, and she realized he was not as calm and collected as he seemed. "Ethan?" She prodded him, desperate to hear more.

He shrugged. "The truth is that I felt safer telling myself you were like a sister to me. It kept me from doing something stupid."

"Because you thought if we hooked up, I would want more, and you weren't ready to settle down."

He nodded slowly. "Something like that." His head was bent now, his gaze focused on their clasped hands. "For the next few days after Sherry and I talked, all I could think about was you and why I had never admitted to myself how special you were . . . how happy I was when we were together. I was kicking myself for losing something so precious and wondering if there was any hope of getting it back."

"And then?" Maybe this was called leading the witness, but she couldn't help herself.

He released her hands, took her face in his big palms, and kissed her softly. "Then the first break-in at your shop happened. I spent a night in your bed, and I found myself head over ass intrigued and sexually attracted to the woman who used to be my best friend. And I knew from that first night that if I'd ever kidded myself you were like a sister to me, those platonic feelings were long gone. You've mesmerized me, Jane . . . fascinated me . . . made me ache to be inside you, beside you. . . ."

Her heart actually shivered. She felt it in her chest. And the deep, urgent sincerity in his words made her eyes wet and her throat tight.

She tried for levity. "Well, I sure as hell never looked at you as a brother. You would have been shocked if you knew what I was thinking back then."

He grinned, a cocky, arrogant, you-can't-resist-me smile that made her want to climb over the table and rip his clothes off. "I *am* shocked, Jane. And here all these years I thought you were such a restrained little thing."

"Little?"

He put their hands together, palm to palm. Hers looked delicate against his, small and defenseless. He leaned forward and kissed her again. "It's a term of affection, sweet thing. I can't help feeling the need to protect you and coddle you."

Her heart light, she dared to tease. "I was hoping for something a bit more wicked and carnal." He might not have said those three important words yet, but she saw what she was looking for in his eyes. And she was reassured.

He stood up and pulled her close for a hug. "Where do you stand on morning whoopee?"

She pursed her lips. "With dirty dishes waiting to be washed and put away?"

He raised an eyebrow, saying nothing, the glint in his eyes promising endless delights.

She shrugged. "I suppose I could be persuaded."

He picked up the bottle of syrup with a naughty waggle of his eyebrows. "Shall I take this along?"

"Eeew, no." Laughing, she coaxed him down the hall. Halfway to the bedroom, he had already shed his shirt and was working on her layered tops. They paused, breathless, to kiss long and deep.

Jane was expecting urgent passion. He gave her long, slow, tender loving, his hands stroking her back, her rib cage, the curves of her breasts.

When she would have unfastened his pants and hurried things along, he took her wrists behind her back and bracketed them with one big hand. And then he proceeded to kiss her senseless.

It might have been minutes, hours, or even days. Jane lost all concept of time. Ethan was staking a claim, imprinting his firm touch, his masculine scent, his unique taste by coaxing her mouth to open to his, her tongue to tangle with his, her lips to cling to his.

She was dizzy, and she broke away long enough to suck in much-needed air. Ethan looked as rattled as she felt, his hair in disarray, his eyes slightly unfocused.

"Bed?" She gasped the question on a half breath. He didn't answer. He merely bent his head to suckle her bare breasts, all the while backing her toward his room.

They fell on the mattress and undressed each other. Unlike recent times together, they were languid in their movements, slow . . . unhurried. The heightened sense of expectation built. Her pulse beat in her throat; her hands shook as she touched him.

It was different this time, perhaps because she knew what she was going to ask him to give her. Forever. That was all. And if Ethan couldn't say yes to that, these shiningly beautiful moments might be their last.

When they were both nude, they tumbled like children on the bed, laughing softly, learning new ways to make the other curse and gasp and cry out.

But eventually, need could no longer be denied. Ethan grabbed at the box of condoms on the floor and groaned when he shook it and found it empty.

His face tight with arousal, he pointed. "The drawer. Your side. Hurry."

With his hand on her ankle, Jane reached across to the bedside table nearest her. She yanked open the top drawer and froze. A coiled copperhead would have been no more alarming than what she found. Five colorful valentines.

She couldn't move. Couldn't think. Couldn't speak. Except for the last one, they were creased and worn, as though he had read them repeatedly. And they were tucked away in his bedroom, where he slept.

As if in a dream, she saw herself pick them up. "What are these?" Her voice was dull . . . her happiness teetering on the brink of extinction.

Ethan reacted visibly. And his automatic response tore at her composure. He frowned. "Those are nothing, I swear."

She stared at him. "But why do you have them?" Before he could stop her, she opened one. "Who sent you these?"

Ethan was a smart man, and he knew trouble when he saw it. Damn it to hell and back. Why hadn't he shown them to her and explained? Why hadn't he thought to move them? It was a bad oversight on his part.

He stroked her leg, wincing when she jerked it out of reach. "They're nothing, Jane. Just some weird mail from a stranger."

"Why didn't you throw them away?"

He felt guilty for no good reason, and that made him mad. "I thought the sender might be dangerous. I kept them for evidence."

"What do they say?"

He shrugged. "They're poems . . . sex stuff, love stuff."

He was sweating now. No way was he going to let one stupid misunderstanding ruin things with Jane.

Despite the distraction of seeing her breasts, her slender waist, the puff of hair at the top of her sex, he managed to stay focused. He was in deep shit with no help in sight.

Her eyes were huge, her expression hard to read. "Was it good poetry?"

He nodded slowly. Might as well tell the truth. She could read them for herself. "Yes. In fact, a little too good. Some nights they made me think of you, and I got even more horny."

"For a woman you don't even know. A woman you wanted to find."

"No." He denied it flatly. "I had no interest at all in whoever sent those notes other than to ascertain whether or not she might pose a threat to me or to you."

"And you hid this from me because . . ."

He studied her face. He couldn't tell if she was angry. But she sure as hell wasn't happy. Her body language was rigid.

He shrugged. "I was afraid you would get the wrong idea, and I didn't want to hurt your feelings . . . not again."

"You thought I would be jealous and pitch a fit?"

"The first, maybe yes . . . the second, no. But I was afraid to do anything that might make you walk away again. That's the only reason I didn't tell you, I swear. Plus, I was afraid she might be dangerous, and I wanted to protect you."

Her gaze lifted from the valentines to his face. "You're going to have to learn to trust me, Ethan. And if you ever keep secrets from me again, I'll have to castrate you."

Her expression had lightened, and the tightness in his chest eased. He blurted out his first thought. "I thought you'd be a lot more angry than this."

She rolled her eyes. "The valentines are from me, dumb ass."

There was a roaring in his ears and his throat went dry. Words and phrased flickered through his brain. He'd read the notes so many times they were as familiar to him as his name and address.

*Dreams hot and deep . . .*
*Snug velvet glove . . .*
*My thighs will spread wide . . .*
*What's right under your nose . . .*
*True love can't be forced . . .*
*Marry me . . . marry me . . . marry me. . . .*

He put his hands over his face. God, he deserved to lose his badge. The evidence had pointed to Jane from the beginning, but he'd been too blind to see it. Hell, he'd even watched Jane mail one of the notes, and he'd still found a way to convince himself it wasn't her.

He sat back on his haunches and dropped his hands. She was perched on the far side of his bed, her eyes wary, her arms tucked protectively over her breasts.

He held out his arms. "Come here, woman."

She hesitated only a second, and then they were wrapped in each other's arms. He rained kisses over her face and, after managing to retrieve a condom after all, moved between her legs. "I love you, Jane."

Her smile was luminous. "Ditto."

He nudged his cock inside her warm, welcoming passage, groaning when her body made good on that "snug velvet glove" promise.

He fucked her slowly at first, trying to show her how he felt. He was shitty with words. Unlike his precious Jane who had wooed him so sweetly.

But then his baser instincts took over, his breathing quickened, and his control snapped as he thrust wildly, lost in the wonder of knowing she was his. Seconds before he came, he drew back, panting.

Jane protested and wrapped long legs around his back to pull him down. "Don't stop."

His breath rasped in his heaving chest. "One thing you should know."

Her blue eyes were hazy, unfocused. "What?"

"You jumped the gun and ruined my big surprise. I was planning to propose to you on Valentine's Day."

# Epilogue

**February 14**

Ethan stood, spine straight, at the front of Jane's small country church and waited for his bride. His gaze drifted over the small crowd of well-wishers. Mr. Benson beamed from three rows back. Yesterday, in a shocking surprise, the old man had deeded Jane's building to her as a wedding gift.

Sherry and Randy sat on the front row, hand in hand. In a couple of weeks, they planned to fly to Florida and introduce Randy to Debra and vice versa. After that, they would be setting their own wedding date.

There were no attendants at the altar, not even a maid of honor or best man. Only the minister flanked Ethan. Jane had said, and Ethan agreed, that since they were each marrying their best friend, no other fuss was necessary.

It was one of the shortest engagements on record, but neither Jane nor he had wanted to wait. Though her parents were shocked, they had known Ethan for years, and once they got used to the idea, they gave their blessing. In lieu of planning and paying for a large, expensive wedding, Jane's disappointed mother and dad had flown her to New York overnight and insisted she buy a designer gown. Ethan hadn't laid eyes on the Vera something-or-other dress, but he'd be able to have his first glimpse very soon.

The music changed as the swinging wooden doors at the back of the room opened wide. There, framed against a simple archway stood Jane.

She took his breath away. Her hair was caught up on top of her head in a pretty, artful tangle of curls. Her graceful neck was bare save for the platinum-and-diamond necklace he'd given her as an engagement present. The dress was worth every penny her parents had paid.

It was an off-the-shoulder design that showcased tempting amounts of her cleavage, emphasized her narrow waist, and ended in a fairy-tale skirt of tulle and satin.

He had to clear his throat and blink back hot moisture from his eyes.

Music played, but in his head she walked to him in hushed, reverent silence. The carpeted aisle seemed to stretch on forever. When she was close, he stepped forward and took her arm, sharing the last two steps to the altar. Her blue eyes were serene, her smile sexy and sweet.

As they paused and faced the minister, Jane slipped a small envelope into his hand. "Put in your pocket," she whispered.

He barely moved his lips, conscious of the roomful of eyes on them. "What is it?" Discreetly he tucked the note in his tux jacket.

Jane squeezed his hand. "It's the last valentine I promised you, number six."

His lips twitched. "I can hardly wait."

The minister gave them an admonishing glance and began reading the familiar, oft-repeated words, " 'We are gathered here today . . .' "

Ethan tuned out for a moment, unable to concentrate on anything but Jane's profile. She faced the minister, her eyes intent as she listened to the beginning of the ceremony.

His hungry gaze roved over her face—her soft lips, her stubborn chin, the curve of her cheek, her pretty nose.

All of it was so familiar to him, and yet today . . . on the threshold of something brand-new and faintly alarming, she was an enigma, a beautiful, wonderful puzzle.

The minister's voice pierced Ethan's preoccupation. "Do you, Ethan, take Jane to be your lawfully wedded wife, to have and to hold in sickness and in health, from this day forward, until death do you part?"

There was moisture on Ethan's brow, and his hands weren't quite steady, but he cleared his throat and answered firmly, "I do."

Again, he spaced out, inhaling Jane's delicate feminine scent, noticing absently that she had transferred her engagement ring temporarily to her right hand so he could place a simple platinum band on her left ring finger.

Joy swelled in Ethan's chest . . . and he sent a rush of jumbled, grateful, prayerful words to the man upstairs. Not everyone in life was lucky enough to fall in love with their best friend. Ethan swore on the spot never to take the gift for granted.

Somehow he said the right things at the right time. He remembered holding Jane's hands, repeating vows in a choked voice, listening to an ancient blessing.

And then it was over. The minister smiled benignly, his voice gently amused as he said, "You may kiss your bride."

Ethan faced the love of his life, toe-to-toe, eye to eye. When he placed his lips over hers, there was an earthquake of some sort beneath his feet. He heard bells ringing, and then Jane was breaking the kiss and laughing softly.

She hooked her arm in his and started for the back of the church. "Come on, Chief. Any more of that and we'll be arrested."

He stopped halfway down the aisle and kissed her once more to the accompaniment or raucous hoots and hollers. When he lifted his head, Jane had tears in her eyes.

"I love you," he said gruffly. They might as well have been alone for all the notice he took of the people surrounding them.

Jane's eyes sparkled, sapphire blue. "And I love you, my dearest Ethan. Happy Valentine's Day."

It was as beautiful a holiday occasion as anyone could have wished. And as the bride and groom exited their wedding reception a short time later, the guests pelted them with small, colorful candy hearts: *Hey, Hot Stuff. Will You Be Mine? Kiss Me. I'm Yours.*

If you love sexy stories like *Hot Mail*, then look for
Janice Maynard's next sizzling tale of seduction

*Mating Game*

On sale in July 2009 from Signet Eclipse

Read on for a sneak peek. . . .

"You have to be married to inherit. It's as simple as that."

Nola stared at her grandmother's lawyer, trying to ignore the knot in her stomach. His expression was sympathetic, but his words were unequivocal.

She licked her lips, searching in vain for some sense to this madness. "Couldn't I go to court and argue mental incompetence?" If Marc were here, he'd have whispered in her ear, *Hers or yours?* He had a wicked sense of humor and loved to tease her.

It was only one of the many things at which Marc excelled, not the least of which was his ability to prove to a woman that she was multiorgasmic, despite all previous evidence to the contrary.

The lawyer shook his head. "She wrote her will five years ago when she was in full possession of her faculties. No judge anywhere will be able to break it. She may have gotten a bit fuzzy there at the end, but she knew what she wanted for you."

Nola's bottom lip quivered, and she bit down on it, not willing to make a scene in her favorite Starbucks. She gazed blindly at a grungy teenager two tables away who was swallowing great gulps of cappuccino from a cup in one hand while texting with his other.

The depth of her grief took her off guard. Since the day her grandmother had taken orphaned ten-year-old Nola into her home to raise her, the two women had butted heads over virtually everything. As an adult, Nola traveled south at least quarterly. She had spent time with her grandmother at Christmas just four months ago, but it was a strained visit, compelled by a sense of duty.

Now guilt and loss made uncomfortable bedfellows in her gut. She brought her attention back to the lawyer. He'd been her grandmother's legal counsel since the late sixties. His worn three-piece suit with the vest tightly buttoned and his dated, almost embarrassing tie made him stand out. He'd have been right at home on a rerun of the *Andy Griffith Show*, but not so much amidst this trendy downtown crowd.

Nola suspected that the decision to fly here and break the news to her in person was more for his benefit than hers. There wasn't much to do in Resnick, Georgia, and this impromptu trip to Chicago would probably be the highlight of his year.

Nola cleared her throat. "I can't believe she's gone." *And it was just like the cantankerous old biddy to demand she be cremated and forgo a funeral.*

The lawyer frowned slightly, as if he had read her mind. "I tried to argue with her about the final arrangements some time ago. It didn't seem fair to you. Funerals are for the living, and they're an important ritual . . . part of saying goodbye."

For the first time, he looked uncomfortable. "We can talk later about where and how she wanted her ashes spread, but let's get back to the matter at hand. You have thirty days to find a husband, or your grandmother's entire fortune—house, land, everything—will go to another beneficiary."

Nola raised an eyebrow. "Who . . . or what?"

He shook his head. "I'm not at liberty to say."

"Probably something stupid." Nola slapped her hand over her mouth, aghast at her ill-timed sarcasm.

But the lawyer just chuckled. Again, sympathy gleamed from his faded blue eyes. "Believe me, Nola. I understand how absurd this seems. But unfortunately, the will is completely ironclad." He paused and took a sip of his plain black coffee. "Surely there's a man in your life. . . ."

Nola nodded slowly. Marc *was* a man. And he was definitely in her life. But a suitable candidate for matrimony? Doubtful.

She sighed. "Tell me again about the residency requirement."

"You have to live full-time in Resnick for a minimum of six months."

"*After* I'm married?"

He shook his head. "Not necessarily. You could start that immediately. And there's no time limit on the marriage. Technically you could marry and then divorce as soon as possible. There's nothing in the will to stop you from doing that."

Except common decency and morality and a basic sense of ethics. She looked him in the eye. "If I decide to do this, I intend to stay married."

The lawyer smiled. "Your grandmother would be very proud. She spoke most highly of you."

Nola rolled her eyes. "Not to me, I can assure you."

He grinned. "She bragged to anyone who would listen about your life and your job. She even had brochures made up with your Web site in case anyone wanted to fly to Chicago and have you shoot their portrait."

Nola's heart sank again as she thought about leaving Chicago and her thriving career. It had taken her a half dozen years after college and a master's degree in fine arts to establish herself as a locally notable photographer. She wasn't in the big leagues yet, but she made a nice living.

At one time she had dreamed of having a studio in her grandmother's house. But the two women could never have coexisted as adults. And besides, how many people in Resnick could afford, or would even want, to have their portraits professionally done?

The lawyer spoke again, perhaps sensing Nola's ambivalence. "It's a hell of a lot of money to walk away from."

Nola stared at him bleakly. "The money is one thing. The house and land are another. I'm the last of the Graingers. How am I supposed to turn my back on that legacy? My family has lived in that house since the early eighteen hundreds." And she knew every one of the oft-told ancestral stories. During the War of Northern Aggression (as Nola's grandmother called it until the day she died) a savvy Confederate Grainger widow had bartered her body in exchange for being bypassed by Sherman's rampaging army. Was Nola about to do the same? Could she prostitute herself to save a house and a few hundred acres of land?

Not without love. Or at least the semblance of it. In that moment, she knew what she had to do.

She had to find a man. Someone she could respect, and look at across the breakfast table every morning, and—above all—someone she could enjoy hot, satisfying sex with. Definitely that last one. Marc had spoiled her that way. He'd taught her things about her own body that still made her blush. She wasn't about to enter into some farcical platonic marriage of convenience.

She wanted a man who would love her and lust after her and understand why she had to protect her grandmother's legacy.

Marc had a fortune of his own, but he was a player. Nola was merely his flavor of the month. And from the beginning, she'd recognized their passionate liaison as temporary and superficial.

So he wouldn't be a viable candidate. But if not him, then who?

She wanted tenderness and respect from her husband, as well as raw, raunchy sex. Was that too much to ask? And was she willing to dangle her fortune-to-be as the carrot? Could a woman ever really love a man who was in it for the money?

She stood up, and the lawyer did the same. Nola smoothed her skirt. "Thank you for coming in person. This would have been tough to hear over the phone." It was still surreal and upsetting, but she was trying to cope.

He gave her an odd little half bow. "If you wish to make other arrangements for your own legal counsel, I certainly understand."

She shook her head slowly. "No. You knew my grandmother. You know the town and the life. I'd say between the two of us we can work things out."

He gathered his umbrella and the newspaper he'd been reading on the train. "It's a hell of a situation, my dear. But I'm sure in the end it will be worth it."

They paused on the sidewalk, preparing to part in opposite directions. Nola's skin felt supersensitive to the thin April sunlight. Early-morning thunderstorms had given way to a tentative springlike warmth.

The lawyer shook her hand. "You're a very attractive woman, Nola. Any man would be lucky to have you."

She adjusted her purse strap on her shoulder. "From your mouth to God's ears." Then she wrinkled her nose. It might be a tad sacrilegious to ask the Almighty's help in shopping for a husband under such base and selfish circumstances.

As the lawyer disappeared toward the subway station, Nola stood irresolute, the crowds of harried pedestrians parting on either side of her as though she were an easily overlooked obstruction. She glanced at the men—old and young, fat and thin, handsome and homely.

Could she do this? Could she deliberately stalk and capture a male beast, drag him home, and let him put his hands on her body? The sheer gutsiness of what she was contemplating sent a little tingle of anticipation into her abdomen and below.

In her own conflicted way, she would miss her grandmother, but the old lady had thrown down the gauntlet, and Nola was not about to disappoint generations of Grainger ancestors by wimping out.

She had thirty days to find a man. And the clock was ticking. . . .

# About the Author

*J*anice Maynard came to writing early in life. When her short story "The Princess and the Robbers" won a red ribbon in her third-grade school arts fair, Janice was hooked. Since then, she has sold more than a dozen books and novellas. She holds a BA from Emory & Henry College and an MA from East Tennessee State University. In 2002, Janice left a fifteen-year career as an elementary school teacher to write full-time.

Janice lives with her husband in beautiful East Tennessee, and they have two grown daughters, who make them proud. She can be reached via e-mail at JESM13@aol.com. Visit her on the Web at www.janicemaynard.com and www.myspace.com/janicemaynard.